HEIR
TO
EVIL

An Inheriting Evil Novel

Paris Hansen

Also By Paris Hansen

Crime Fiction
Inheriting Evil Series
The Broken Doll
Beloved
Heir to Evil
Prodigal Daughter

Romance
Finding Love Series
Restless
Powerless
Speechless
Breathless
Priceless
Harmless

CHAPTER ONE

Growing up he'd always been told that patience was a virtue. Even back then, he knew the saying was bullshit. As an adult, he realized it was just a way for his parents to control him. Instead of taking what he wanted, when he wanted, he did everything on their time. But now he knew better. There was nothing virtuous about waiting to slit someone's throat. Nothing virtuous about waiting to torture someone because it gave you the rush you couldn't get any other way.

No, patience wasn't a virtue. But, it was a means to an end. Good things would come to those who waited. He believed that one wholeheartedly, and he'd seen proof of it over and over again, even more so throughout the last few months.

Waiting to look into the circumstances of his birth showed him what he'd been missing his entire life. Had he tried sooner, he would have come up empty-handed; he would've never learned the answers to the questions that had plagued him since he was a child. Patience not only got him those answers but gave him a sense of belonging, a sense of purpose. Now, he knew who and what he was, and it was finally time to tell the world.

Of course, he'd have to wait just a tad bit longer to do that. There were steps he had to go through before he could make himself known. And one of those steps was sitting in the woods, bored out of his damn mind being eaten by mosquitos while he waited for an old man to leave the comfort of his stupid cabin.

If the old man in question hadn't been a highly decorated Army veteran, he would've marched right up to his front door without hesitation. But between the man's skills and the retired Army dog that belonged to that stupid bitch Sloane Matthews, he decided he'd rather be safe than sorry. Odds were the guy had more than one gun in his cabin, and while he wasn't a fan of them because they killed too quickly, he knew his target wouldn't hesitate to pull the trigger on a stranger. His plan was too important to risk being offed by a gun-toting geriatric asshole.

From now on, he had to be smart about everything he did. His life finally made sense. He no longer questioned the voices in his head or the desires he tried unsuccessfully to satisfy in other ways. Everything was finally falling into place, except for one small piece.

Sloane Matthews was a thorn in an otherwise perfect life.

And he intended to remove her.

His plan thus far had been fun but not very effective because of the FBI. He wanted to toy with her, drive her crazy until she was on the verge of losing her mind. Yet that was damn near impossible when she had no idea he even existed.

Everything he'd left behind for her had been kept hidden away. At first he'd been angry about their interference. His gifts were for her, not them. Now, he found humor in the situation knowing that the dumbasses in the FBI actually thought the items he left behind were proof that Sloane was involved. Like she could ever bring herself to torture and kill innocent human beings.

She was a disgrace to her family, to the DiSanto name. She didn't deserve to live, her presence a reminder of everything he was entitled to but would never have. Sooner or later, he'd get the chance to rid the world of her, and they'd all be better for it.

In the meantime, he had a game to play, and now that she knew the people she trusted had been lying to her for months, it would only be a matter of time before he got her where he wanted her. Eventually, she'd realize he'd been so close to her they'd even had a conversation. He could've snuffed her life out right there at the coffee shop, but where would the fun be in that.

The joy was in the chase, after all, which was part of why he bugged not only her best friend's house but also the apartment of the stupid agent that sniffed around her like she was a dog in heat. So much easier to stay one step ahead of them if he knew what their plans were. Between the bugs and his insider at the FBI, he didn't have to work too hard at keeping Sloane in his sights.

Knowing Sloane was on her way home made him positively exuberant. She would never forget the present he planned on leaving for her this time. Of course, the old bastard needed to leave his damn cabin soon in order for him to make it all work.

If he took much longer, he'd have to alter his plan, something he didn't really want to do if he could help it. At least the camera he set up in the eave over her porch was in place so he wouldn't have to worry about taking care of that and delivering the package to her front door before she arrived.

It was the little things that made a plan go right. It was also being able to make adjustments on the fly, which he obviously needed to do if he planned on getting what he came for. Instead of waiting for the old man to come to him, he was going to need to make things happen. Walking through the clearing between the woods and the cabin had him admittedly on edge. For all he knew, the old guy had a gun on him at that very moment. When he approached the steps and hadn't been shot, confidence seeped back into his bones.

As he knocked on the door, he felt like he was invincible. He felt the same thing every time he was about to take a life. The snarling dog and the cocking of a gun heard through the door did nothing to break his resolve. As the door flew open, he struck quickly, the blade he'd been hiding in his pocket finding purchase in the old man's chest before his obvious threat could even leave his lips. He pulled the knife free and batted away the gun as quickly as he could before slamming the blade back in.

The gun clattered to the ground just as the dog lunged for him. This was the part he'd been dreading. He might have been a monster, but he wasn't the kind that hurt animals, even ones that were out for blood. He also couldn't just stand there and let the beast rip his face off. It was a no-win situation. He reared back and kicked out with his right leg just in time to connect with the dog's jaw. A yelp filled the room, followed by another snarl that raised the hair on the back of his arms.

"I don't want to kill you," he grumbled.

Not that the dog cared about his intentions. He wasn't just protecting himself; he was protecting the old man who was currently bleeding out just inside the door of the cabin.

He kicked at the dog a few more times, hitting him in the face and ribs, then threw the bag he'd brought with him over the dog's head. Holding it in place, he muscled the dog into the bedroom and closed the door. Before heading back to the body, he checked for any open wounds the dog may have left behind. He didn't feel anything, but he knew from experience that adrenaline was an excellent painkiller. Once he was sure the dog hadn't bit him, he moved back to the living area to finish up. The last thing he wanted was to leave behind evidence, at least not the kind of evidence that could be used against him later on.

While the dog barked in the bedroom, he went back to the living room so he could retrieve the present he had in mind for Sloane. Despite the two stab wounds, the old man still had a little fight left in him, so he took pity on the veteran and slit his throat.

There was no fanfare, no thrill. It felt nothing like his usual kills. This one was a means to an end, nothing more. If the old man didn't mean something to Sloane, he'd have gotten to live out the rest of his days in his dump of a cabin. But unfortunately for Richard Briggs he was the perfect target since he was the only friend of hers not under the watchful eye of federal agents.

It took twenty minutes and the help of an ax he found outside next to a pile of firewood to get what he came for. Once he'd removed the old man's head from his body, he searched the house for a new way to transport it back to Sloane's cabin. Eventually, he opted for a thick black pillowcase which was a much better option than the bag he'd used on the dog.

Looking around the cabin one last time, he smiled at the mess he was leaving behind. He'd created one hell of a picture. Paired with what he was setting up at Sloane's, he knew she'd never be able to forget him. He was about to leave a very lasting impression, and he couldn't wait to watch her fall apart.

Then when he was ready, he'd tear her apart. He would prove to her and the world that he was to be feared. He was the evil that went bump in the night. He was everything wrong in the world and then some.

Before it was all over, everyone would know his name, while the blight known as Sloane Matthews would become a distant memory.

CHAPTER TWO

Rage coursed through her, setting her veins on fire. On the flip side, sadness was doing a bang-up job of chasing the anger away, so she couldn't seem to find any kind of emotional balance. Though if she had a choice in the matter, Sloane would definitely pick the veins on fire. She wanted the fury, the desire to hurt whoever did this to Richard, to fuel her movements. She needed it. Otherwise, there was a good chance she'd break, and she couldn't break. Not now.

Tears welled in her eyes, but she tried to blink them back. Crying wouldn't help her situation. There'd be time enough later on for more tears. What she needed now was to calm down and get herself together. She needed to call Reid or Cade or the local cops, and then she needed to find her dog.

"Oh god..."

Panic engulfed her at the mere thought of Apollo. Her chest hurt so bad she couldn't breathe. Black spots danced around the edge of her vision. She tried to concentrate on calming herself, all while her brain rattled off one question after another.

Was he out in the woods, hurt, or worse, dying? Was he already dead? How the hell had someone gotten close enough to Richard to take him out with Apollo by his side? Not to mention the years of Army training Richard had under his belt. The man had withstood three different wars only to be taken out at home by someone obsessed with her.

Richard deserved more than to be a part of some sick game only a few people even realized was being played. He was a hero and a great friend. He should've been able to go out on his own terms, not wind up with his head in a box, left behind as a present for her. What kind of sick fuck did something like that?

Sloane would find the person that hurt her friend, and she would avenge him. But first, she needed to forget that the situation was happening to her. She needed to look at it as if she was an outsider looking in. Like she would have if she was still an agent.

Just the mere thought of the FBI sent a shot of anger through her. Would Richard still be alive if she'd been told about the bodies and notes sooner? Would she have been able to save her friend? She might've been the reason Richard was killed, but his death was the FBI's fault. Reid and Cade and everyone else that kept her in the dark.

They should've told her someone was leaving pictures and notes for her pinned to bodies all over the country as soon as they started showing up. Maybe she could've helped them figure everything out before so many innocent people had to die. Instead of being focused on her, they should've included her.

Could've.

Should've.

None of it really mattered now. What was done was done. Richard was dead. A mad man was still stalking her, his sick and twisted game just barely beginning. There was a great chance her previously believed to be dead mom was actually alive and well, killing and taking other psycho killers under her wing. Her dog was missing and quite possibly dead.

The shit had hit the fan, and there was no way to go back in time to turn the fan off. She would have to pick up where they were and help the FBI clean up the mess. She would find the killer, find her mom, and bring them both to justice even if it killed her.

Staring at her cabin through the windshield of her car, she let her thoughts drift to a whirlwind of revenge and memories of Richard. Sloane allowed herself to sit there for a few more minutes before shutting it all down. She needed to stop thinking and actually do something. The more time she wasted, the further way the killer got. Not that he'd go too far or anything. She was the object of his obsession, after all, and everything he did was to torment her. She was his endgame.

Picking up her phone, she quickly considered her options. The local Hope's End police were wholly unequipped to deal with the situation. In the four years Sloane had lived on the island, not a single person had passed away. The only dead bodies the people of Hope's End ever saw belonged to animals. A head without a body would be far too much for them.

She knew she should call the county Sheriff or the Seattle FBI, but instead, she pulled up her recent call log, then called the first number on the list. Setting the phone on speaker, she put it on the dash and wiped at her eyes.

"Sloane, I'm glad you called. Did you go home? Emily said you didn't come back to her place, so we took the chance you went back to Seattle. We're on our way there."

"Cade..." she could barely get his name out as she stuttered around a sob.

No matter how many times she tried to convince herself to stop, the tears kept coming. She'd been able to hold them back for a little while, but now hearing Cade's worried voice through the phone set her off again.

"Sloane, what's going on?"

"Rich...head...box..." Sloane stopped talking to take a few deep breaths.

She knew she wasn't making any sense, but forming words around the sobs was harder than she thought it would be. Her breathing was ragged, her throat raw. None of that mattered, though. She needed to calm down enough to tell Cade what was happening so he could send help. Closing her eyes, she focused on her breathing, forcing herself to slow down instead of gulping in air. Once she felt steady, she opened her eyes again and let her gaze focus on her cabin.

"There...there was a box on my porch."

"Shit."

"There was a note. I know...I know I shouldn't have opened it, but I needed to. There was blood. I could see it...smell it."

"We just got on the road. We're about an hour out, but Reid says he can cut that time down. Where are you right now?"

Sloane let out the breath she hadn't realized she'd been holding. Soon, she wouldn't be alone. Though she didn't understand why they were headed to her house. How could they have been sure she'd gone home?

"I'm inside my rental in my driveway. Why are you coming here? How did you even know where I was?"

"It was an educated guess, and we wanted to bring you the notes and pictures. We wanted to talk. And I didn't want you to be alone," Cade admitted, his tone softening as he delivered the last part.

Sloane didn't know what to say to that. Though she had to admit she was damn glad the two men were pushy as hell. If things had gone according to plan, she might have been pissed when they showed up on her doorstep. Now, she'd be glad for their presence.

"Stay in your car. We'll be there soon. In the meantime, Reid's already on the phone with the Seattle field office. They're sending in a team from Poulsbo, and we're calling the Sheriff's office too. You shouldn't be there alone. Whoever left the box could still be there."

"It's Richard," she choked out. "His head in..."

"Jeezus, Sloane. I'm so sorry."

Closing her eyes, Sloane let her head fall back against the headrest. Memories of Richard played through her head. The man was the epitome of an old curmudgeon, but he'd taken Sloane under his wing like she was the daughter he'd never had. He protected her even when she didn't need protection. He loved spending time with her and Apollo. It had been a friendship she never expected but one she absolutely cherished.

And now he was gone. She'd never get to tell him how much he meant to her.

A sob wracked her body again, the sound catching Cade's attention. He promised to stay on the phone with her until someone got there to secure the scene or until he and Reid got there, whichever came first. Sloane didn't really know what to do with herself, so she did as she was told and waited in the car. When the air became too oppressive, she started the car and turned on the air conditioning.

At some point, she must have dozed off because the next thing she knew, someone was knocking on her car window. The man outside was in a Jefferson County Sheriff's uniform, but she wasn't sure she could trust it. Looking in her rearview mirror, she found a couple of patrol cars and three more deputies in uniform securing the area.

"Sloane, there should be a few of the Sheriff's deputies at your place now. We're about ten minutes out."

If it had been anyone else on the other line, she would've been surprised that they'd stuck to their promise to stay on the line until help arrived. But that wasn't the case with Cade. Despite the situation with the notes, she knew deep down she could trust him. Would he put his job before her again? Only time would tell. But until then, she'd give him the benefit of the doubt. Or, at the very least, she'd try to. She'd need to be able to trust him and Reid if they were going to catch whoever killed Richard. She planned on being involved every step of the way, and if either of them thought otherwise, then she'd just have to go around them.

"They're here. I'm going to get out now so I can talk to them."

"Stay close to one of them until we get there," Cade demanded before saying goodbye and disconnecting the call.

Sloane suddenly felt very alone even though people were waiting just outside her car for her. Taking another calming breath, she turned off the car, then opened the door and climbed out. The officer standing next to the car held out his hand to help her, but she brushed him off. Her catnap had done wonders for her resolve.

She was done being a victim and back to being pissed the fuck off.

"Ms. Matthews, I'm Deputy Cochran. We've secured the porch, and we're just waiting for reinforcements before we secure the surrounding area. The FBI is on their way, as well as your friends. Is there anything you need while we wait?"

Sloane shook her head and looked around her front yard. Aside from the tape blocking off her front porch and the patrol cars blocking her driveway, everything looked normal, though she knew it was anything but. She'd always know.

Her friend was dead, and some psycho left his head on her porch. She didn't want to wait for backup before heading out into the woods. The reasonable part of her knew the killer was long gone, but she didn't want to be reasonable. She wanted to find the asshole that did this. She needed to find him. And she needed to find her dog.

Running into the woods wouldn't help the situation, though. It would only make matters worse in the long run. Even though she knew he was gone, she couldn't put the officers' lives around her at risk on a hunch. There was a small chance he was out there watching her, which ultimately put them all in danger just by virtue of standing in her front yard, but there was nothing she could do about that. Staying put was the right thing to do, no matter how much she yearned to do otherwise.

Before she knew it, more cars were pulling down her gravel driveway and coming to a stop around her house. The one in the lead came to a screeching halt, throwing gravel at the ankles of everyone nearby. Cade jumped out of the passenger seat before Reid had even had a chance to put that car in park. He ran to her, pulling her into his arms as soon as he reached her. He didn't seem to care who was around to see them.

She should've pushed him away, told him she would be okay, and that they needed to find the person behind this, but she couldn't find the strength or the voice to do either. Instead, she welcomed the crush of his body against hers. She relished the strength he poured into her. His whispers of hope were helpful, almost as helpful as his strong arms wrapped around her. Sloane allowed him to hold her for a minute longer than necessary before pushing him away.

"We need to find who did this, but first, we need to find Apollo. He's out there somewhere," she said, her words sounded calm, but she wasn't. "Cade, I need to find my dog."

He nodded. "Reid's rounding up a few people to go with us. We want to secure the trail between your cabin and Richard's. Hopefully, we'll find Apollo at his house, or if he ran away from the killer, he'll see you and come running."

Sloane swallowed down bile as she thought about what Cade wasn't saying. "What if he's..."

"Don't go there, Sloane. You don't need to think about that right now. Focus on being the guide we need through the woods."

"Can I get my gun out of the house?"

Despite being surrounded by FBI agents and Sheriff's deputies, the thought of having a way to protect herself made her feel better. Sloane didn't like depending on other people for her safety. Not when she was more than capable of taking care of herself.

"Does your cabin have a backdoor?"

"No. Fuck," she muttered, understanding why he asked.

"The techs are still on the way, which means you can't get into the cabin until they've fully processed your porch. After that, we'll want to go in and make sure the unsub didn't leave anything else behind."

"Jeezus...I didn't even think...he could've been in my goddamn house, Cade. I..."

Sloane turned to look at her cabin once again. It didn't even look like her sanctuary anymore. It was tainted beyond recognition, and that was before knowing whether or not the killer went inside. In the five years she'd lived there, she'd never allowed anyone inside other than Richard. At least not until Reid landed on her doorstep a couple of months earlier, asking to be let in.

She should've known his showing up was a bad omen, but never could she have imagined she'd end up with her yard and porch filled with law enforcement officers, her friend's head in a box against her door. There was no way she'd ever feel safe in that building again. It was no longer where she found the solitude she sought years ago, but instead, it was a place violated by a monster.

Cade took a step closer, another attempt to comfort her, but this time she didn't need it. This time she wouldn't fall apart in his arms. Now was the time to step up, figure out who did this, and make them pay. Once that was done, she could mourn the loss of her friend and her safe haven.

Until then, she had shit to do.

CHAPTER THREE

When he'd gone to bed the night before, he hadn't expected his day to turn out quite like this. Never in a million years would Cade have guessed he'd fall asleep next to the woman he was falling for, then end up at her cabin in the woods dealing with a head in a box the next morning.

How it had turned into such an utter shit show so quickly, he wasn't sure. He knew he was partly to blame. Instead of insisting on having a conversation first, he let his hormones and his dick lead him into a situation that only made the bigger picture worse. Even so, he couldn't, hell he wouldn't, regret what happened between him and Sloane the night before. Eventually, he'd make it right, but he needed to remember to keep things professional until then.

Something that was obviously easier said than done when all he wanted to do was pull Sloane into his arms and keep her there. Thankfully, she didn't need, nor want, his comfort. She wanted justice, and she wanted revenge. And he wanted all of that for her. He just wished he'd been able to talk his boss into letting him tell Sloane about the notes sooner. Maybe then they would've been closer to catching the guy. Or better yet, their unsub, or unknown subject, would be behind bars where they belonged, and Sloane wouldn't be standing in her front yard mourning her friend and the life she'd built in Hope's End.

Even though it wasn't reasonable, Cade felt responsible for everything that happened, and he had a feeling there was a part of Sloane that blamed him too. Logically, she'd understand he was only doing his job, but emotionally, he was the asshole that got her friend killed. Cade wasn't sure there was enough groveling in the world to fix the damage his involvement in Richard's death had done to their burgeoning relationship...or whatever it was. All he knew was he would do everything he could to fix things.

"Here comes Reid. Does that mean we can go now?" Sloane asked, her gaze directed over his shoulder.

Cade turned to look behind him and found Reid Morgan and another agent approaching them. They were joined by one of the responding deputies. All three had somber looks on their faces, and despite their history together, Reid seemed to be looking around at everyone and everything except for Sloane. The man needed to own up to his own role in the way things went down, but Cade wasn't sure that would ever happen.

Agent Reid Morgan liked to throw the blame around as long as none of it ever stuck to him. Throwing Cade under the bus the night before was what started the mess they were in. Any tiny modicum of respect he had for the man was thrown out the window when he showed up at Cade's apartment in the middle of the night and proceeded to blow everything up. Sure, he didn't know when he got there that Sloane was in the bedroom, but no amount of telling Reid to get lost had worked.

Cade knew he should have tried harder to tell Sloane about his case sooner. He should've insisted when she showed up at his apartment, but he could tell talking was the last thing she wanted to do. Waiting until the morning to tell her about the notes would have made things easier. But Reid had to rush in like he wasn't complicit in the entire thing. He pointed fingers like a kid tattling on his sibling, which made everything worse.

"We're ready to go when you are, Cade," Reid announced as he and the other two men approached. "We've got a group of agents covering the ground to the right of the driveway, moving south, and another group moving to the east. We'll head north toward Richard's cabin. We'll have to have one of the groups double back and check the area west of the cabin, but since there are fewer woods through there, we figured that area could wait."

Sloane started to speak, but before anything could leave her mouth, Reid continued.

"I've alerted everyone to keep a lookout for Apollo. Each group is equipped with a radio to stay in contact if necessary. We don't know if our guy is still out there somewhere, so we should try to keep our communications to a minimum. No need to give him any more help to figure out where we are."

"I want to know right away if someone finds him, Reid. To hell with the unsub. He's probably long gone by now anyway. I don't think he's stupid enough to hang out in the woods crawling with cops and the FBI. He wants to face off with me at some point. He wouldn't want to get caught spying."

Reid let out a heavy sigh of exasperation worse than that of a toddler. "Fine. I'll spread the word. If anyone finds the dog, they'll come straight back here to you."

"I'm not staying here."

"Yes, you are."

"Fuck you, Reid. I'm not staying here. I'm going to Richard's cabin. With or without your permission," Sloane said through clenched teeth.

Her face was red with anger, her eyes though still puffy from crying, were narrowed at her ex. If looks could kill, Cade was fairly certain Reid would be a dead man.

"Morgan, that's not what we discussed. She's coming with us. She knows the way better than anyone, and she'll know if something at Briggs's cabin doesn't look right."

Cade tried his best to sound neutral, like the voice of reason, but it was harder than he thought it would be. Honestly, he wanted to shake the man in front of him for trying to change their plans. They both knew what Sloane was capable of. They also both knew she'd do whatever she wanted to and that the only way to stop her was to shove her in the back of a patrol car so she couldn't get out. The hell they would have to pay if they pulled that wasn't worth the hassle. They needed her on their side. And they needed her out in the woods.

"She's unarmed, and it's not safe."

"That's the most bullshit excuse I've ever heard, Reid. Just because I can't get at my gun right now doesn't mean I can't take care of myself. Plus, I'll be with you and Cade and a bunch of other people with guns. How much safer can I get?" Sloane asked. "Stop being an asshole, and let's get this show on the road. All of this shit you're pulling right now is wasting precious time, and that's time Apollo might not have."

Holding back a smile, Cade reached out to grab the radio from Reid's hand. The other man didn't try to fight him for it, which was surprising. Then again, being told off by a civilian in front of the local cops and other agents was probably enough embarrassment for the moment. He didn't need Cade to pull rank in front of them too.

"Alright, everyone, let's head out," Cade called out to the people gathered around them.

He waited for the other two groups to move out before he turned to Sloane and motioned for her to lead the way. She truly was the best asset they had at the moment. Not only did they need to be on the lookout for the killer and any evidence he left behind, but they needed to find Apollo and the rest of Richard's body. Odds were, they'd find Richard in his cabin, but that wasn't a guarantee, and if they didn't, she'd know best where to look next.

Sloane moved forward but didn't walk too far ahead of him. She seemed to slow up so they could walk side by side, which eased some of the tension in Cade's shoulders. He needed to be able to focus on their surroundings, a feat that would be far too difficult if she was in his line of sight. Plus, with her at his side, protecting her would be a lot easier.

Too late, he realized he should've insisted they find Sloane a bullet-proof vest before they headed out. Not that he expected their unsub to take her out from afar or anything. It was pretty obvious a confrontation with her was the ultimate goal. Everything he'd done so far was to call her out, so she'd leave the sanctuary her cabin provided.

Unfortunately, it worked.

Cade knew Sloane's life on Hope's End was over the second she found what the killer had left behind for her. She'd always see the box on her porch, her friend's bloody head inside. She'd always know this was the place a psycho killer had dropped the gauntlet, challenging her to face him.

The fact that someone inside the FBI was the reason her identity was discovered, the reason the unsub was able to find her, pissed him off. She should've been safe with them looking out for her. It was the second time the FBI had done Sloane Matthews wrong. Now they owed her, and he hoped he'd be the one to pay up.

Cade didn't plan on leaving Sloane's side until they caught whoever was after her. Then he planned on sticking by her until they caught her mom. It didn't matter that she would argue that she could take care of herself, and it didn't matter that he knew she was more than capable of doing so. The FBI owed her, and he owed her. Sloane deserved more than the circumstances she'd been dealt, both as a child and now as an adult.

And Cade planned on making sure Sloane got everything she deserved. Even if she ended up not wanting anything to do with him when all was said and done.

CHAPTER FOUR

"Where have you been?"

Despite knowing she couldn't see him, he fought back the urge to roll his eyes at the tone of her question. She hadn't even said a greeting when he answered the phone, just immediately jumped down his throat like he didn't have better things to do than listen to her. He shouldn't have even answered the phone in the first place. Avoiding her calls had gotten easier the longer he did it. By swiping his thumb over the answer icon, he'd thrown away a week's worth of progress.

"I told you I had a work trip."

The lie slid off of his tongue effortlessly. It should. It had been his go-to for months, but for some reason, she no longer seemed to be buying it.

"I know you're lying. You've never been gone this long. Where are you really?"

The way she was speaking to him was beginning to piss him off. He wasn't a child she needed to keep tabs on. And he sure in the hell didn't need her to scold him for disobeying her. He would do what he wanted, whenever he wanted. If she didn't like it, too fucking bad.

He had no doubt she'd probably checked on him while he was gone. Maybe she even talked to his boss and found out he'd taken a leave of absence from his mind-numbing day job. He needed time to focus on what mattered, and that definitely wasn't peddling pills to doctors all over the country. Sure, he made great money doing it, and it allowed him to travel unchecked from one corner of the US to the other, but it was a waste of his time and his talents.

"If you must know, I took some much-needed time off of work, though I feel like I already told you this last month."

"Don't get smart with me. You know very well you didn't tell me shit, and we both know why. Are you in Seattle?" she asked, the words clipped like she was biting back more than anger. "I told you not to go there. I told you to leave her alone."

He laughed. "And I told you I'm not a little boy. You don't get to tell me what to do."

The sound of her teeth grinding together made its way through the phone line, making him wish he could see her face. She didn't like to be talked back to, nor did she like to be dismissed. Grace Baldwin was an alpha through and through, and while other men and women may defer to her, that wasn't something he'd ever do.

He was not her dog to heel.

Someday, she'd finally realize that. Then she would be the one deferring to him just as it should be.

"I told you she was not your concern."

"And I told you I wanted to see her because I wanted to play a game with her. I really think she's going to enjoy playing with me."

"What did you do?" she asked through clenched teeth.

"Don't worry. I didn't hurt your precious Isabelle. I just left behind a couple of things for her to find. For now, anyway."

She didn't say anything for a long while, her breathing the only sound coming through the phone. Tired of waiting for her to lecture him, he pressed the speakerphone button, then set the phone in the console next to him. He had a plan he needed to get to, and sitting in his warm car waiting for her to continue spouting off bullshit, was messing with his schedule.

He loved Grace, but he didn't worship her the way everyone else seemed to. She couldn't manipulate him into giving her whatever she asked for. Maybe it was because he still held onto a bit of the pain and hatred that came from being abandoned. Or perhaps it was because he wasn't interested in what she usually gave out in return for obedience.

No matter what, he wasn't backing down. There was nothing she could say to get him to change his mind and nothing she could do to get him to leave Sloane or Isabelle alone. It was so damn confusing what he was supposed to call the bitch. But it didn't really matter. His plan was already set into motion, and even if it wasn't, he wanted to fuck with the stupid bitch more than he wanted to obey Grace.

"You don't know what you're doing messing with her."

He laughed again. "Oh, I think I do. I've seen her in action. I'm not sure you know who she really is. Your darling Isabelle will be easy to take down."

"Then why are you even bothering with her? Don't you want a more formidable foe?"

Smiling, he resisted the impulse to tell her who his real foe was. By going after Sloane/Isabelle, he was taking them both on, and he knew it. Grace needed to be knocked down a peg or two, so she realized which of them was truly in charge. She had her time.

Now it was his turn.

He would prove to her that he would continue the DiSanto legacy his way. She could tag along if she wanted, but he wouldn't let her stand in the way of what he wanted. And the first matter of business in his rule was getting rid of Sloane.

Then maybe, if she didn't fall in line, he'd take care of Grace, too.

CHAPTER FIVE

She'd walked through the woods around her cabin more times than she could count and had never been on edge. Even in the dead of night, with no light shining through the trees, she'd always felt safe and secure.

That feeling was long gone, ripped away from her like her friend was.

It would never be the same. The woods. Her cabin. Her life.

Sloane had seen a lot in her nearly 37 years. Death and destruction. Blood and betrayal. Her parents were two of the most prolific serial killers in the United States. She had a career in the FBI, where she hunted down bad guys of all shapes and sizes, con artists, terrorists, serial killers, and child rapists. There wasn't a lot that fazed her after all of these years.

Until now.

Maybe she'd been fooling herself all this time, thinking she could run from her past. For decades, her worst nightmare had been coming face-to-face with her mother after she supposedly died because of Sloane. Now it seemed her nightmare was coming true, and not only was she going to have to face her mom, but another person was also in play. A stranger, a wild card, someone Sloane was going to have to figure out before it was too late.

The fact that she felt like she was on the first chapter of a book that everyone else had nearly finished didn't give her much hope that she would make it through the situation unharmed. And that was how she felt before she found the present on her porch. Now, she felt like she was slogging through quicksand, trying to find something to hold on to before she sunk to the bottom.

After everything that happened, Sloane wasn't sure if she wanted Cade to be her anchor. As she walked next to him through the woods, she realized it didn't matter what she wanted. Cade's role had already been decided. The only time she didn't feel like her world was completely falling apart was when he was so close to her they were nearly touching or when he reached out toward her, letting his pinky brush against her. The little gestures let her know he was there for her, even though he was still commanding a team searching the woods. Having him by her side gave her the little dose of security she needed to focus on the task at hand.

It would've been easy to start falling apart the closer they got to Richard's cabin. Every step they took brought them closer to the rest of his body, or at least where the soul of the man she loved like a father, hopefully, rested. At this point, thinking about Richard just made her angry because she knew without a doubt her friend was dead. On the other hand, fear and sadness filled her whenever she thought about Apollo since she had no idea where he was or what happened to him. The pain in her chest worsened as they got closer to their endpoint, yet still hadn't seen a single sign of Apollo. If he was dead, she hoped he'd gone quickly and had taken a piece of his killer with him.

Same with Richard.

She hoped he fought back as long as he could, but that in the end, his death was swift and relatively painless. Though, she wasn't going to hold her breath. Anyone who took the time to sever a head from a body wasn't going to be nice about it. Hell, the person was likely a disciple of Rosalie DiSanto. Torture might as well have been her middle name, and it seemed like she'd passed that fondness on to whoever killed Richard.

"How much further?" Cade leaned over and asked her, his voice barely above a whisper.

"At the rate we're walking, another ten, fifteen minutes," she told him, then looked behind them where Reid walked with one of the deputies.

Most of their team was spread out to the right and left of Sloane and Cade to cover more ground. Reid had decided he needed to stick close to her and watch her back for some reason. His hot and cold attitude was nothing new for her, but that didn't make it any easier to deal with. He was a giant pain in her ass and her head. She never knew if he would insult her or try to protect her. Hell, half the time, even when he was protecting her, he was insulting her in some fashion. His intention never really mattered in the long run.

"I wonder if anyone else has found something. Do you think he really told them to radio in if they found Apollo?" she asked Cade, though she wasn't expecting an answer.

"Honestly, I have no idea. Normally, I'd say he wouldn't risk alerting the unsub over something like a dog, but it's you, so he's not nearly as predictable. From what little I know about Reid, he likes to play by the book, and most of what I've seen proves that. When you're involved, he's either so far in the book, he's making shit up, or he's throwing caution to the wind and doing shit that endangers others. Your guess is better than mine at this point."

"Well, that's comforting," she muttered as she glanced one more time over her shoulder.

Her gaze met Reid's, and he scowled, so she flipped him off. Probably not the most mature reaction, but more often than not, the man pissed her off just by breathing, so he was lucky all he got from her was the bird. The way they reacted to each other now made people wonder how they could have ever stood each other long enough to get married. Sometimes Sloane wondered the same thing, but then she remembered how he listened to her about the conspiracy at the Richmond field office when no one else would, and about the three-week European vacation he took her on for their second wedding anniversary.

Reid Morgan hadn't always been a selfish bastard. She liked to believe that sweet man was still inside of him somewhere. Maybe after all of this was over, she'd give him a chance to tell her why he did what he did. Since she filed for divorce and fled California, he'd begged her more than once to sit down and let him explain himself. She was just too stubborn to give him what he wanted after he helped ruin her career and their marriage.

Maybe it was time to let that shit go.

Maybe it would be easy to do now that she had someone new to focus her anger on.

Exhaustion weighed down her limbs and shoulders. Her bones felt like they were made of lead. She couldn't remember another time in her life she'd been so tired. It wasn't just physical fatigue. It was emotional and mental, too. Every part of her needed to rest, but rest wasn't an option. And she had a feeling it wouldn't be for a very long time.

Not when Richard needed to be found. Not when Apollo could still be out there alive. Not while the unsub was still out there killing.

And then there was her mother. Rosalie DiSanto wouldn't be easy to find. Especially not after twenty years of staying off of everyone's radar.

They were getting close to the clearing surrounding Richard's cabin, which meant Sloane needed to start paying attention to what she was currently doing and forget about what came next. None of that mattered until the rest of her friend was found.

Cade stopped before she could walk through the final set of trees, putting his hand on her arm. Then he put his other arm up in the air letting the rest of the searchers know to stop as well. Walking into a wide-open space with little to no cover wasn't the smartest move, but in this case, it was necessary. They'd just have to be smart about it.

The odds of the killer still being in the woods were pretty slim, but they needed to be cautious anyway. For all they knew, he had other partners besides Sloane's mom. Hell, they couldn't even be sure that the unsub was a man. Despite her gut saying otherwise, there was still a chance her mom was behind everything. There were still so many things they didn't know, and Sloane hated being in the dark.

It felt like it took forever for the rest of the team to spread out further along the perimeter. Sloane was eager to get moving, and she knew Cade could feel it. As soon as everyone was in place, he motioned for them to move forward. He kept his hand on Sloane's arm until most of the team was in the clearing, then removed it so she knew she could make her move.

The moment she cleared the tree line, she felt it. A wrongness filled the expanse between them and the cabin. The air felt different and smelled different. It made her skin crawl, while the rest of her wanted to turn and run away. Sloane wasn't sure she'd ever be able to shake the feeling.

Despite the evilness that seemed to imprint itself on the clearing, nothing seemed to be amiss at first glance. Richard's truck was parked in its usual spot, mud caking the tires, the back license plate still slightly crooked because he refused to fix it. Sloane smiled as she remembered the rant he went on the day he got pulled over and told he needed to take care of it. She wondered if the deputy who stopped him was part of one of the search teams and if he remembered the interaction with the cranky old man.

The area around the cabin was eerily quiet as they moved forward. Even the birds knew they needed to steer clear. Once she was close enough, Sloane noticed the door to Richard's cabin was slightly ajar, and drops of blood dotted the stairs. She didn't want to go into that cabin, but she had to.

Before she could run up the stairs, Cade put himself in her way. She narrowed her eyes at him but didn't try to move around him. Sloane knew he was right to stop her. Rushing into things could not only put herself in danger but the rest of the team. It also led to potentially ruining evidence. She'd never stop blaming herself if she did something stupid that kept Richard's killer from being brought to justice. It was bad enough she got the man murdered.

Sloane waited for Cade to tell them what the plan was. Reid was so close behind her she could feel his breath on her neck. As annoying as it was, it was also oddly comforting to be surrounded by two people who not only wanted to keep her safe but also wanted to catch the bad guy as badly as she did.

"I'm going in first. Sloane, I'd tell you to stay out here until we clear the place, but I know you won't listen. Stay glued to me. Where I go, you go. Morgan, you're our backup. We all need to be careful and alert. We don't know what the unsub left behind, if anything."

"Got it," Sloane and Reid said at the same time.

"How many rooms are in the cabin? Is there anywhere less obvious than a closet to hide?"

Sloane closed her eyes and tried to picture the inside of Richard's home. It was pretty similar to hers, but when Richard built it, he added extra storage space to hold the items he brought back from his time in the Army.

"It's got an open concept kitchen and living room, but it's not a very big space. There's only one bedroom with a tiny closet and a single bathroom. Richard did add in a storage closet of sorts at the end of the hallway. It looks like a cupboard but actually goes deeper than that. It's kind of like an attic, but instead of being above the house, it's behind the walls. It would be a bit of a tight fit, but someone could hide in there if they needed to."

Cade nodded, then turned back toward the stairs and drew his gun out of its holster. Being careful to avoid any of the blood left behind on the steps, he moved as close to the railing as he could get, then made his way up the stairs. He moved slowly to avoid any noise, though she knew there wouldn't be any. Richard checked the stairs every other month to make sure they stayed squeak-free. It was another one of his eccentric behaviors that she'd grown to love over time.

He was quirky as hell, but she adored him. Every memory she had of him made her heart ache more, the pain nearly bringing her to her knees. Sloane hated it. Never in her life had she felt such intense sadness. None of her physical injuries could ever measure up to the agony she felt now.

The closest experience she'd ever had was when her father tried to kill her when she was thirteen. At the time, she didn't understand why her dad wanted her dead. The stab wound, the betrayal, all of it had made her wish she'd died that night. Now, she knew what she felt then was barely the tip of the iceberg of the pain she could handle.

As they ascended the stairs, she could barely hear anything over the thundering of her heart, which was why she was confused when she started to hear what sounded like moaning coming from inside the cabin. When Cade pushed the front door open, she tried to peek around him to see where the noise was coming from, but he blocked her view of the floor.

"Sloane..." Cade said her name slowly and quietly, sending a chill down her spine. "I'm going to open the door wide enough for you to stand next to me, but you can't go into the cabin, and you need to stay as quiet as you can, no matter what. You got that?"

She nodded, then realized doing so was stupid since Cade couldn't see her. "Yeah, I got it."

The second the words were out of her mouth, her head started to spin.

What the hell could be in the cabin that would make Cade call an audible? Especially when there was still a chance, small though it was, that the killer was inside.

Then it hit her.

There was only one thing that could stop Cade in his tracks. And only one reason he'd open the door so she could see inside, but not allow her to enter. Her dog was in there, and Apollo was alive.

CHAPTER SIX

When he pushed the door to Richard Briggs's cabin open, Cade expected to find a gruesome scene. Given the open concept, he figured the man's decapitated body would be the first thing he'd see as soon as walked in. He hadn't expected to find a very angry, potentially injured German Shepherd covered in blood and growling at him. Apollo's muzzle was cleaner than the rest of him, but his very sharp teeth held remnants of blood. Whether it was his or Richard's, there was no way to tell until they got it tested.

"Oh god," Sloane whispered as she stepped out from behind him and to his right.

Her dog's gaze moved from him to Sloane, to Richard's body, then back to Sloane. He let out a sad bark that sounded a bit like a yelp, then laid his head down on the torso of his friend. A sob escaped Sloane, and it was all he could do to stop himself from putting his arm around her so he could offer her some comfort. They needed to hurry up and clear the cabin so she could check on her dog.

"I need you to keep him calm while I clear the rest of the cabin, okay? Morgan, keep an eye on her."

Sloane turned to look at her ex. "You will not hurt my dog."

"I'll do whatever I need to in order to keep you safe."

"You. Will. Not. Hurt. My. Dog," she repeated, punctuating each word.

"Sloane..."

She turned her narrowed gaze to Cade. "Look, Apollo won't hurt me, and he won't hurt either of you as long as you stay away from him, and you don't lay a hand on me. He's only trying to protect Richard. Just leave him be. Please."

The last thing he wanted to do was hurt an animal, and he was pretty sure Reid felt the same. But then again, neither of them wanted anything to happen to Sloane either. They'd have to trust that she was safe with Apollo despite everything the poor dog had recently been through.

Cade nodded. "Let's go."

He moved in slowly, going left while Sloane walked straight into the cabin toward her dog. Reid moved right, his eyes scanning the room. Cade waited a moment, watching as Sloane dropped to her knees a couple of feet away from her dog and her friend's body. He knew the situation had to be impossible for her, but she was holding it together better than he probably would have if the situation had been reversed.

While she whispered to the dog, Cade continued into the cabin. He cleared the bedroom and the closet first, then the tiny bathroom. The home was well lived in and definitely a bachelor pad. It was precisely the kind of place Cade could see himself retiring to someday.

Eyeing the cupboard at the end of the hallway, Cade braced himself before he threw open the door. When he discovered the storage space was empty, he let out a sigh of relief, then pulled the radio out of his pocket.

"This is Agent Cade at the decedent's home. This is the primary crime scene. The body is here as well as the dog. Send the crime scene techs over as soon as they're free. In the meantime, we'll try to coax the dog out. We don't know yet if he's injured or not. Is there anyone on site that's good with animals? We're going to need to process him as well."

"This is Agent Daly. I'll see what I can find. We're nearly done here, so we'll be over soon."

As soon as he had things moving along, Cade turned back toward the cabin's living area. He knew getting Sloane to leave wasn't going to happen, not until she had the okay to take Apollo with her. While they waited for the techs to arrive, he watched her talk to her dog. Every once in a while, she'd scoot closer, but not too close, always careful not to compromise any evidence left behind. Apollo whined back at her, whether out of pain or sadness Cade couldn't tell, but he really hoped it was the latter.

When it was finally time to transport Apollo to a local vet, Sloane went with him. There was nothing anyone could do to stop her. Cade sent Reid with her so she wouldn't be alone, even though it meant he had to take charge of both scenes and nearly thirty agents and deputies by himself.

It took nearly four hours for them to finish up both cabins and the woods surrounding them. Occasionally, he'd get a text with an update about Apollo, but otherwise, it was radio silence between him and the other two, which felt both weird and unsettling. Even though he wasn't a big Reid Morgan fan, he felt like they'd become a team of sorts over the last few months. And with the little they'd found at either scene, he could have used the other man on hand to help him see what he was missing.

Cade had no idea how they were supposed to track down the unsub with absolutely nothing. Even the camera the unsub left behind on Sloane's porch would come up empty, at least that's what he assumed. Whoever they were, they'd been eluding the FBI for months, even longer if they added in the time he killed before he started leaving notes for Sloane. Their killer was intelligent, and he'd been trained by the best. They were going to have their work cut out for them with this one.

The only thing that might work in their favor was that this unsub wasn't trying to go unnoticed like Rosalie DiSanto had the last two decades. This killer wanted notoriety, and they wanted attention. Even before they started leaving taunts for Sloane, they'd marked their victims with Roman numerals so that everyone could keep track of their kills. Whoever was behind this wanted the world to know who they were, but more than that, they wanted Sloane.

After seeing the anger mixed with grief in Sloane's eyes before she left, Cade had a feeling the killer was going to wish they never started this war. He just hoped he could keep her from doing something she'd end up regretting. The last thing Sloane would ever want is to become like her parents, but Cade could see just how easy it would be for her, or anyone in her position, to cross over the line. She'd done it once before for a little girl that was a mere stranger. Killing in the name of her beloved friend would be easier to justify.

While he watched the crime scene techs pack up their tools and the little bit of evidence they were able to collect, a yawn broke free before he could suppress it. He tried to cover his mouth with his hand, but it didn't make a difference; a second one followed not long after. It had been a long damn day.

After getting less than an hour of sleep, being woken up by Reid a little after three in the morning had set Cade up for a sleep-deprived day. Sloane finding a severed head on her porch was just icing on the sleep-deprivation cake. And it seemed like there was no end in sight. Would he end up sleeping somewhere in Washington for the night, or would he find himself back in California before the day changed over? He honestly had no idea.

"Agent Cade, we're all set here. Not sure how quickly we can get results for you, but we'll try to put a rush on what we've got. Especially the camera."

When Agent Daly arrived on the scene, Cade found her no-nonsense approach to her job refreshing. She was in charge of the entire ERT team but also had no problem getting right into the muck with the rest of them. Nothing seemed to faze her, which was the kind of person they needed on their team when they were chasing a killer who was already five steps ahead of them.

"Thank you. Keep Agent Morgan and me up-to-date with whatever you get. I won't hold my breath that he left anything useful behind, but stranger things have happened."

Daly and her team began filling their vehicles with boxes while Cade coordinated patrol efforts with the Sheriff's department. On the off chance the unsub revisited the scene, they needed to keep an eye on both cabins, at least for a day or two, until they had a better idea what he was up to.

The only thing left for him to do was figure out what their next steps were. Cade knew Sloane would want to come back and grab stuff from her cabin for her and Apollo, but after that, he had no idea where they were going to go or what they would do.

The only thing Cade knew for sure was that he planned on keeping Sloane as safe and protected as possible. It was unsettling how focused the killer was on her, which meant eventually he'd tire with the taunts and surrogate victims. He'd want to confront her in person, and Sloane would be more than happy to walk into the lion's den and give him exactly what he wanted, especially if it meant saving the people she loved.

Cade desperately hoped to keep that from happening, and there was only one way to make sure he got his way. He had to find the killer first, and he had to make sure he never had the opportunity to hurt Sloane again.

CHAPTER SEVEN

Leaving an injured Apollo at the vet proved to be one of the hardest things Sloane had ever done. The weight of the guilt she carried was nearly debilitating. Leaving him behind was what got him hurt in the first place. But she knew sitting in the waiting room, not even able to see her dog while he rested, was a waste of her time. She needed to get some rest too.

And then she needed to figure out what the hell to do next.

She didn't talk to Reid on the drive back to her cabin. Once there, she didn't speak to Cade either. She needed time to process things before she could have it out with them. They gave her some space while she packed up a few things, which surprised her. Even so, she appreciated the gesture.

As soon as she walked into her cabin, the hair on her arms stood up. The space felt wrong. Though she couldn't tell if anyone had been inside, it didn't matter. What he left for her outside was enough to ruin the cabin forever. The place made her skin crawl.

Sloane threw everything she needed and the few things she didn't want to lose into her suitcase. Anything she left behind could be sold right along with the property for all she cared. All that mattered was that she never had to step foot in the place again.

With her suitcase rolling behind her, Sloane walked toward the front door. Reid took the bag from her while Cade waited for her to shut and lock the door. Her cabin had been her happy place for a long time, and now it was tainted by evil. Anger hardened her heart as she turned to walk toward the car. She bypassed the spot the box had rested, ducked under the police tape strung across the stairs, then walked toward Cade and Reid's rental car. She didn't look back at the cabin, not even when she was in the backseat of the car, ready to be taken somewhere less vile.

"I booked us rooms at the hotel down the street from the hospital. Figured you'd want to be close to Apollo," Reid said as he glanced over his shoulder at her once the three of them were in the car.

"Thanks."

Sloane didn't have it in her to say anything more than that. She was on the verge of something, but she wasn't sure what it was. An emotional breakdown, a rage-filled tirade, a grief-induced blackout. If she got to choose, she'd take the last one. It was the better option for all of them. When they finally sat down to talk, she wanted to be calm and level-headed. She was far from either at the moment, and Sloane knew they'd accomplish nothing if she dealt with them when she was feeling the way she was.

"How's Apollo doing?" Cade asked though he was looking at Reid when he did.

She didn't know how he did it, but Cade was a hell of a lot better at reading her than her ex ever was. It both unnerved her and fascinated her. At the moment, she was just thankful that she could sit back and zone out for the trip to the hotel. It wouldn't take them long to get there, but just the thought of making small talk, even about her dog, made her unreasonably angry.

"He's a damn lucky dog," Reid answered, then decided to elaborate. "A few broken ribs, a hairline fracture along his lower jaw, and some broken teeth. Doc said he was probably kicked a few times. I don't get why the guy didn't just kill him too. I mean, if his whole thing is torturing Sloane, he'd have to be stupid not to realize her dog would be just as important, if not more so, than any human."

"Some killers, no matter how depraved, have lines even they won't cross. Maybe hurting animals is this guy's line. Not all serial killers start off torturing animals as children," Cade pointed out.

"Fuck that. I don't want to think about this asshole having some kind of moral compass."

Sloane actually agreed with Reid. While she was thankful Apollo was ultimately okay, she didn't want to believe it was because the killer spared him. Whoever the killer was had to be heartless; it was the only explanation for the things they'd done.

"Knowing that the unsub doesn't hurt dogs gives us insight into the killer's mind that we didn't have before. He..."

Reid groaned. "Can this wait until tomorrow? We need to get some rest. It's been a long damn day."

In the backseat, Sloane scoffed. Reid was one to talk about it being a long day. He was the reason everything went to shit in the first place. If he hadn't shown up at Cade's in the middle of the night, they'd all be back in San Francisco enjoying a day filled with less drama and fewer dead bodies. She and Cade would have had their conversation this morning, where he told her all about the notes. Of course, she would be mad that they'd been keeping things from her, but she liked to think she'd have reacted better if she'd been told in a less hostile way. Unfortunately, they had no way of knowing since Reid ended up forcing Cade's hand.

The rest of the drive to the hotel was blissfully quiet. Once checked in, Reid handed her the key card for her room, then handed one to Cade. Without waiting for them, she made a beeline for the elevator, then pressed the button so the door closed before the guys could get in. It wasn't a huge setback for them, but it afforded her a nice, private ride to their floor, instead of the awkwardly slow ascent she would've gotten had they joined her.

By the time Sloane heard them outside in the hallway, she was peeling the comforter off the bed and falling face-first across the queen-sized mattress. Thankfully neither of them knocked on her door. She wouldn't have answered anyway. Not when she was so close to drifting off to sleep for the first time in over sixteen hours. Nothing short of the killer coming to visit her would keep her from getting the rest she needed.

Which was why she didn't make an appearance until noon the next day. She'd slept soundly through the night, only waking a couple of times to call the vet to check on Apollo. Her fatigue had been strong enough to keep the nightmares at bay. Given what she'd seen and learned that day, Sloane had expected them to hit her hard but was more than thankful they didn't.

When she was finally ready to start the day, Sloane made her way to Cade's room. Unsure of what to expect when she came face-to-face with both men, she hesitated a second before knocking on the door. She didn't have time to pussyfoot around her feelings. Cade may have kept the situation a secret from her but at least he'd tried to tell her. Even if it was a little late in the game. Instead of sitting down and talking, she shot him down so they could have sex. Because of that, her friend was dead.

She couldn't change the past, so she had to live with it. Odds were, Richard would've been killed even if Cade had told her before they hooked up. The only thing that would've saved her friend was if Cade or Reid had told her about the unsub a hell of a lot sooner. Knowing that didn't change anything and dwelling on it only made her feel worse.

She couldn't change the past. Though, if that was one of her superpowers, she wondered how far back she'd go. Maybe to a time before her dad tried to kill her. Or to the day she took her mom's journals to the police station and turned her in. Or maybe the day her mother fell off the bridge to her supposed death.

Thinking about the what-ifs and the maybes did nothing. She needed to focus on the here and now and make sure nobody else got hurt. To do that, she needed to see the notes left for her and forget about her feelings for a while.

"Hey. I was just getting ready to check on you," Cade said as he threw the door open and stepped back so she could enter.

Sloane stared at him, their eyes meeting briefly before she looked away. The attraction was still there. It probably always would be. The feelings she had for him were there too, but she had no idea if they'd ever be the same or if they'd always be wrapped up in what she lost and the part he played in it.

"I must've needed sleep. Sorry to keep you waiting."

She wasn't surprised to find Reid sitting in the room since she figured Cade's room would act as their makeshift office until they could figure out their next steps. It didn't matter to her where they were. All she needed was a place to sit, and a copy of everything that was left for her.

"How's Apollo?"

Cade's question followed her into the room as he shut the door behind her. Instead of following her, he leaned against the door and waited for her to get comfortable. She could feel Reid's gaze on her as well, but she didn't look over at him because she didn't trust herself enough not to give him a piece of her mind. She shouldn't have been surprised by the way he acted, but she was, and that was on her. Yet, it still stung. All of it. Both his part in everything and her decision to ignore her instincts.

"He's doing as well as can be expected. They think I should be able to take him home later today, though I have no idea where that is at the moment."

"We were actually talking about that when you knocked."

It was the first thing Reid had said since she entered the room, and for some reason, it felt like a bad omen. She didn't like it when people decided things for her. Wasn't that what had gotten them into this mess in the first place? By the look on Cade's face as he moved further into the room, she knew she wasn't going to be happy about whatever came out of Reid's mouth next. She also knew that whatever he said would be mostly what he wanted and very little of what Cade thought was a good idea.

Sloane didn't need to see that written all over Cade's face to know it to be true. That's just the way things went with Reid Morgan. He always thought he knew what was best for everyone else.

"We think you should be in protective custody until we catch this guy."

And now she knew he'd lost his fucking mind.

CHAPTER EIGHT

He'd never been much of a morning person. He knew it was probably because he spent a lot of time out at night, hunting, killing, and enjoying every second of his extra-curricular activities. Sometimes, he wouldn't crawl into bed until three or even four in the morning. Getting up at seven to make it into the office by eight was a chore, especially as he got older. It was a task he was happy to give up so he could focus on his calling.

Surprisingly, he'd been excited to jump out of bed that morning. It didn't matter that he'd rolled in close to four a.m. It didn't matter that he'd expended more energy than usual, putting his plan into motion. For the first time in a long time, he had something to look forward to. The vision he'd been working toward was getting closer to becoming a reality. And it felt really damn good.

He was finally on the path he was always meant to be on. Getting rid of Sloane Matthews was the one thing standing in his way. Once he was done with her, the world would be his for the taking. He could do what he wanted when he wanted. Taking out Sloane would prove that he was a force to be reckoned with once and for all. Grace would never be able to doubt him again.

Looking at the clock on the bedside table, he realized he needed to get a move on. There was a lot he had to get done in order for everything to work out the way he planned. He stretched, allowing his back to crack and his muscles to ease, then he got out of bed and went about his morning routine.

Once he was done getting ready, he switched on the TV to check the news. He wasn't sure if it was too early for his latest victims to be found, but he had to check. If he was lucky, Sloane and the world would have his note in hand. It would take everyone else a bit to figure out the meaning behind it, but Sloane would see it right away. He didn't like her much, but he knew she was smart enough to read between the lines.

His plan only worked, though, if the FBI gave her what he'd left behind. At some point, he'd need to check in with his friend. He'd be able to tell him if the FBI had gotten wind of what he'd been up to the night before. And he needed to know if Sloane had his earlier letters and pictures yet or if the FBI was still holding back.

What he really wanted to know was if he'd broken her by killing her friend. He didn't think one act would do it, but he wasn't worried. He had a lot more up his sleeve where she was concerned.

A thrill coursed through him. That was what his entire plan was all about—breaking Sloane. Taking her down piece by piece, showing everyone what a weak, pathetic person she was. She wasn't worthy like he was. She was nothing.

He was going to enjoy the hell out of showing everyone what he could do. Grace would regret the day she told him to leave Sloane alone. Everyone who thought he was nothing would realize how wrong they were. They would realize just how stupid underestimating him had been.

He watched the news for a while longer, then turned it off and gathered his things. There was nothing on there about the couple he left behind. He knew it was because they hadn't been found yet. It was too soon, but knowing that didn't make him any less antsy. The game couldn't begin until Sloane knew about them and his latest note. Her friend and everything that came before was merely their story's prologue. The couple was chapter one, where the villain and the mystery were introduced for the first time. He wasn't quite sure just yet how the rest of the chapters would go, but he knew exactly how the story would end.

This was a delicious tale of good versus evil, after all.

Only this time...evil would prevail.

Paris Hansen

CHAPTER NINE

"No."

"Sloane."

"No."

"We can't..."

"Look," she interrupted before her ex could say anything else. "I get your reasoning. You don't even have to tell me what it is because I get it. But no. I will not hide from this guy."

"Or girl."

She rolled her eyes at Reid's interruption. "Whatever. I will not hide from this person. Guy, girl, Martian. I don't care who the fuck they are. I will not hide from them. I do agree protective custody is a good idea for Emily and Tally. And your mom and Cooper should go with them. Maybe even Greg and Nancy."

Saying her foster parent's names in conjunction with a serial killer felt weird. They'd been so far removed from the life she'd lived before she ended up in the system they never even

52

knew the truth of where she came from. They didn't even realize she'd joined the FBI. She'd wanted to keep all of that away from them.

She couldn't be sure if her mother or the unsub knew about them, though she had to assume they did. Putting them in protective custody would open their eyes to a world she never wanted them to know about. But if she didn't, and something happened to them, she'd never forgive herself. At the very least, she needed to give them the option. Whether or not they took it would be entirely up to them.

"I'll make the call," Reid said, his gaze meeting hers.

He held the look far longer than was comfortable for either of them, but she knew he needed to. It was his way of checking on her without actually asking her if she was okay. Though they hadn't been together in years, and on a good day, she wanted to cause him bodily harm, they were still connected by the love they both had for his family. She would do anything for Emily and Tally, and Reid knew that.

"We knew you'd refuse protective custody. It's not your style to sit back and hide, but we had to at least try. Instead, we're hoping you'll agree to stick with us. We know you can take care of yourself, but three is usually better than one. Plus, if we're together, we can work the case. We need you, Sloane. We all know we aren't going to get anywhere without your input."

Sloane smiled at Cade, knowing Reid would never in a million years be able to admit any of what was said. Cade didn't have the same kind of hang-ups. If he was wrong, he was wrong. If he needed help, he needed help. His ego wasn't too big to allow anyone else in.

"As long as you guys don't try to shove me in a closet when we figure out who we're looking for, then I'm in. Otherwise, I'll take the copies of the notes you promised me and be on my way."

Cade looked over at Reid, then back to Sloane. "Equal partners. We've got your back, and you've got ours. How's that sound?"

Sloane laughed. "Too good to be true."

"Fair enough. I promise, Sloane, everything we know you'll know. But I expect the agreement to go both ways. Don't go shoving us in a closet if you get a lead we don't. I know how you work. No running off to be the hero."

"Fine," Sloane said reluctantly. She fought the urge to cross her fingers as she did so.

She was not in a hurry to face down another serial killer by herself, but in this situation, she was the one he was after. If facing him alone meant saving the lives of the people she cared about, she'd do it. Cade and Reid would just have to deal with her decision.

She looked back over at Reid, who was taking notes on a pad of paper next to him then typing on his phone.

"Reid, can you arrange for Apollo to go wherever Tally and Emily go? I know they'll take care of him, and he won't let anything happen to them."

Something passed over Reid's face as he acknowledged her request. It was so quick she nearly missed it, but it was there. Appreciation, relief, a little of both, that she would ask for her dog to go with his family so he could protect them. She cared more about her best friend and her niece than she cared about herself. If she had to take a bullet, real or metaphorical, to keep them safe, she'd do it without question.

While Reid went back to typing furiously on his phone, Cade walked over to the desk and grabbed a manila envelope. He took a few steps toward her, then held the envelope out to her.

"This is everything the unsub has left behind before yesterday's incident. If you want some time alone to look at them, you can take the envelope back to your room."

Sloane thought about it for a minute. Would she like time alone with the pictures and notes? Yes. Did she need it right at that moment? No. They needed her to glean whatever information she could from the only evidence available to them. She couldn't allow herself to dwell on whatever was in the envelope. For now, she needed to leave her emotions out of it. There'd be plenty of time to go down that rabbit hole once they knew what they were going to do next.

She shook her head, taking the envelope out of his hands, then looked around the room for a place to sit. The only available surface was Cade's neatly made bed. While it felt a little weird after what happened between them less than 48 hours earlier, she didn't have any other choice. Once she was situated on the bed, she set the envelope down next to her, then closed her eyes and took a deep breath.

She could do this. She could look at what was in the envelope objectively. She would help the investigation.

She repeated the three sentences in her head like a mantra until her lungs started to burn. As she exhaled, she hoped like hell it was enough. When she felt steady enough to look at what was in the envelope, she pulled the stack out and set it on her lap.

"Do you want any background information at all while you go through those?" Cade asked.

"No. I think I know enough for now, but I might have questions."

Looking down in her lap, she read the handwritten note that had started it all.

You never should've forgotten where you came from.

As far as letters from a serial killer went, the words were relatively innocuous. If it had been left behind anywhere other than on a dead body, it likely would have been ignored. There was nothing overtly threatening about the words. Nothing that screamed the start of a deadly plan.

Combined with the picture also left behind and the murder victim, the story changed. Add in that the victim belonged to the Roman Numeral Killer and things escalated quickly.

Even though this note didn't scream danger and the picture likely wouldn't either, Sloane knew the rest of what was left behind would gradually intensify, culminating in a severed head and a promise of revenge. For what, she still didn't know, but maybe once she'd gone through everything, she'd have a better idea.

She did know that whoever they were dealing with not only enjoyed what they were doing, they took pride in it. They'd worked hard on their plan, and she knew that would show in every note and picture she flipped through. Their ultimate goal with what was left behind was psychological torment. Once she was significantly broken down, that's when they'd move in for the kill.

Knowing she needed to get a move on, Sloane flipped to the next page, discarding the face-down note onto the bed next to her. Most people would have looked at the photo and gotten emotional. Sentiment would have gotten the best of them. But Sloane wasn't like most people, and this wasn't the time to get sentimental. She scrutinized the black and white photo wondering why the unsub used it in his plans.

It was a beautiful shot and one she'd seen nearly every day for the first sixteen years of her life.

A woman and her brand-new baby. The love was obvious for both the woman in the photo and for whoever took the picture. If she didn't know any better, she would have believed that the image belonged to a picture-perfect happy family.

But she did know better. They may have been happy at one time, but the DiSantos were anything but picture perfect. They were cold-blooded killers, even while a framed version of the photograph followed them everywhere they went. It lived on top of the boxy TV in their living room when they were at home. On the road, the picture was taped to the dashboard of her father's truck or the RV, frame and all. Her parents loved the picture because of how happy her mom looked. Once upon a time, she had loved it too, but now it made Sloane feel bitter. The photo was a reminder of the lie her childhood turned out to be.

Just with this one picture, Sloane knew her mother wasn't behind the notes. No matter how mad about the past she might have been, she wouldn't use family pictures to torment Sloane. Rosalie wasn't into games. If she wanted to make Sloane pay for what she'd done, she'd do it in a more direct manner. Of course, Reid and Cade would need more than her gut to believe her, so she moved on, adding the picture and the ones of the crime scene to her discard pile so she could read the next note.

Some people would kill for a family like yours, yet you threw them all away. You're an ungrateful bitch who didn't deserve what you had.

Sloane read the note again, then a third time for good measure. Once she'd nearly committed it to memory, she flipped the page over to look at the picture it accompanied. It was another one she'd seen a lot during her childhood and one she remembered being taken. One of her favorite things growing up was getting the chance to travel across the country in her father's semi. Sometimes they didn't have time to make many stops, but other times they did. Whether they could check out the sights along the way or just watched the world pass by through the window, it didn't matter much to her. She loved every second of it.

The picture she held in her hands was from one of the times they got to stop and check out one of the attractions. In High Point, North Carolina, the World's Largest Chest of Drawers stood towering over everyone, and Sloane had been so excited to get her picture taken in front of it with her dad. Before her mom could take the picture, another tourist had offered to take one of the family for them, which had made her day. The smile on her face as she sat atop her father's shoulders while holding her mother's hand was nearly blinding.

The giant chest behind them filled the entire background, but it was an afterthought whenever they looked at the picture. All they ever noticed was the happiness on their faces.

Seeing the picture after all these years was unsettling. Not because of the image's content, but because she thought it had been lost years ago. So many of their belongings back then had either been ruined or collected as evidence by the FBI. Sloane never knew what happened to the rest of it, and she'd never cared to know.

Apparently, her mother did, though, and whoever her mom's new partner was.

It still hadn't quite sunk in that her mom was actually alive. It was a nightmare come true that Sloane was far more surprised about than she expected. Deep down, she'd always suspected she was alive, but fears like that rarely turned into reality.

Not wanting to dwell on it too much, she flipped to the next note. She had too many more to go through to get lost in thought with each one.

She looks so sweet and innocent. No one could have known she'd betray the people that loved her without a second thought.

The picture was of her at the age of six, a giant gap-toothed smile on her face. Her long dark hair was in two carefully crafted braids, a pink dress fluttering around her legs. It was a moment caught in time long before she learned who and what her parents really were. Of course she looked sweet and innocent. She was clueless about what was happening around her and she had loved her parents more than anything.

There was a tiny part of her that still did, even after everything they'd done. She couldn't help it. They were her parents, and they were a piece of her, whether she wanted them to be or not.

For years, Sloane spent hours talking to a therapist about that very subject both before and after joining the FBI. They assured her it was normal, but she always felt anything but, which was why she never admitted her feelings to anyone other than her therapist. Not Reid, not Emily, and even though she'd told him other things she'd never admitted out loud, she doubted she'd say anything to Cade about her feelings.

Sloane rubbed at her chest to dull the ache that had taken residence there. She hated that the pictures brought up so many feelings and memories. She'd spent so much time putting it all in a box and shoving it so deep inside of her she'd never see it again. For nearly two thirds of her life, she'd worked on forgetting where she came from and how it affected her. Now it was all twisted up inside of her, trying to find cracks it could leak through.

But none of it mattered. Her feelings wouldn't change how she looked at this case. She would find her mom's new friend, and she would find her mom. And then she would have a hand in putting them both away.

"My mom isn't behind the notes."

"How do you know?" Reid asked, not bothering to try to hide the skepticism in his voice.

"If she wanted to confront me, she would've done it by now. Fucking with people isn't her thing, and she doesn't play games."

"Maybe she changed her tune. She's had twenty years to think about this and plan it out. Provoking you with pictures of your past and notes would allow her to prolong whatever torture she hopes to inflict on you and others."

Sloane shook her head as she looked over at Reid. "She wouldn't use pictures of our past against me. If she did decide to play with me, she'd have used things that she knew would hit home. Pictures from my childhood wouldn't do that. No matter how happy we seemed, and maybe we were, she knows how I feel about all of it. I told her right before I turned her in. I told her I hated her for lying to me."

She glanced over at Cade, who stayed quiet, then back at Reid, who looked like he wanted to say more but was smart enough not to. With a renewed focus, she flipped through the rest of the notes and pictures. The letters were of no consequence, just more ramblings about how she'd betrayed her family and was the rotten piece of the DiSanto family tree. Whoever the unsub was, they had it bad for her family, which gave them a pretty open field to start looking for suspects.

The next few pictures were more of the same. The family in front of the RV when she was nine, her and Rosalie at her father's funeral when she was thirteen, a picture of her mother smiling brightly at the camera, taken with the new camera Sloane had gotten for her sixteenth birthday. Three shots chosen to distract her with her feelings.

They might have done the trick, too, if she hadn't warned herself to stay numb before she'd started going through them. She couldn't give the unsub what he wanted. Her focus could not wane while she fell back into distraught daughter mode. Especially not while she still had three pictures left, ones she knew proved to Cade and Reid that she wasn't involved in what the unsub was leaving behind. How anyone could have thought that after reading the notes, she didn't know, and she didn't care. They were on the same page now, and that's what mattered.

She stared at the picture of her and Apollo on her cabin steps and felt the ache in her chest grow. This was where the unsub would hurt her most. He'd hit the mark by invading her space and privacy—by ripping her sanctuary and her friend away from her so brutally.

The following picture was of her and Cade at the coffee shop in San Anselmo. Knowing the unsub had been that close to her, and she hadn't felt like she was being watched, was downright scary. He could have taken her out whenever he'd wanted, yet hadn't. He could have confronted her whenever he'd wished to, yet she still didn't even know what he looked like or if he was even a he.

Sloane knew the last note and picture were the reason the FBI finally decided she needed to be told about what was happening. Until they were left behind, Tom Anderson, the asshole overseeing the case, had deemed her the bad guy. She wouldn't be surprised if he still thought that even though she clearly wasn't.

The note was short and simple, two words that were both innocuous and threatening at the same time.

It's Time.

Paired with the picture of her with Emily and Tally, the words took on a more sinister meaning. The unsub intended them as a threat, a promise, and he certainly delivered. She just didn't know why he'd gone back to Seattle to take out Richard when they were both in California. How could he know she'd go home when she did?

He was playing a game she didn't quite understand, which made him even more dangerous than she initially thought.

Even knowing that, she wasn't going to run and hide.

The stupid fool had no idea what he'd done. If he planned on taking her down, he was going down with her. He might have fired the first shot, but he wouldn't get the last.

That pleasure would be all hers.

CHAPTER TEN

Watching Sloane silently process the pictures and the notes was torture for Cade. He couldn't do anything to comfort her or help her, and he couldn't do anything to take away the torment they were causing her. Instead of standing around, he paced from one end of the room to the other, not caring if it annoyed her or Reid, who was still busy arranging protection for his family. He felt helpless, but at least while he was moving, he was doing something. Each time he was near Sloane, he could see how hard it was for her to look through the pictures. The pain she was feeling was written on her face. Then again, so was the anger.

He knew she wouldn't let go of that anger any time soon, and he was pretty sure she'd use it to fuel her movements going forward. Whoever was behind Richard's death and the threats lobbed at her family was going to regret ever messing with Sloane Matthews. What Cade didn't know was how things would go down. Who else would end up losing their lives in the process?

Who else would get caught in the crossfire?

He would never have thought things would work out this way. He knew he wasn't to blame for what happened to Richard Briggs, but that didn't stop the guilt. If he'd had any inkling that the unsub would go after someone Sloane loved, he would've said to hell with the rules and to hell with the FBI. He would have told Sloane everything, even if it meant he lost his job.

Now he understood why Sloane still held onto the guilt about what her parents did even after all these years. While he didn't plunge the knife into Richard's chest, he might as well have. There wasn't anyone who could absolve Cade of what he was feeling except maybe Sloane, though he'd never let her. His job was to make sure she didn't add Richard's death to the baggage she was already carrying. He'd carry all of it for the both of them.

If he knew anything about Sloane after nearly two months, it was that she would blame herself for everything that was happening. In her eyes, if he'd never met her, then Lt. Colonel Richard Briggs would still be alive. The man had fought in multiple wars for his country only to die at the hands of a madman, or woman, in his own home. It really fucking sucked.

But the only ones to blame for his death were the person who killed him, Rosalie DiSanto, and the FBI.

What made matters worse was that more bodies would drop before all was said and done. All because Tom Anderson hated Sloane so much he couldn't see what was happening right in front of him. All Cade, Sloane, and Reid could do now was play catch up and hope they could figure out who was behind it all before it was too late.

Cade was exhausted just thinking about what lay before them. They most definitely had their work cut out for them. Even with Sloane's insight, they wouldn't have much to go on. Their unsub was a ghost, and so was his mentor. Neither of them had left anything worthwhile behind, and he didn't see that changing any time soon.

Sloane sighed. "I don't get it. What's this guy's endgame? What is the point of all of this?"

The sound of Sloane's voice broke through his depressing thoughts, bringing his attention back to her. The pictures and notes were back in the envelope, her hands resting in her lap. She looked tired and worried and maybe even a little defeated. It made everything he was feeling worse. He could only do so much to help her shoulder the burden of what was coming, even though he'd take it all if he could.

"Nobody's been able to figure him out," Reid admitted. "Half of the agents working on this still think it's you behind it. The other half think it's a copycat of your parents. Then there's the tiny group that believes it's someone your mom took under her wing."

Sloane smiled at Reid and shook her head. "Let me guess. This tiny group you speak of is just the two of you, right?"

"Well, us and Jennings. But she's much smarter than the rest of the assholes, so that's not a huge surprise."

"She'll make one hell of a director someday," Sloane mused. "I'm glad she's on my side."

"We are too. She's doing everything she can to help us. Now that she's got the director's attention, we're hoping she'll be able to get Anderson off of our case. The man has a very strong distaste for you," Cade told her, though he probably didn't need to.

"No need to sugar coat it. He hates my guts, and if it helps any, the feeling's mutual. He nearly got me killed when I first started with the FBI, and I've never forgotten that."

"Me neither," Reid grumbled, his hands curled into fists on his thighs. "The guy is a total prick who never should've been given the supervisory position on this case in the first place. He was never going to play fair. He doesn't give a fuck about finding the person really behind this. He just wants to pin everything on Sloane, and he almost made it happen."

"So, what do we do now?" Sloane asked, her uncertainty clear as day.

"We've always been three steps behind this guy, and it's really fucking frustrating," Reid said as he pinched the bridge of his nose. "I know you said you don't think your mom's involved, but..."

"I didn't say that," Sloane interrupted him. "I said she's not the one behind the notes or even Richard's death. She's one hundred percent involved, though. I have no doubt she taught the bastard everything he knows. Whether they're still traveling together or not, they were at one time. She's his mentor."

"How does knowing that help us?" Cade asked.

He didn't want Sloane to get too wrapped up in her mother's involvement if it did nothing to help figure out who they were chasing. Even if finding out her long-dead mother was actually alive was one of Sloane's worst nightmares, Rosalie DiSanto was the least of their worries at the moment.

They needed to focus on the person out there actively killing, not ghosts from the past.

Sloane stood and stalked her way to the desk where Reid sat. She threw the envelope down on the table with enough force that the contents spilled out over the notepad Reid had been using earlier. The smirk on her face sent a chill down Cade's spine.

"Once upon a time, she taught me a thing or two as well. It's about time I used that knowledge for something," she said before turning to look at Cade. "Can we get access to all of the case files for the murders you think belong to her and this guy? I'd also like to see her file from before."

"You've gone over that file several times already. Why do you need to look at it again? Shouldn't you have it memorized by now?" Reid asked, concern filling his voice, despite his attempt at sarcasm. "What good could looking at it again do?"

"Over the years, I've worked hard at compartmentalizing all of the shit I saw and heard as a kid. It's time I let it all out. I need to in order to catch my mom. To make that happen, I need to relive what my parents did, and I need to go back to the beginning."

"I don't think..." Reid started but was once again interrupted by Sloane.

"I know, but I have to."

Cade felt like he should say something, but he didn't know which side to take. He had no doubt reliving her past was a terrible idea, but he also knew it wasn't his or Reid's decision. Sloane needed to do what she needed to do, and nobody was going to get in her way. With or without them, she'd make it happen.

"I can get you what you want," Cade said, even though he knew Reid would be pissed. "Let's focus on this guy first. Then we can worry about Rosalie."

Whether Cade agreed or not, it didn't matter. It was better to have Reid be pissed at him than having Sloane be even angrier at the both of them than she already was. If anything, they needed to make sure they kept her happy. If they didn't, if they kept things from her again, she'd go rogue, and that was the last thing they needed.

Cade knew the other man would eventually see reason no matter how stubborn he tried to be. Not that it mattered what Reid wanted. Until they found whoever was after her, Cade would do whatever he could to help her, even if it cost him his job. It was the right thing to do, and he owed her for not doing it sooner.

No matter what, Cade wouldn't let her down again.

CHAPTER

ELEVEN

She'd probably wondered about her mother's fate a million times over the last twenty years. No matter how hard she tried to fight it, her thoughts shifted to her mother at least once a day. It might have been her greatest fear to learn her mother was alive after all this time, but deep down, she knew the truth. It explained why she still dreamed about her even though she should've faded into the memories of the past. It's why she started writing crime thrillers after her FBI career fizzled out. Even though her parents were gone and her previous life was over, she couldn't let it go.

She could try to deny it all she wanted but there was still a small part of her that wanted to prove herself to her mother.

Sloane would never be a killer like her parents, the child murderer she took out at the end of her career notwithstanding. That didn't mean that the little girl who desperately wanted to be enough wasn't still alive deep inside her. She'd always wanted to be loved enough for her mother to give it all up. She wanted to be more important than whatever drove her need to kill innocent human beings. Why was it so easy for Rosalie to throw away her flesh and blood for the literal flesh and blood of others?

She hated that she genuinely wasn't over it after all this time. She'd moved on, but the disappointment and heartbreak were still there, buried down deep with the things she'd seen but never really knew what they meant until it was too late.

The melancholy feeling that shrouded her like a blanket was the reason Reid didn't want her looking at her mom's file again. But the despair, anger, and disgust were the very things that were going to keep Sloane going until they got what they were after, which was Rosalie and her new partner behind bars finally paying for everything they'd done.

It didn't matter what it took, Sloane vowed to herself that she'd take them down or die trying. No matter what, she was done with the games and waiting for them to pounce. It had to end. And it had to end now.

She just had no idea how the hell they were going to take them down. The FBI hadn't been able to figure out who Rosalie's friend was or who Rosalie was for that matter, and they had a few months' head start on her. Going back to the beginning seemed like the best chance they had, but she had her doubts it would work. Rosalie wouldn't be that easy to crack.

"Do you have it in you to meet with Jennings for a minute? She'd like us to check-in," Cade said, interrupting her thoughts.

While Cade started working on what she asked for and Reid went back to working on arrangements for his family, Sloane laid down across the end of Cade's bed, letting her thoughts wander. She'd wanted to head back to her room to decompress after the heaviness of the pictures, but they couldn't get any work done if she was in another room. And they had a lot of work that needed to be done, including meeting with Jennings.

"Not that I have a choice, but sure. Maybe she can help expedite the things I need."

Cade only nodded, then grabbed the laptop Sloane hadn't even noticed on the desk next to Reid. As he joined her on the bed, she sat up, wishing at the last second that she could have checked herself out in the mirror before the call. Within seconds Diane Jennings's face filled the screen. Although she still gave off that no-nonsense demeanor that Sloane appreciated, she could see the concern and empathy in her gaze.

"I'm sorry about your friend and your dog, Ms. Matthews. I hope you know this isn't the outcome any of us expected or wanted. If it weren't for that asshole Anderson, we would've told you what was happening weeks ago. Still, we never expected this person would double back and attack your loved ones in Washington."

Sloane nodded. "Thank you, Agent Jennings. I appreciate your honesty, and please know I understand what you were dealing with. And I get it. I've looked over what you have, and I wouldn't have seen it either. Why follow me to San Francisco, get close to Tally and Emily and even Cade, then go all the way back to Hope's End? It doesn't make any sense."

"At this point, I think you can go ahead and call me Diane, and I'll forgo the Ms. Matthews crap if that's okay with you. I have a feeling we're going to lean on each other quite heavily before all is said and done. You have to know at the moment we're on our own. I'm still trying to get the director on our side, but Anderson was already a step ahead of us. Like he knew something was going to happen before it did."

Reid grumbled a few choice swear words under his breath, then came around to Sloane's other side so Diane could see him. Sloane could feel the anger radiating off of him. Hell, she could feel it coming from both of the men in the room, and it gave her hope that they were really and truly on her side and not just telling her what she wanted to hear.

"Do you think that's possible?" Reid asked, then looked across her at Cade. "Could that dickhead be in on it? Is that why he was so hellbent on pinning things on Sloane? Sorry, ma'am."

Diane let out a slight chuckle. "It's okay, Reid. I have thought and said out loud worse things about the man in the last few days. I don't know if he's somehow involved or, at the very least, hindering the investigation in some way, but I wouldn't put it past him. Tom Anderson hates Sloane, and he isn't afraid to admit it. There are some things about what's going on that I can't explain, and when it comes down to it, he's the common denominator."

"That son of a bitch," Reid growled. "How the fuck?"

"We don't know what he's done at this point, and until we can prove he's broken the law, he's untouchable. But that's not what you guys need to focus on right now. Leave him to me. In the meantime, tell me what you need. Sloane, did you get anything from the pictures and the notes that maybe we didn't see?"

While Cade went over Sloane's thoughts about the evidence and what she needed moving forward, Sloane tried to grasp the bomb that was just dropped. The idea that someone so high up in the FBI could be a part of what was happening was baffling to her. She didn't understand why Anderson was suddenly willing to risk his career after holding on to his anger and desire for revenge for over a decade. Was whatever he gained by framing her for murder worth everything he'd worked for? She had no idea.

Did it all just go back to him wanting to prove he was right about her? Could it be that simple? It scared her to think that someone with the kind of clearance Tom Anderson had hated her enough to team up with a serial killer. Or, at the very least, he was willing to play fast and loose with the truth, keeping anyone from seeing what was happening behind the curtain. He waved his hands around and threatened jobs to keep people from realizing there was absolutely no real reason to suspect Sloane in the first place.

She couldn't imagine spending so much of her life hating one person, especially since his hatred stemmed from things that weren't her fault. It started when she was sixteen, and she turned her mother in. Anderson didn't get to arrest the last remaining member of the Cutthroat Couple, and it made him unbelievably bitter. Then when she was a brand-new rookie at the FBI, she exposed a cover-up happening right under his nose that nearly cost him his job.

Was he trying to pay her back after all these years? Did he think ruining her life and taking the lives of those she loved was the way to do it? He couldn't be that petty and cruel, could he? Or was there something else he was getting out of all of this?

"Is Anderson married?" she asked suddenly, her question interrupting the conversation Cade and Reid were having with Diane.

The other woman raised an eyebrow as uncertainty flashed across her face. "I'm not sure where this is going, but no, he's not. At least not anymore. His wife left him not long after the fiasco at the Richmond field office."

"Yikes, no wonder he hates Sloane. She cost him the biggest collar of his career, then made him look like a fool which in turn cost him his wife," Reid pointed out.

Sloane wanted to argue that uncovering the plot in his field office did not cost him his wife, but she didn't bother. What she thought didn't matter; what Anderson believed was what counted. If he saw her as the reason his marriage went downhill, then that just added another layer to his hatred of her. It added motive to his actions.

"Why did you ask about his marital status?" Diane asked. "What could that have to do with anything?"

Sloane shook her head. "I don't know that it does, but I was just thinking about what he could get out of all of this. Is it just his need for revenge? Does he just want to see me pay for humiliating him? Why now? Why risk his career at this stage in the game? Did he come up with this plan, or did someone else take advantage of the need for revenge he's had simmering under the surface all these years?"

"So you think maybe someone's been whispering in his ear, getting him not only to divulge who you are but where you've been?" Cade asked.

Shrugging, Sloane looked over at him. "It's not that far-fetched. He might not have even realized he was helping a killer at first, and now maybe he sees it as a means to an end. He wants to get rid of me bad enough he's willing to sacrifice everything. It would be really easy for my mom to seduce a man like Tom Anderson. He wouldn't know what hit him."

"He does seem to have an unhealthy fixation with you," Diane added. "If someone were trying to get information about you, it wouldn't be hard to get him to start talking, especially if he was plied with alcohol first. If sex was involved, he'd be an open book."

Reid grumbled a few more swear words. "I seriously fucking hate this guy."

"Join the club," Cade said, his voice harsher than usual. "How can we prove any of this? This isn't a small thing we're accusing him of. If we tell anyone about this and we're wrong, it'll mean our careers and likely Sloane's freedom. Anderson won't hesitate to take it out on her."

"Fuck."

Reid took the word right out of Sloane's mouth. They were stuck between a rock and a very hard place, and there were only a few people they could trust to help them figure things out. In the meantime, they also had a killer on the loose and not a single idea where to start looking for him.

It felt like the walls were closing in on her. Like no matter what she did, things would never be the same for her and the people she loved. They had to make a move soon because she was sick and tired of being two steps behind everyone else. Maybe she could figure out a way to get the unsub to come to her. She wasn't a huge fan of using herself as bait, but if it was the only option, she'd do it in a heartbeat.

She'd do anything to make sure she protected the people she loved, even if she had to give up her life to do so.

CHAPTER TWELVE

Watching Sloane with Apollo was almost as eye-opening as watching her with Tally. She had a tough exterior and a badass personality to go along with it. When she was working on a case, she had a take no prisoners attitude to finding the killer. But when she was with Apollo and Tally, she was a completely different person. Her soft side came out, and she didn't give a shit who saw it.

The love she had for her dog was so bright at the moment it was nearly blinding. Cade hated that she had to say goodbye to him so soon after he was released from the emergency vet. If things were different, maybe they could have kept the dog around. He might have been an asset to the team goal of keeping Sloane safe. But he was injured and Cade didn't want to put pressure on the poor dog. He and Reid would just have to make sure they did their job.

Apollo's next mission would be to keep Emily and Tally safe wherever they were. Having the three of them together would ease some of Sloane's concern. Unfortunately, there were still a hell of a lot of things to worry about.

Sloane laughed as Apollo licked at her face. She'd bent down to give him a treat but barely gotten the item out of her pocket before the dog was attacking her. They were supposed to be taking the dog on a walk around the block while they waited for Agent Daly to come to pick him up, but they'd barely made it to the other side of the business next to the veterinary hospital. Dog and human were so happy to see each other they couldn't help but stop every couple of steps to love on each other.

Cade didn't care if they made it all the way around or if they stayed where they were as long as he could hear Sloane laugh. She needed the levity of the moment, no matter how brief it ended up being. After this, there was no telling how long it would be before she'd feel light enough to laugh again.

"He's lucky to have you," Cade said when she stood again and started walking.

"We're lucky to have each other. We've both been through a lot, and we've seen a lot. It's like we get each other even though we can't communicate the way humans can. I know that sounds stupid, but..."

"It doesn't sound stupid at all. Dogs are intuitive animals, and they understand far more than most people realize. It's why they're chosen as therapy animals. They know when you need an extra bit of help getting through the day. I see it in the way Apollo is with you right now. It doesn't matter to him that he's been through a traumatic event and that he's hurting. He wants to make sure that you're okay."

Sloane sniffled, then cleared her throat. He didn't bother to look over at her, knowing she wouldn't like an audience to her moment of vulnerability. It didn't matter if he saw it or not; he knew she was on the edge of breaking down. She'd do her best to keep it inside until after Apollo was gone and they were back in their hotel rooms, then she'd let it go. Better to keep everyone else from realizing where her soft spots were. Of course, Cade already knew.

"I wish I could keep him with us," she admitted. "I hate having to send him off again. Hopefully, he understands why and that it's not because of what happened with Richard."

"Just keep telling him what his duty will be, and I think he'll be fine."

"Plus, he loves Tally, so I think he'll be excited to see her. But he'll be sad I'm not going with him."

"I bet those two get into lots of trouble together," Cade said, hoping the slight change in the topic would help lighten the weight Sloane was carrying.

At least for a moment.

"Hopefully wherever Tally is has a huge backyard; otherwise, the FBI might have to replace a few of the items in the house," Sloane laughed. "They love to chase each other around until Tally inevitably falls to the ground giggling too hard to keep running, then Apollo will pounce on her and lick her until she's laughing so hard she can barely breathe. Then it's rest and repeat until they both decide it's time to lay down on the couch and take a nap."

Cade laughed, picturing the scene easily. Tally was a force of nature with more energy than anyone he'd ever met before, and that included his niece and nephew. She was all giggles and light, and just spending a few moments with her was enough to chase the darkness away for a while. He hoped she'd never lose the vibrancy that made her who she was.

"I wish we could bottle up her energy. We'd never have to work again."

"Right? We wouldn't even have to work hard to market it. Just show a brief clip of her running around or her laughing hysterically, and boom, instant sales," Sloane agreed.

"We would be rich, though we'd probably have to share some of the profits with Tally and Emily, but even still, hello retirement."

Sloane stopped walking, but instead of squatting down to pet Apollo, she turned to look at him while the dog sniffed around.

"Is that something you think about? Retirement?" she asked.

There was a hint of uncertainty in her voice like she was afraid to ask the question. Or maybe scared to hear the answer. Cade wasn't sure, but there was a part of him that liked it all the same. That part was the one hoping she was thinking about the future, one where the two of them had something to live for. He'd never allow himself to get his hopes up, but the tiny spark would always be there, right beneath the surface, no matter how things worked out.

"I've thought about it a lot over the last few years. I don't know if I can make it to forced retirement, not as an agent anyway, and I have no desire to take on the responsibility of someone in charge. Leading isn't my thing," he admitted.

"I don't think you'd be all that great at the politics part of it either. Not that you wouldn't try."

Sloane's observation was pretty damn spot on. He hated politics with a fierceness that could easily get him into trouble. Case in point was the situation with that asshat, Anderson. They shouldn't have had to jump through hoops to do their jobs. It was one thing obeying the law and doing everything they could to make sure they got their conviction. Dealing with the egos of other agents and those in charge was altogether different and a part of the job Cade despised.

"You're not wrong. I'm not a fan of pussyfooting around, so I don't step on some asshole's ego."

She let out a snort of laughter but tried to cover it up with a cough. "Working with Reid's been a lot of fun for you, hasn't it?"

"He's not all bad, but man, the ego on that guy," Cade laughed. "I'm surprised he can fit through the door sometimes."

"When we first met, he was the hotshot of the field office. He'd only been on the job for a few years, but in that time, he'd worked hard to prove himself. He wanted to be the greatest, and the other agents were happy to let him do all the work. Some were lazy and over it. Others we found out later were involved in the cover-up I discovered. Reid didn't care to uncover why. He was just happy to be given a chance to prove his prowess as an agent. There are times, though, where it still goes to his head, and it gets tough not to nut punch him."

Loud, obnoxious laughter burst out of him, startling Apollo, who gave him a sharp bark of disapproval. He apologized to the dog, who was staring up at Sloane like he was ready to move on.

"As much as it pains me to see other guys get hit in the junk, can you promise me if you ever lose the fight and decide to punch him that you will let me watch? I kinda need to see the guy get knocked down a little."

"I'll see what I can do, but you know most of the time, those things are spur of the moment, so I'm not going to promise anything," she said before starting to walk again.

Cade followed after her, chuckling at her honesty. "I accept that. I wouldn't be able to hold back just to get you either."

They both laughed as they continued to walk behind Apollo who was enjoying the sights and smells of the block. Cade checked his phone and realized that their respite was almost over. Soon, they'd drop Apollo off with Agent Daly, and then he and Sloane would be right back in the thick of things. There would be very little if any, lightheartedness where they were headed.

Knowing that, he packed the walk away in his memory banks so he'd have something to help him through what was to come. He hoped Sloane was doing the same thing. What they went through next would be a hell of a lot harder for her than it was for him. All he could do was hope his presence was enough to get her through the heart of the darkness they were about to step into.

Otherwise, they'd be in serious trouble.

CHAPTER

THIRTEEN

Waiting around for the other shoe to drop fucking sucked. Especially when the other shoe was another dead body she'd take the blame for even if she wasn't the one who killed them.

Falling back onto the bed, Sloane let out a heavy sigh. After talking to Special Agent-in-Charge Diane Jennings the day before, they'd all decided that staying put was their best option. They had no idea where their killer had gone. For all they knew, he was still near Hope's End, waiting to make his next move. Sloane doubted that was the case, as did Cade, but without knowing for sure, they'd just be chasing their tail if they left the area.

It had been two days since she'd found Richard's head on her front porch. Two days of silence and two days of nothing to go on. It didn't feel right. She would've sworn that he was escalating by taking out someone she loved. And if that was the case, he'd never go dormant, not now that he had her attention.

But as Reid liked to point out, there had been plenty of time between victims when he was leaving the notes and pictures behind. Why would he accelerate his timeline now? Wouldn't it be just as torturous for him to play the long game and draw things out?

It would be worse.

Sloane didn't know what she'd do if she had to wait days or weeks for him to kill again. She was already going stir crazy locked inside a hotel room with only her ex-husband and the last man she'd been intimate with as her company. What had her life become that this was her reality? Being taunted by a mad man, learning that her mother was indeed still alive, all while dealing with the drama of her love life, if that's what it could even be called.

It was so bad she hadn't even been able to bring herself to face them yet, though she'd been up and about for hours. She'd had room service deliver breakfast while she went through the pictures and notes one more time. Then she started to go through the file the FBI had started on the Roman Numeral Killer on the FBI-issued laptop the SAC arranged for her.

Having everything at her fingertips allowed her the time to go over the files and evidence at her own speed. She knew diving deep would give her a perspective she didn't have before. And that was even before she had a chance to dig into her mother's file.

So far, what she'd seen had solidified what her gut had already told her. There was absolutely no doubt in her mind that Rosalie had mentored the Roman Numeral Killer. It was also evident to her that he was no longer seeking Rosalie's attention. Not in the usual sense anyway. He wanted her to see him, but not how Sloane initially thought. He wanted her to recognize him as an equal or even a threat to her dynasty. It's why he started marking his victims, so they were separate from hers. And why he'd gone after Sloane.

She hadn't told the guys or Diane her theory yet, but the more she thought about it, the more it rang true. The why of it was the part she couldn't figure out. Why did he care about her at all? She didn't want her mom's attention. Hell, she didn't even want her mom to know who she was. Changing her name when she was 16 wasn't just so the weirdos wouldn't know where Isabelle DiSanto ended up. It was to keep her safe from Rosalie if her worst fear ever came true.

And it had. Yet changing her name hadn't done a bit of good. Rosalie knew who she was and now her protégé did too. But why couldn't they leave her be? Why did they both feel the need to fuck with her life? Maybe if she confronted them both, they'd leave her alone. If she died in the process, then so be it, but at least her friends and family would be safe.

Or would they? Would he stop just because she was out of the picture, or would he finish what he started? And Rosalie, would she leave them alone knowing that they were the reason she sacrificed herself?

"Fuck."

If only she could figure out what the hell was motivating the two psychopaths, then maybe she could end things once and for all. Sloane didn't want another person to die just so she could set her sights on the unsub, but it seemed like that was the only way they were going to catch a break. If she could, she'd put herself in the place of whoever his next victim was, but instead, she'd have to wait for him to make a move while she planned his destruction.

She would end him, and then she would end her mother because until they were both dead or locked up, Sloane knew she'd never know true peace. She would spend every day looking over her shoulder for the next protégé or the woman herself. That wasn't the life she wanted to live, and neither was the one she was currently living, holed up in a hotel room, waiting around for another body to drop while the world went on without her.

Something had to give. And if it didn't happen soon, Sloane was going to have to make some moves of her own. Moves the FBI wouldn't like.

But Sloane no longer gave a shit what the FBI liked and didn't like. She would team up with them as long as it was convenient for her. Otherwise, they could fuck right off while she ended things once and for all.

CHAPTER FOURTEEN

Cade rubbed at his eyes for the millionth time in the last hour. He needed to get the hell away from his computer before he did permanent damage, but there wasn't anything else he could do with his time. They were in the hurry up and wait stage of their investigation, and he was starting to go a little stir crazy.

It didn't help that he was worried about Sloane. She was avoiding him, and he didn't blame her, not after everything that happened. Not after she learned about his involvement in her friend's death, but knowing that didn't make the silent treatment any easier to deal with. He wanted to sit down and talk it out with her. He wanted to make things right.

Unfortunately, it was not the time nor the place to take care of that business. They had a couple of cold-blooded killers to catch first. Then maybe if they made it out the other side, he could tell her how sorry he was for everything he was a part of.

"I'm over this hotel room."

Cade's gaze focused on the man sitting at the desk, the spot he commandeered as soon as they picked Cade's room as their home base. Reid Morgan was a pain in the ass, to be sure, but he was a damn good agent. Even still, Cade wished they didn't get to spend so much alone time with each other. Not that they couldn't work by themselves in their own rooms, but it was harder to collaborate that way. A big part of the work they had to do was bouncing ideas off of each other. He just wished they could convince Sloane to join them. Three heads were better than two, right?

"I am, too," Cade admitted.

"Would it be a terrible idea to go next door and have dinner at the diner? I don't know how much more room service I can take."

Another thing Cade could easily agree with. He was no stranger to a room service menu, but the one at the Victoria Hotel in Port Townsend didn't have a lot going for it. The food was bland, and the number of items was limited. It would do for a short period, but having to eat breakfast, lunch, and dinner off of it wasn't ideal—especially not when there was a diner that looked pretty popular right next door.

The question was about safety. Was it safe to leave the hotel? What if Sloane didn't want to go with them? Would it be safe to leave her here alone? Maybe getting their order to go was a better idea. They'd have a different variety of food, at least, if not a different locale.

Odds were the unsub was long gone, moved on to his next victim instead of waiting around for Sloane in sleepy Port Townsend. He wanted to inflict as much pain as possible before he confronted her. Cade was sure of that much. What he wished he knew was where the hell the guy was headed. If he could just figure that out, they wouldn't have to sit around twiddling their thumbs.

"Maybe we should just get takeout. I don't know if we should all leave the hotel."

Reid scoffed. "You know she won't come with us. I want out of this room, man, and I think going next door and having a quick meal is fine. But I guess if you don't want to go, I could go, have dinner, then bring back something for you and Sloane."

Sighing, Cade shook his head, then shut the lid of his laptop. "No, you're right. A quick meal isn't going to hurt anything. We'll just let her know so she can be on alert. I need to get out of this room too."

While Reid packed up his stuff, Cade sent a text to Sloane letting her know what they were doing.

Cade: *We're headed to the diner next door for dinner. Want to join us?*

Sloane: *No thanks. I'm already in my pajamas.*

Cade wasn't sure he believed her excuse. Then again, changing into something other than his rumpled suit sounded like a great idea.

Cade: *Here's the link to their menu. Let us know if you want us to bring something back for you.*

Sloane: *Thanks.*

When she didn't add anything else, Cade knew he wouldn't hear from her again. No matter how hungry she was, she'd rather eat the same room service meal over and over again than deal with him or Reid more than she had to. At least not yet. What he didn't know was whether it was because she was still pissed at them for keeping secrets from her or because she was too focused on the unsub to worry about anything else. Or maybe it was both.

"She's not coming," he told Reid as he shoved his phone in his pocket and grabbed his coat from the top of his bag.

Reid shook his head but didn't say anything. Neither of them spoke as they took the elevator downstairs and crossed through the lobby. The air outside the hotel was a tad on the chilly side, even though it was June. Washington state didn't start warming up until around July or August, but even then, it was never too warm around the water.

Inside the diner, they were told to seat themselves, so Reid led them to a table next to the window facing the hotel. Cade glanced at the sticky menu that was tucked in between the napkin holder and the ketchup bottle, even though he already knew what he was going to get. It was just something to do to distract him while they waited for their waitress.

Why he thought going out to dinner with the man sitting across from was a good idea, he didn't know. Eating alone in his room, zoning out on some stupid TV show, would have been far more comfortable than the awkward silence they sat in. What in the hell were they supposed to talk about? The case wasn't something they should talk about in public, and Sloane seemed like the worst possible topic of conversation for the two of them to have.

They hadn't been on the same page about her since the day they met, and it had only gotten worse the deeper they got into the case; the deeper Cade got involved with Sloane. Now they were both angry at their situation and blamed each other when they were both the reason everything went to shit.

It didn't take too long for their waitress Tess to take their order, a bacon cheeseburger with onion rings for Reid and a patty melt for Cade. They both ordered coffee and water, hoping the caffeine would help them with the hours of research they still had left to go that night. Cade had a feeling every night moving forward was going to be a coffee-filled long night, at least until they got a better handle on how to find their unsub.

"I'm worried about Sloane, man."

Not only was Cade surprised by the fact that Reid was trying to instigate a conversation, but he was taken aback by the man's choice of topics. As a general rule, they tried to avoid talking about Sloane unless it pertained to the case. Even then, they didn't tend to talk about their feelings because an argument almost always broke out. Lord knew they had already argued enough without bringing their emotions into the mess. Just the facts were sufficient to have them at each other's throats.

"Honestly, I am, too," Cade admitted.

"The entire situation is already enough of a shit show, and letting her dig into her mom's file will only make things worse. We need to try to keep her distracted enough that she doesn't go down that rabbit hole."

Cade sighed. He didn't have the experience with Sloane to know just how well she'd handle diving back into her past, but what he did know had him agreeing with Reid. It couldn't be good for her mental health. Especially not while she was dealing with the rest of the bullshit she was dealing with. He did know, though, that they couldn't stop Sloane even if they tried, so if she was determined to work through her mom's file, she was going to do it, with or without their approval.

"We can try, but we can't afford to push her in whatever direction we see fit. It has to be her idea. Otherwise, we're going to lose her, and she's going to do what she wants on her own timeline. If that means burying herself in her past right now, then we'll have to deal with it. Hopefully, we can appeal to her sense of wanting to catch this guy, and she'll hold off on her trip down memory lane."

Reid took a long sip from his coffee. "She's probably the most stubborn person I've ever met, but you're right. As much as she wants to find her mom, we'll be able to get her to focus on the person who killed Richard first. He's the more imminent threat. The only problem is we can't seem to figure out what the hell his plan is. That might end up frustrating her enough that she starts focusing on something she can control."

"We'll just have to figure out a way to keep that from happening. But if it does, and she inevitably starts in on her mom's file, we need to figure out a way between the two of us that we can keep her grounded. We can't let her lose herself in the past."

"Agreed."

Before he could add anything else to the conversation, their waitress was setting their dinners down in front of them. They each focused on their food, but in the back of his mind, Cade was working on a plan. It didn't bode well for them if Reid was worried about Sloane. The man had known her far longer and had shared an intimate relationship with her. If he was concerned, then that meant Cade's concern was warranted and not an overreaction.

The question now was how the hell did they keep an eye on her when she was avoiding them like the plague. How could they keep her safe from herself when she didn't see herself as a danger?

Cade didn't know the answers, but what he did know was that he wasn't going to give up on her. She might not want anything to do with him. She might not be ready to forgive him, but none of that mattered. He'd vowed to keep her safe from the unsub and her mom, and now he was promising to keep her safe from herself. He wouldn't let her do more damage to her already low sense of self-worth. He wouldn't let her take on more guilt or put more weight on her shoulders that she couldn't carry alone.

Whether she wanted him to be or not, Cade was going to be with her every step of the way until there was nothing left to threaten her well-being. Even if it cost him his chance to be with her in the end. Nothing meant anything to him if she didn't make it through this, mentally, emotionally, and physically. Sloane was all that mattered to him. Everything else, including his career, could be collateral damage, and he wouldn't care, as long as she was okay.

He would throw everything away as long as Sloane made it through whatever hell was coming for her.

CHAPTER FIFTEEN

Trying to stay on schedule when nobody else realized you were on a schedule was maddening. He'd thought his plan was perfect, but now that it was in motion, he realized exactly where the flaws were. He never should've let things happen organically. When he'd first worked out his plan, he thought there'd be more urgency at the law enforcement level to put together the pieces of evidence he'd purposefully left behind.

He should've known better.

The minute he killed the first couple, he should've sent the information to the press himself. The police weren't going to do him any favors by actually entering evidence in a timely fashion, and even if they did, they likely wouldn't compare it to federal crimes. He would just have to help things along so everyone could put two and two together.

Thankfully, he had copies of everything he'd left behind. He'd planned to use them later on so he could admire his handiwork, but they'd serve a different purpose now. He had one last thing to do, but then he'd take matters into his own hands. Dropping off what he had at the local news station was a risk and a detour he hadn't planned on, but he needed Sloane to know what she'd made him do. He needed her to chase him, and she couldn't do that if she didn't know where he was going.

If you wanted something done right, you had to do it yourself. And he would, just as soon as he was finished with the couple in the atrociously decorated room. Garish wallpaper adorned the walls, giving him flashbacks to elementary school when he stayed at his best friend's grandmother's house for the weekend. The resemblance was so close he half expected to see doilies covering nearly every surface.

The rest of the house was just as bad and would probably lead someone to believe the couple living there was in their seventies or eighties, but they weren't.

Not that it would matter much longer.

Mr. Bad Taste was already gone, his blood seeping into the mattress below him. The gurgling sounds only lasted for a few minutes after he drew the knife across his throat. Mrs. Bad Taste, however, was still whimpering, occasionally gasping for breath around the gag he stuffed in her mouth before he stripped her naked then tied her up. She wasn't pretty by any means, but with her arms and legs tied to the bed and fear dancing in her eyes, she was a vision.

The scene laid out in front of him wasn't half bad, terrible decorating aside. Blood, death, fear, and soon sex. It was close to what he set up for himself whenever he went out hunting. He might have hated her with a passion, but Sloane was a pretty decent author. At least where the murder and mayhem parts of her books were concerned.

He'd read each of them multiple times since learning who she was. For someone who'd tried to distance herself from her family roots, she sure wasn't doing a very good job of it. Even if she didn't go out at night and find someone to kill, she murdered just the same. Her brain was wired for it. Just because she did it on paper didn't make her any less sick in the head.

Grace had always wanted Sloane to join the family business. She thought her books were proof she could hack it. But he always knew the truth. Just because she played out her killer fantasies in her books didn't mean she could stomach it in real life. If she could, she'd be out there. She would never have turned her back on her family.

But that's exactly what the stupid bitch did. She threw her mother's love back in her face and got her killed. He didn't understand who could do something so cruel.

A muffled attempt at a scream and the squeak of mattress springs reminded him he was in the middle of something. He focused his attention back on the woman waiting for him. Tears streamed from her eyes, coasting down the side of her face to the pillow below her. The right side of her body was decorated with her dead husband's blood; the tiny droplets on her face and chest taunting him.

While he was technically copying the kill straight from Sloane's first book, the entire scene was set up similarly to his normal kills. Though he didn't usually do couples and definitely didn't kill people in their homes, the rest was almost exactly like what he learned from Grace. It was further proof that Sloane was more like her family than she wanted to admit.

Climbing on top of the bed, he positioned himself between Mrs. Bad Taste's legs, then smiled when she squirmed beneath him. He could feel her thigh muscles contracting on either side of him as she tried to close her legs. She was going to be more fun than he expected.

With the knife he'd grabbed from their kitchen, he traced a path from her right ear to her chin, then down her neck and collarbone to the valley between her milky white breasts. He didn't press too hard, only breaking the skin occasionally, allowing tiny specks of blood to break free. His pulse quickened at the sight. Man, he loved what he did.

He leaned over until his mouth was near her ear, then remembered the part of the book he refused to do. Licking his victim's face was just asking for trouble. He did everything he could not to leave DNA behind. Even now, when he wanted the world to know who he was, he didn't want them to figure it out because of a stupid mistake. He couldn't afford to be caught. Not when he needed the high of the kill as badly as a junkie needed their drug of choice.

Instead of licking Mrs. Bad Taste's face, he whispered in her ear with great detail what he was going to do to her. His dick twitched as her heart felt like a jackhammer beneath his hands, and tears fell from her eyes faster. She'd stopped squirming, but he figured that was only because he'd told her how much it turned him on. She couldn't fight against him much, but being still was one way to do it.

Whether she moved or not, he was going to have fun taking what he wanted from her and then some. Then he'd have fun rubbing the woman's death in Sloane's face. He would make sure she knew it was her fault this poor woman suffered as much as she did. The guilt would weigh her down with each body he left behind, and eventually, she would break.

But he couldn't break her with only a few bodies. He needed to get the show on the road and have his fun with the woman beneath him so he could move on to the next step. He had places to go, people to kill.

A bitch to torture.

Pulling a condom from his pocket, he left the knife resting on her chest so he could undo his pants and pull his cock free. He rolled the latex down to the painstakingly groomed base. The manscaping wasn't an act of vanity or because it made his dick look bigger or some bullshit like that. It was yet another measure he took to keep from leaving anything identifying behind. The embarrassment from getting caught because of a drop of semen on a sheet or a stray pubic hair would be more than he could bear.

Once he was ready to go, he smiled down at Mrs. Bad Taste, then picked up the knife and drew the tip down over her stomach. His heart beat frantically against his chest as he positioned himself and his knife right where they needed to be. Then between one beat and the next, he entered her, just as he plunged his knife into her body. She screamed against the gag, but it was useless and only added to the bliss coursing through him as blood seeped out around the knife.

He paused for a moment, reveling in the taste of her fear in the air. His cock throbbed inside of her, waiting for him to find his release. Finally, he began to move, over and over. With every pump of his hips, he drove the knife into her porcelain skin until he was well and truly spent, and she was covered in bloody wounds.

Some were shallow, some were deep, but all were exactly as they were meant to be.

But he wasn't finished with the scene he was creating just yet. There was still one last thing he had to do before he could leave Mr. and Mrs. Bad Taste behind. Wiping the knife off on the sheet below them, he climbed off the wife, taking care of the condom by wrapping it up in a paper towel he had in his pants pocket, then shoved the entire disgusting package into a plastic baggy. He'd burn it later, along with any other evidence he took with him.

Once he was tucked back into his pants, he made his way to the foot of the bed and carved a crude Roman numeral into the heel of her left foot. Then another into the heel of her husband. He admired his work once he was done, and though the lines weren't perfect given the size of the knife he was using, they would do the trick. He wanted the world to know how many deaths he was responsible for. That's why he started tagging his victims with the Roman numbers. He wanted to keep his kills separate from Grace's. He wanted to hold himself apart from her.

Usually, he'd take a picture for his collection, but these bodies weren't for him. They were for Sloane. As was the last little piece that would set the stage perfectly.

Taking one last look around the room, he verified everything was as it should be, and he hadn't left anything behind he hadn't planned to. When he was satisfied things were exactly how he wanted them to be, he pulled the note for Sloane out of his pocket and unfolded it. He smoothed out the creases as best he could, then set it carefully at the foot of the bed, making sure it was safe from the blood that coated the scene. He hoped the note wouldn't be disturbed when the first responders stormed the room, but since he planned on taking this note to the media with the rest, it didn't matter in the end.

He quickly removed the latex gloves he'd put on before entering the house and shoved them into his pocket next to the baggy with the used condom. He picked up the long black trench coat he'd left by the door and put it on, making sure it covered most of his blood-spattered clothing before he hid the bloody knife in one of the pockets. Then with another job well done under his belt, he made his way out of the house and to the van he rented and parked a few blocks away.

He didn't bother running away from the scene or even walking too fast. Anyone who might be out at this time of night, or even those glancing outside while grabbing a glass of water at two in the morning, would remember seeing someone moving faster than usual. Instead, he walked with an almost sloppy drunk stagger. Nobody would even think twice about someone stumbling home drunk at that time of night.

Climbing into the back of the van, he changed his clothes, adding the new discarded ones to the pile of things that needed to be burned, then got into the driver's seat to plot out where he was going next. After heading out into the woods to burn his evidence, he'd have to make a detour to the nearest news station. After that, his next stop was pretty simple.

All too soon, he would reach the end of his journey, which was a little disheartening, but it also meant he'd get to play out the grand finale he'd put together, and for that, he couldn't wait. With his body humming from not only the sexual release but also from the release of his need to kill, he started the van and pulled out onto the road. He was ready to move things along so he could finally come face-to-face with the woman who didn't even know he existed.

The moment was a year in the making but 37 long years past due. Wouldn't Sloane be surprised when she learned she wasn't the only one with a legacy to uphold?

CHAPTER

SIXTEEN

DLegacy76: *I need to know where she is.*

He'd sent the message to his contact hours ago when he realized that just alerting the media to his presence wasn't going to be enough. He needed to make sure Sloane had a package of her very own. It was the only way he could be sure she knew what he was up to. If only he could see her face when she realized what he'd done.

He was starting to get impatient and angry. His contact should have gotten back to him by now. It might have been a little after two in the morning when he sent the chat, but his contact was on the east coast. They should've checked the secure chat on the dark web by now.

For a moment, he wondered if maybe his contact had gotten himself caught. It would suck if that were the case, but the show would still go on no matter what. He'd just figure out another way to get the information he needed.

Checking the chat again, he smiled as a new message popped up on his screen.

DiSantoisaKiller: *She's at the Victoria Hotel in Port Townsend, room 314.*

DLegacy76: *Thank you. We're so close to the end. Your help has been invaluable.*

DiSantoisaKiller: *As long as you fulfill your end of the bargain. That's all that matters to me.*

DLegacy76: *You'll get your wish eventually.*

DiSantoisaKiller: *Good. Once the world is rid of her, we'll all be in a better place.*

It was apparent his contact had no idea he'd sold his soul to the devil. He was so blinded by his hatred for Sloane and the need to see her suffer that he didn't care who he was working with. Whatever she'd done to him was nothing compared to what he was capable of, and one day the dumbass would realize that. In the end, his contact would regret deciding to work with him, but that wasn't his problem. His problem was dealing with Sloane and making sure she didn't miss his news.

While he waited to find out where to find her, he stopped at a copy shop so he could make a second set of everything to send to Sloane. He added a couple of other items in the package just for her, then sealed the envelope with a glue stick he bought at the copy shop. The one thing he didn't know was how he would get the package to her. If she was close by, he might be able to deliver it himself, but if she was anywhere else, it would be a little more complicated.

Once he got word she was still in Port Townsend, he checked into one of the overnight delivery places, but they wouldn't be able to get Sloane her present in time. Knowing most places would be the same, he knew he needed to figure out a more creative way to get what he wanted. Which is how he found himself in the parking lot of said delivery place, a blond wig and baseball cap covering his head and a pair of sunglasses on his face waiting for a sucker to show up. He knew he'd be able to find someone that would take what he was offering. Everyone had their price.

When a heavy-set man stumbled out of his vehicle, his hair disheveled and his eyes a little glassy, he knew he'd found his man. He quickly got out of his car and approached him, trying not to come off overeager.

"Excuse me, I hate to bother you, but I need some help."

"We don't open for another couple of hours, man."

The answer was exactly what he expected, but the slur of the man's words wasn't. This was indeed the perfect person to make things happen. He was still drunk, or at the very least hungover, from the night before, which meant he could easily pass off an excuse to his boss. And it was likely he'd need the money he planned to offer him. He looked around, making sure no one else in the parking lot would find their conversation interesting.

"I know, but I can't wait that long. I've got a thousand dollars with your name on it if you can help me."

The man stopped abruptly, finally turning around so he could see who was talking to him. "A grand? What could you possibly need done that would earn me a grand? I'm not going to suck your dick, dude. I'm not into that kind of shit."

He laughed. "I would never pay a grand to have my dick sucked, my man. I don't have any trouble making that happen. What I need from you is much more important anyway."

The guy looked at him like he was a little bit crazy, but he could also tell he was intrigued. He fought back a smile, knowing he had him right where he wanted him. He glanced around the parking lot again, then back at his mark.

"I need this package delivered to a hotel in Port Townsend in the next few hours."

"That's like a four-hour drive."

He smirked and nodded his head. "That's exactly why I'm offering you a thousand dollars to make it happen. Five hundred now and five hundred once you show me the package has been delivered. That's more than you'd make in your entire shift for today and then some. You could go in there, tell them you're too sick to work, then come back out here. I'll give you five hundred in cash and the package."

"Are you fucking with me, man?"

"No. I'm one hundred percent serious. I just need a package delivered quicker than it'll get done if I go through official channels. You'd be helping me out," he said, laying on the helplessness as thickly as he could.

"And how would I get the rest of the money?"

He had him, hook, line, and sinker. There was no way he'd back out now.

"Once you get to the place, take a picture of the package at the door, send it to me, and I'll forward you the other five hundred in the cash app of your choice."

For a couple of minutes, the man thought about it, sweat beading on his forehead. Whether it was from the detox he was currently going through or the stress of the situation he'd been put in, he didn't know or care. No matter how hard the guy considered his options, they both knew he would deliver the package to Port Townsend; before long, Sloane would have proof that he wasn't done with her, and he wouldn't be until she was completely out of his way.

Eagerness tore through him, almost ripping a giggle from his throat. Thankfully he was able to tamp it down before he scared off the jittery man in front of him. The last thing he needed was to show the guy how scary he was. He didn't want to find someone else to do the simple task for him. Not only was it a waste of time, but it was annoying having to try to talk someone into easy money. Only an idiot passed up a thousand dollars for a few hours of work.

"Fine. I'll do it. Just stay here while I deal with my boss."

He nodded at the guy and waited while he slowly made his way to the backdoor of the warehouse. Once he was inside, he walked back to his car. Good things were about to happen. He could feel it. Which was the only reason he wasn't irritated with how long it took the guy to talk to his boss. Once the package was delivered, the game would begin, and then he'd really be having fun. You could only enjoy yourself so much when there was only one player. Now there would be two. Sloane would do exactly what he wanted her to and chase after him, and he would give her a run for her money.

He pulled up the secure chat again, hoping he could get information from his contact regarding someone else that would be vital to his plan.

DLegacy76: *Now I need to know where they're keeping her friend and that cute little girl of hers. I know they're in protective custody somewhere, so find out where and let me know.*

DiSantoisaKiller: *You can't hurt them.*

DLegacy76: Don't pretend you get to tell me what I can and cannot do. Don't worry, though. I don't plan on hurting them. I just want to use them in my plot against her. I'm sure you can understand that better than anyone.

DiSantoisaKiller: Fine. I'll see what I can find out.

DLegacy76: Remember, I'm just doing what you wanted. Not much longer, and she'll be out of the way for good.

DiSantoisaKiller: That's all I want.

The guy was so damn easy.

Smiling, he put his phone away and leaned against his car. It didn't take much longer before his driver was back outside. His pallor had changed to a grayish-green color which probably helped with his "too sick to work" story. He certainly had picked the right dude for the job.

Ten minutes later, the guy was long gone with his package for Sloane, and he was on his way to the local news station. He kept his disguise on as he approached the building with an envelope addressed to Tracy Wagner, one of the morning newscasters. She was gorgeous, the kind of woman made for TV. Blonde hair, blue eyes, a set of breasts that would make any man weak. And she was the one he wanted to tell his story.

He knew they'd have to scan the package for explosives and make sure there wasn't anything else life-threatening inside, but in the end, she'd read what he sent her on air. If not before the morning newscast was over, then definitely during the news at noon. Before the day ended, everyone would know what he'd done and who they could blame for it.

In the meantime, he had more work to do, and he couldn't wait to get started.

CHAPTER SEVENTEEN

Sloane stared at her friend for longer than was probably necessary as tears formed in her eyes. She was the reason Emily wasn't safe in her own home. She was the reason someone had threatened her and Tally. She'd never forgive herself if something happened to either of them. Until they were safe, she wouldn't stop hunting for the unsub. He didn't know it yet, but the second he set his sights on her best friend and her niece, he'd forfeited his life.

"God, Em, I'm so sorry about all of this."

Emily's eyes narrowed, her lips dipping down into a frown. "You have nothing to be sorry for. It's not your fault you were born to psycho parents or that your psycho mom hooked up with a new psycho who's got a hard-on for you."

Sloane bit back a laugh. Her friend knew how to frame things in a way that made sense and lightened the mood. She hated that Emily was the one trying to make her feel better when Emily was the one who couldn't go home. It should've been the other way around.

"I..."

"Nope," Emily said as she held her hand up. "Repeat after me...I. Am. Not. A. Psycho."

Emily paused and looked at her expectantly. Sloane fought the urge to roll her eyes. She did not want to repeat after her, and she didn't want to say she didn't feel responsible because it would be a lie. But what was a little lie between friends if it made Emily feel better?

Sighing, Sloane shook her head and smiled. "Fine. I am not a psycho."

"Good," Emily smiled. "My psycho mother is not my fault."

"My psycho mother is not my fault," Sloane mimicked.

"You're such a brat."

"You're such a brat," Sloane repeated.

They both laughed, the sound music to Sloane's ears. It felt like years since she'd been able to laugh about anything, even though it had only been a couple of days. No matter what Emily said, she would always feel guilty for the position they were all in. It was Sloane's fault their lives were in danger, and they were in hiding. No one could ever tell her otherwise.

"You know very well that wasn't part of it, but thank you for the laugh," Emily's smile nearly lit up the computer screen.

Sloane smiled, though it was half-hearted at best. "It's the least I can do. Are they taking care of you? How's Apollo doing?"

As if he knew they were talking about him, an excited bark rang out through the house behind Emily. Sloane's heart clenched at the sound of her boy. She missed him something fierce but was so glad he sounded almost like his old self.

"Apollo is still healing, but he loves the attention he's getting from everyone, especially Tally. She's taking care of him like he's her baby, and he's soaking it up. She's the next best thing to you, I think. Though it also might be all the treats she insists on giving him for being the 'goodest boy.' I hope that's okay."

This time Sloane's smile was the real deal. "Of course, he can have all the treats he can handle. He deserves it. I'm just glad he's with you guys. Even injured, I know he'll protect you with his life, though it shouldn't come to that."

"It won't," Emily shook her head. "We're going to be just fine."

"And what about you guys? How are you doing?" Sloane asked again, ignoring how confident Emily sounded about being safe.

"They're taking great care of us here. Tally's in heaven, though it's easier for her since she doesn't know what's really going on. She thinks we're on a family vacation. The safe house we're in has a castle with a slide in the backyard. She says she's finally officially a princess but wishes she'd remembered to pack her crown. Cooper, on the other hand, he's going a bit stir crazy..."

"I'm..."

"Don't you dare say you're sorry again, or I will smack you the next time I see you. Do we need to go through your new mantra again?" Emily scolded her the way only a mom could.

Seeing the look on her friend's face told Sloane she better behave or she'd be in some serious trouble. If they made it through this, she'd gladly let her best friend ground her, scold her, or whatever else she wanted to do to punish her. She'd do anything as long as she got to see them again.

"No."

"Are you sure? I am not a psycho..."

Sloane laughed. "I'm not going to say anything more about it, Em. I promise. Now, how are you doing? Don't think I haven't noticed that you've conveniently left out how you're holding up."

Emily shrugged, but Sloane could tell the situation was taking its toll on her. The beginning of dark circles under her eyes told a completely different story. She was just as stressed and worried as Sloane and Reid were. Knowing her friend was trying to put on a brave face, made her want to apologize again, but she wouldn't. The last thing she wanted was another lecture.

"Would I prefer to be surrounded by the comforts of my own home or working with you guys to find this bastard? Yes, but if I've got to be in FBI protection, there are worse places to be. At least we're safe and together. I wish I could say the same about you and my brother and Cade."

Sloane's gaze drifted from the computer on her lap to the wall that connected her room with Cade's. She'd been avoiding him most of the day, only leaving her room long enough to have breakfast with him and Reid in his room, then pretending like she had a headache and needed to go back to bed for a while. Really she just wanted to be alone.

"I promise you we're being safe. Right now, I feel like we're just waiting around, watching the clock, which is absolute hell. I have no idea how the hell I'm supposed to find this guy when he's always got the upper hand. I thought he was calling me out. I thought that he was saying he wanted to face me somehow, but the longer we go without hearing a single peep from him, the more I'm not sure what he wants."

Emily gave her a comforting smile, which was quickly replaced by her "get your shit together" face.

"Look, I know it's hard waiting around, but this is the time to use your big brain. Stop moping and start thinking. Why you? Why now?" Emily raised a finger with each question she asked. "I know next to nothing about what's going on, but I know you can figure this out. Have you guys accessed the dark web yet? Maybe there's chatter there about someone with an intense dislike for Isabelle DiSanto."

Sloane had asked herself the same questions over and over again but hadn't been able to come up with anything that made sense. But she hadn't thought to check the dark web, which was a colossal failure on her part. How could she forget the one place the scum of the earth hung out? In all likelihood, that was probably where Rosalie and her protégé hooked up. At the very least, it could be where they were getting the information about Sloane.

"You're a genius, Emily."

"I know," she smirked. "Now, is there anything else I can help with? How are things with you and the guys? Have you forgiven Cade yet for doing his job? And what about my dumbass brother. He's not being an asshole, is he?"

Laughing, Sloane shook her head. "No more than usual. As far as everything else goes, I have no idea what the heck I'm doing. I have no idea what to do about Cade. I'm not mad at him. Not really anyway. I know he didn't have a choice, and we've only known each other for a couple of months. Still it stings and my pride is a little bruised, but I'll get over it. If we all make it through this bullshit, I'll give it some thought, but until then, I have to focus on finding the bastard that killed Richard."

A loud crash and a sharp bark startled them both. Emily looked behind her then got up to investigate the noise, leaving Sloane to stare at the empty spot on the couch. Her heart hammered in her chest. Had the killer found their hiding place? Was her family in danger?

"Oh, Tally, what happened?" Emily finally said, the amusement in her voice alleviating Sloane's anxiety.

"I'm sorry, mommy. Apollo and I just wanted some lemonade, and I thought I could get it down without help."

"Don't cry, Tal. How about you and Apollo go out and chat with Auntie Sloane while I clean up this mess."

Sloane could picture how upset Tally was about the mess she'd made. The little girl was a sensitive soul, and her heart ached for her niece. The sound of running and giggles replaced the sniffling as Tally did just what her mom suggested. Sloane's mood lifted as she realized she was about to see her favorite little girl and the goodest boy ever. They would make everything better.

"Hi, Auntie Sloane!!!" Tally squealed as soon as she reached the living room even though she couldn't see her yet.

Sloane laughed as she waited for Tally to get situated on the floor in front of the couch. She kneeled between the sofa and the coffee table, then leaned forward until she was far closer to the camera than she needed to be, but Sloane didn't mind at all. After being around her niece for two months, she was going through withdrawal not getting to see her face every day. All she wanted to do was wrap her up and squeeze her until Tally told her to stop. Then she'd pepper kisses all over her precious little head as she giggled.

Tears pricked at her eyes as she wondered briefly if she'd ever have the chance to do that again. Or was the last time she hugged her quickly as she ran out the door the last time she'd ever get the chance to wrap her arms around the little girl?

Sloane vowed not to let that happen.

"Hey, sweet girl! I miss you. How's your vacation going?" Sloane asked, trying hard not to let her emotions seep into her tone.

"This place is the best. There's a real castle in the backyard. Did you know that?" Tally asked but didn't wait for Sloane to answer. "Now I'm a real-life princess, and mommy is the queen, and Cooper is the king. I made Apollo a knight because he is protecting me. He's so good at his job. He even sleeps in my bed with me at night."

Sloane blinked rapidly, hoping to clear the tears from her eyes before Tally could see them. "Oh honey, that's so great. I love that you're enjoying yourself, and Apollo is keeping you safe."

"I wish you were here, though. You and Uncle Reed and Sara and Cade. It'd be way funner if you guys were all here too."

Sloane laughed. "We wish we were there too, sweetie. It'd definitely be more fun than the boring work we have to do. Maybe when our work is done, we can stay at that house with you for a while."

"Yay! That would be so cool, Auntie Sloane. We could get dressed up in fancy dresses so we look like the princesses in the movies. And Cooper and Uncle Reed and Cade can wear nice clothes like princes and twirl us all around."

"I think that sounds amazing. Will you help me pick out my fancy dress? I'm not really good at that sort of thing."

Tally gave her a big smile that made her heart feel like it was being squeezed in her chest. "Of course. I'm the bestest at picking out dresses. Oooooh, and then mommy can do our hair all fancy too. We'll look bootiful."

Sloane laughed. "Yes, we'll look absolutely beautiful. I can't wait."

"Do you think it'll be soon?" Tally asked, the question bringing tears to Sloane's eyes again.

"I don't know, but we'll try to make it soon, okay?"

"Okay!!"

Sloane listened to Tally chatter on for a while longer before Emily came back into the living room. She sent the little girl and the dog off to the backyard with the cup of lemonade she'd asked for. After an excited squeal and a 'bye Auntie Sloane', Emily retook her seat on the couch, a somber look on her face.

"What's going on?" Sloane asked as soon as she heard the screen door slam shut.

"I just got a text from work. There's...well shit, Sloane, you need to turn on the news."

Closing her eyes, Sloane fought back the bile that crawled up her throat. Something had obviously happened, and now the news was on top of it. That couldn't be good. So far, the FBI had been able to keep the entire situation from the press. They'd only been able to do so because the Roman Numeral

Killer had been killing all over the U.S. Now, he was spending most of his time in a concentrated area. It was only a matter of time before they put things together.

"He told them."

Sloane's eyes popped open. It was like Emily had read her mind. "What?"

"He told them what he's done."

"Holy shit."

Emily grimaced. "Oh, Sloane, it's worse than that. You need to get the guys and turn the news on. I'll let you go. Please check in later, though, so I know you're okay."

Sloane nodded, then said a quick goodbye, her voice cracking on the word. What the fuck had Emily so freaked out? What could the unsub have said or done that brought on her friend's reaction? This wasn't Emily's first foray with a serial killer. Hell, she'd nearly been the victim of one only a few days earlier.

Whatever he'd said or done, Sloane knew things were about to change again, and she wasn't sure she was ready for it.

Unfortunately, she didn't have a choice.

CHAPTER EIGHTEEN

They were on day four of trying to figure out the unsub's plan and find Sloane's mom, and Cade was beginning to wonder if they were ever going to catch a break. It seemed like he lived in a version of that movie Groundhog Day where every day was exactly the same. He'd been on lengthy investigations before where things didn't move at the speed he wanted them to, but this one was different for many reasons. The most important of which was because it had become personal. Not just because he had slept with Sloane, but because he'd gotten close to her.

No, he hadn't just gotten close to her. He was falling for her.

Boy, would his colleagues have a field day with that information, especially since she'd been a suspect when his investigation started. Cade didn't regret anything that had happened between them, and he didn't regret his feelings. What he did regret, though, was the fact that he couldn't end this nightmare for her. He was just as stuck as she was, and it was killing him slowly.

"Do you think she's ever going to come out of her room?" Reid's voice drew his attention back to the present and to the other man in the room with him.

They'd been locked away in Cade's room all day. They'd even had their meals delivered to them there. For the most part, it had been just the two of them, though Sloane had joined them for a quick breakfast, and they'd had a video call with their boss Special Agent-in-Charge Diane Jennings not long after Sloane left them. Other than that, he'd spent far too many hours with a man that drove him crazy and made him feel mildly violent at times.

Cade shrugged as he glanced at the clock next to the bed where he sat.

"You know better than I do that we won't see her until she wants us to, which could be close to never at this point. We probably got our daily Sloane sighting this morning for breakfast. Unless we get something, we probably won't see her until tomorrow."

"But it's almost dinner time. She has to eat, right?" Reid sighed. "I wonder if Emily's heard from her."

Reid picked up his cell phone and typed out what Cade assumed was a text to his little sister. She'd been given a burner phone when she was placed in protective custody, but thanks to some fancy FBI technology, text messages that were sent to the phone she left behind were routed to the burner. It was the one concession they were willing to make that would get her to agree to go into hiding.

Cade had never met two more stubborn people than Sloane and Emily. They were like two peas in the same headstrong pod. They were forces to be reckoned with, and he'd grown quite fond of Emily and her daughter Tally over the last couple of months. He really fucking hoped he'd get to keep them in his life once everything was said and done.

"Shit, shit, fuck."

The tone of Reid's voice was immediately concerning, the swearing not so much. Cade watched as his reluctant partner looked around the room frantically, then rushed over to the bedside table and picked up the TV remote. As soon as the TV was on, he started flipping through the channels, mumbling more swear words as he did.

"What's going on?" Cade asked even though he knew Reid wouldn't answer him right away. He was in some kind of frenzy that didn't allow for questions or anything else at the moment.

He wondered if he should go next door and get Sloane. If Reid had learned about whatever was happening from Emily, then it probably involved Sloane. Then again, maybe it didn't. Though, he couldn't fathom Reid being as frantic as he was if it didn't involve Sloane or their case. Instead of going next door, he watched the other man flip through the channels until he landed on the local news. A breaking news banner scrolled along the bottom of the screen.

Cade was really tired of seeing those damn things.

"Just a few short hours ago, Tracy Wagner, an anchor with WPDX channel four in Portland, Oregon, read on air the letter she received from the serial killer the FBI has dubbed the Roman Numeral Killer. The letter, along with an envelope filled with other items, was left at the WPDX building this morning before the morning news crew arrived at the building."

The screen changed from the Seattle news anchor to a video of a beautiful blonde woman holding a manila envelope.

"I never thought I'd end up being a part of the news instead of just delivering it. I don't know why this person picked me, but I knew I needed to get the letter on air as soon as I read it. The people need to know what's happening around them. And this Isabelle person needs to know that he blames her for everything."

Cade sucked in a breath and nearly choked on it. "Holy fuck."

"Emily got the information from her office so she could write something up. She was on a video call with Sloane when it came in, so she knows he did something, but I don't know if she turned on the news. I'll see if I can get a hold of Diane. You go get Sloane."

Nodding, Cade headed toward the door, appreciating that Reid was taking charge at the moment. He was still trying to process what he'd just heard. What did the killer hope to accomplish by alerting the news of his presence and his obsession with Sloane? Or Isabelle, in this case. They needed to get their hands on everything he delivered to the anchor in Portland. And they needed to see if there was video footage of him dropping off the envelope.

Cade didn't think the guy would be stupid enough to let his face be seen on camera, but he could hope. Maybe he was getting cocky and no longer cared if he stayed under the radar or not. They'd been working on the theory that he wanted

Sloane to chase him. But how could she chase a ghost? Maybe this was his attempt at throwing her a bone. It wasn't fun to play games when the person you were playing with didn't know the rules.

Opening the door to his room, he stepped outside and turned to the right so he could knock on Sloane's door. Before he could knock, he noticed an envelope leaning against her door that looked eerily similar to the one the Portland anchor had been holding in her interview.

"Reid. I need someone from forensics here, ASAP."

"What? What's going on?" Reid asked as he stepped through the doorway to see why Cade was yelling for him. "Oh fuck. Okay, Diane didn't answer, but let me call the Seattle field office and see what they can do."

Reid went back into the room just as the door to Sloane's room opened.

"What's going..."

"Don't touch it. Just leave it where it is."

Sloane looked down at the package lying half in her room and half outside, then back up at him. The color drained from her face as she looked back down. Her name was on the outside in a scrawling cursive with the hotel's name and her room number hastily written beneath it.

"Let's go into your room," Cade suggested. "Reid's working on getting someone out here to collect the evidence."

"But we should look at what's inside of it."

"We will," Cade assured her. "But we can't take the chance we might disturb something he accidentally left behind. Or what if he put something inside of it that could hurt you?"

Sloane shook her head as she backed up but didn't take her eyes off of the bulky parcel on the floor.

"This isn't how he'd kill me. I know that much, at least. I was right. He wants me to follow him, but there was a flaw in his plan. At least that's what he said in the note he left for the woman in Portland."

Cade followed her into the room, leaving the door open so they could keep an eye on things while they waited. Once she was sitting on her bed, he grabbed the chair from underneath her desk and moved it over, so he was close enough to her without crowding her. He wasn't sure if she wanted comfort or not, but he wanted her to know he was there to give her whatever she needed. All he wanted was for her to know she wasn't alone in this.

"So you watched the broadcast?" he asked once she seemed a little more settled.

"Part of it. It was kind of hard to follow and seemed more about the woman he left the envelope for instead of what was actually in the package. We need to get our hands on that, and we need to see what the hell is in this one. I know it's from him. It has to be."

"Or maybe it's from the FBI."

Sloane scoffed. "You don't believe that."

"No, I don't," Cade admitted. "But it's better than the alternative."

"Which is what? That he knows where I'm at. Where I'm hiding. Yeah," she paused, drawing out the word. "That's a big fucking deal, Cade. I thought we were safe here. I thought only people with really high clearance levels knew where we were."

Sighing, Cade raked a hand through his hair as his gaze met hers. "Me too. All the goddamn arrows are pointing right back at Anderson. They've got someone in custody for the earlier breach, but he swears up and down he didn't do it and that he's never even heard of you. Watching the interrogation video, I have to say I believe him. Plus, he was in custody when we ended up here. It couldn't have been him that leaked your whereabouts this time."

Sloane's shoulders dropped as she let out a sigh of her own. "How the hell are we supposed to compete with an executive assistant director? He has more at his fingertips than we can even imagine having. He can do whatever the fuck he wants, and no one would even know. He can pin all of his wrongdoings on poor unsuspecting rookies, and there's nothing anyone can do about it."

"I wish I had answers for you, Sloane. I really do. But I promise you we're not giving up. We're going to figure this out together. The Anderson thing, the unsub, your mom. We're going to figure it all out."

"I..."

"I know it sucks, and it doesn't seem like we're getting anywhere, but at least now we have a path and some evidence to follow. We will find this guy. I promise. We won't stop until he pays for what he's done."

"You know it means that someone else is dead, right? That's why we have this path to follow."

He did know. And it sucked.

"We can't think of it like that. We can't change the past, Sloane. We can only worry about the future."

She shook her head but didn't say anything because she knew he was right. That didn't make it any easier for her to swallow. Hell, it didn't make it any easier for him either. He'd hoped that Richard Briggs would be the last, but he knew deep down they wouldn't be that lucky.

All they could do now was work their asses off to make sure that whoever the latest victim was didn't die in vain. Their death would lead Cade and Sloane to the man who killed them, and then they'd make him pay.

CHAPTER NINETEEN

Sloane's hands shook, the only outward sign that she wasn't handling the situation as stoically as she used to. She shoved them between her knees, hoping the restriction would help a little. Things had gone from bad to so much fucking worse in a matter of seconds. The fucker who killed Richard had a package hand-delivered to her door in a hotel where no one knew who she was. None of them were checked in under their real names, and while the FBI was footing the bill, that fact wasn't widely known amongst the hotel staff, and it certainly wasn't listed in their registration system.

Which meant their FBI leak was to blame for selling them out.

The thought sent a chill down her spine. How could they trust anyone? How could...

"Oh god, they need to be moved," she blurted out the second the thought hit her.

"What?" Cade asked as he placed a hand on her knee. "Who needs to be moved?"

"If he knows we're here, he can find out where they are if he doesn't know already. Emily and Tally are in danger, they need to get out of there."

Before Cade could say anything, Reid entered the room carrying his laptop with him. Sloane could see Diane Jennings's face on the screen, and the older woman was pissed.

"We need to move Reid's family," she blurted out before anyone else could speak first. She didn't care what anyone else had to say, not until they realized the danger Reid's family, her family, was in.

"I've already got that on my list, Sloane. I'll be taking care of it personally, hand-picking people to keep them safe. No one will be able to get close to them, I promise."

"Tally's going to be so heartbroken. She loved that house and the castle slide," Sloane murmured, not expecting anyone to even notice as they got down to business.

"I'll try to find her something just as magical," Diane promised. "I don't like that this guy was able to find out where you're staying. So from here on out, you guys are on your own. I'm closing ranks, and we're shutting out the FBI. Morgan, Cade, you guys have my permission to do whatever you think is necessary to find this guy and keep yourselves safe. I've got a few people on this side that I know we can trust. Dixon and Mills are going over the footage from your hotel and the new station. Morrissey is going through the evidence, and I'm going to have him enter in false information to throw whoever's watching off track."

Sloane's shoulders sagged in relief. Knowing Agents Lily Dixon, Brian Mills, and Trevor Morrissey were helping out made her feel a little better. They'd worked together on the Mommy Murderer case, and she knew they were strong, dedicated agents. She also knew they would need all of the help they could get. There wasn't a whole lot they could do with just the four of them, especially since Diane would have to be very careful about the things she did on her end. The last thing she wanted was to draw attention to herself. At least not until they had proof of who their leak was.

"There's not a whole lot we can do about covering your tracks through the database, so be careful what you access for now. People will expect you to be in there poking around, and while Mills thinks he can help keep you covered a little bit, he's not one hundred percent sure, so keep that in mind."

"We will," Cade assured her.

"This case has gone beyond Sloane now. He's made everything public, and there are people higher up, including EAD Anderson, who are calling for her head. I can only hold them off for so long, so we've got to get this shit wrapped up soon."

"Have we talked to Tracy Wagner or gotten our hands on the package she received yet?" Reid asked.

Diane nodded. "The Portland office sent over a few agents to take care of that. They should have the envelope and its contents back at their lab by now. Of course, the new station pretty much destroyed any chance we had at possibly getting DNA or touch evidence off of any of it, but they'll still give it a shot. Someone from the Seattle ERT should arrive at your hotel shortly. They've been given strict orders to let you observe and take pictures of what's in the envelope, but you can't take any of it with you."

Calling a member of the Evidence Response Team out from the Seattle office would take time, and Sloane wasn't sure they had much to spare. But she didn't have a choice in the matter. She knew she couldn't take the chance that she could ruin something vitally important by handling the package left for her. What was in the envelope could mean the difference between Richard's killer getting the death penalty or going free, not that she'd ever let that happen.

"Once they're done here, we head to Portland," Reid announced, though Sloane was confident they were all on the same page.

"Then you head to Portland," Diane agreed. "Since this is where everyone expects you to go, we can send one of the jets for you, but after that, if we want to keep you off of the radar, you'll need to figure out your own mode of transportation."

Cade looked over at her, then to Reid, who nodded back at him. "I think we'll go ahead and figure that out now and skip the jet if that's okay with you."

Diane smiled. "Do whatever you think is best. We have to be smart about this so we can get ahead of this guy and whoever his contact in the FBI is."

"Anderson," Reid growled.

"We can't prove that, but I'm working on it. The man is in my crosshairs. He's going to wish he never fucked with us," Diane promised. "His friend has gone on to kill four more people since leaving Sloane's cabin. If he keeps getting help from Anderson, or whoever, we're never going to be able to get out in front of the situation. We can't let that happen."

"Four people? It's only been a few days. He's not just escalating here," Cade pointed out.

"He killed two couples, one in Seattle and one just outside Portland. Since no one seemed to be paying attention to him, he delivered the story right into the hands of the press."

"He isn't going to stop until I give him what he wants," Sloane said, though she was mostly talking to herself.

Four more people were dead because this guy was obsessed with her for some unknown reason. Maybe if she gave herself up, he'd stop the madness. Maybe she could save whoever he had in his sights next if she willingly walked into his trap.

"No. Don't even think about it," Reid scolded her.

Sloane looked up at him and frowned. "You don't know what I was thinking."

"Sure I don't," he scoffed. "I know you, Sloane. I know you'd willingly put yourself in harm's way to keep anyone else from getting hurt. That's exactly what you were thinking just now. *Maybe if I give myself up, he'll stop.*' Well, they don't stop. Once you're out of the way, he'll keep going, but this time, he won't have you to focus on. If that happens, then we're all fucked."

"As much as I hate to agree with Reid, he's right," Cade admitted. "Right now, every move this guy makes is with you in mind. We can make that work in our favor. But if you were taken off of the playing field for some reason, all bets would be off. This guy is demented and out to prove he's the best there is. He will take his game to a whole new fucked up level if you're gone. We can't risk it."

"Listen to them, Sloane. They know what they're talking about."

Sloane sighed. It was three against one, and there was no way she would win the argument. "Fine. I won't do anything, but we have to get this guy. We can't let him keep killing."

"We will," Diane assured her.

"Thank you. One other thing I thought of, could we have Lily or Brian check the dark web for chatter? There's a chance that's where the killer and his contact are meeting up or maybe where he met Rosalie," Sloane suggested.

The second the words were out of her mouth, Diane's face shifted, though it was barely perceptible. She shared a look with Reid, then looked back at Sloane like she hadn't just reacted to her suggestion. There was something she was missing. Something Reid and Diane knew, but she and Cade didn't. Had they started talking before Reid brought the laptop to her room to join them?

Sloane wanted to ask what they were keeping from her, but before she could do anything, Diane signed off, and there was a knock on the door. As she looked over to the ERT member standing in the doorway, she forgot the look, the conversation, and that she was annoyed they were once again keeping secrets from her, and instead, she focused on the envelope.

She needed to know what he wanted her to see. Everything else would have to wait.

CHAPTER TWENTY

It took an hour for Agent Jameson, the ERT member, to painstakingly go through the envelope. For each item he pulled out, he had to bag it, tag it with an evidence number, then take a picture of it for the record. At least she didn't have to wait for them to swab each item for DNA or dust them for prints since they'd do that at the lab. Even so, it took nearly five minutes per item before she could take her own picture of what was left for her.

It was difficult for her to stay focused on her task when all she wanted was to examine each piece of evidence until she figured out what the unsub was up to. Unfortunately, they didn't have time for her to do that at the hotel in Port Townsend. If they wanted to get to Portland before the day was over, they'd need to get on the road as soon as the agent was finished. It was nearly a four-hour drive to the city from where they were, though that was on a good day without traffic. In

Washington, there was always traffic, especially along the I-5 corridor.

While Agent Jameson worked and Sloane watched him like a hawk waiting for dinner, Cade worked on packing up his and Reid's rooms. Reid was out trying to find them a car since they didn't want to use an FBI-issued vehicle for their trek. Between items, she packed up her own stuff, though not much of it had left her suitcase.

By the time they were done packing and the ERT agent was gone, Reid still hadn't returned, and Sloane was getting antsy. She paced from one side of the lobby to the other, her nervous energy not allowing her to sit down for even a second.

"What the hell is taking him so long?" she grumbled on one of her passes by Cade.

She didn't expect him to answer but wanted him to know she was getting more anxious by the second. He sat in one of the lobby chairs surrounded by their bags. He and Reid only had their go-bags and the bags with the laptops one of the Seattle agents had dropped off a couple of days earlier. Sloane had her oversized suitcase nearly stuffed full with clothes and personal items. It wasn't just her stuff in the bag, either. She'd made sure to grab items she knew Apollo would miss once the dust settled.

She'd left behind a lot of material possessions that she didn't care about. They could easily be replaced someday. But the pictures and memories couldn't. Inside the suitcase was a framed photo of herself with Richard and Apollo that used to sit on the mantle above the fireplace. It had been taken by a hiker they'd passed one day while they were out. She'd been hesitant at first, but Richard insisted. From that day on, she'd cherished the picture more than she would ever admit.

She also had pictures of herself with Tally and Emily, photo albums filled with images from the first four years of Tally's life, and a few things from her life with Reid that she couldn't bear to leave behind. She didn't need to leave space for her laptop since it was already at Emily's. Instead, she used the space for reminders of the good times, her gun, and a few boxes of bullets. Then she walked out of her cabin without looking back.

Now that they were heading out, it seemed a little inappropriate to have so much stuff with her. She could have it shipped to Emily's or maybe put it in storage until all was said and done. All she needed was a duffle bag, her gun, and a few changes of clothes, and she'd be set. Looking over at Cade, she realized they needed to do something about him and Reid too. If they were going to blend in, they needed to drop the stuffy agent look and go a little more casual. The suits they had with them made them stick out like sore thumbs, even if they did lose the ties and jackets.

"We need to go shopping. Then I need to find a place to store my bag. I can't lug this thing around while we're searching for a killer, and you and Reid look like FBI agents."

Cade smirked, then raised an eyebrow at her comment. "We are FBI agents."

"You know what I mean," she smiled.

"I do, and you're right. We'll find something along the way, and I'm sure there's probably a storage facility once we hit Poulsbo or Silverdale. Will that work?"

Sloane nodded. "Yeah, I can make that work. This bag has the only things I wanted to keep from my cabin in it, and I don't want anything to happen to them. The clothes can be replaced; the photos and what they mean to me can't."

Ten minutes later, Reid finally showed up in a nondescript brown sedan. It wasn't pretty and probably had no bells and whistles, but it would do the trick. No one would expect two highly decorated FBI agents would be driving around in such a beater. Though she knew it had to hurt Reid just a little to pick up something so old. He'd always been one to enjoy the latest and greatest in automobiles, trading in his car just about every other year back when they were married.

After they were loaded up, Reid insisted on driving while Sloane climbed into the backseat. She needed to go through the pictures more than she needed to see the scenery. It had only been a few days since she'd driven up the peninsula after flying in from San Francisco, and nothing had changed in that time, except maybe a few more piles of garbage added along the sides of the freeway.

Settled into the back, she let the guys figure out where they were headed first. Reid agreed with Sloane about stopping to pick up different clothes and store her things, so she knew she had probably a little less than an hour to go through the pictures before she was interrupted. Next to her on the backseat was the original set of taunts.

There had to be something in what he left behind that would help her figure out who he was. She could already tell he was methodical in how he planned things out. The pictures meant just as much to him as they would to her. Maybe it wasn't just Isabelle that he was obsessed with, but the entire

DiSanto family. Maybe he was jealous that she'd been a part of one of the deadliest families in the United States, and he wasn't.

It was sick and stupid, but she'd seen it before. Many of the DiSanto fanboys wished Rosalie and Michael had been their parents. They believed Sloane didn't deserve her heritage since she'd turned her back on the legacy her parents had built. There were some seriously crazy people out there, but none of them had ever acted on their jealousy until now.

"I wish I knew how she picked him out of the crowd of crazies," she said, not realizing she spoke the words out loud until Cade turned in his seat to look at her.

"What are you thinking?"

"It's just a feeling, but why these particular pictures and these messages? He talks a lot about being part of a family, and I wonder if it's jealousy that's fueling his fire. We've seen it in romantic relationships. Why not familial relationships? Maybe he's mad at me because I threw away the parents he always wished he had."

Cade seemed to think about her observation for a minute, then nodded. "If you're right, then the dark web is likely where they met. People can't be as open and honest about their proclivities on the regular web, not with the way the government scours it looking for threats. Plus, Rosalie wouldn't want to approach anyone that way. It'd be like walking up to them in broad daylight and announcing who she was in a crowded room."

"She definitely wouldn't throw away two decades of flying under the radar like that. There has to be something special about this one that made her reach out to him. She wouldn't risk her new life for just anyone."

That was one of the things they desperately needed to figure out. What made the unsub so damn special that Rosalie would risk everything to team up with him. She'd had a damn good thing going for so long. It didn't make sense that she'd throw it all away on a whim or a stranger.

"I doubt she's going to be too happy about what he's been doing, which might work in our favor," Cade pointed out, hope evident in his voice as his eyes met hers. "Now we know she's alive. We wouldn't have known that without him. We can take them both down, end this once and for all, and you can be free to live your life without looking over your shoulder."

Sloane tried to ignore the warmth that spread through her at Cade's remark. Could it be that easy? Could she go on to live a regular life once Rosalie was caught and she no longer had to wonder where she was and what she was doing? Could she live that life with Cade? There'd been a glimmer of hope that spread through her when he admitted thinking about retirement even though he was still so young. Could there be a future for them if they made it out the other side? Or was that just wishful thinking on her part?

"I don't think it's going to be that easy," Reid said, bursting the happy little bubble Sloane had been trying to create.

Ever the realist, she wasn't surprised her ex had been the one to bring her plummeting back down to the real world. If only he could have waited a little bit longer to speak his mind.

Cade turned around now that their shared moment of optimism was replaced by their crazy reality. It was probably for the best. They couldn't afford to get caught up in the what-ifs and what it could mean for her future. They needed to focus on what they had in front of them, which, unfortunately, was a whole lot of nothing. With any luck, by the time they got to Portland, they'd have a little more.

Sloane just hoped another person wouldn't lose their life before she could figure out who the hell was fucking with her. Sadly, she had a feeling there'd be a few more bodies in the morgue before she uncovered who he was and what her mother had to do with what was happening.

Eventually, she'd catch up, though, and once she did, they'd both be sorry they decided to mess with her.

CHAPTER TWENTY-ONE

His hands itched with need.

He was getting antsy, needing desperately to take the next step in his plan. Now that she finally knew what he'd done and why, he couldn't wait to keep going. He had to show her and the world what he was capable of. He had to make a name for himself before telling everyone who he was. There was so much more he wanted to show them all, yet he was stuck at the moment.

Sitting in a car waiting for a victim to show up wasn't his idea of fun, but it was a necessary evil he had to deal with so he could continue with his plan. He checked his phone for the time and then for any messages he might have missed. Usually, he deleted messages after he read and responded to them, but he'd kept the message from the delivery guy because it made him smile. He was delighted knowing Sloane had his package. She was no doubt freaked out that he knew how to find her and the information inside had to give her pause. If only she knew what else he had in store for her.

If only he could see her face when she finally learned the truth about him. The thought of it almost made him want to rush through his plans so he could get to the best part. But he wouldn't. He needed to terrorize her a little more until she learned the truth about him at the same time as everyone else. It would make the reveal that much sweeter.

God, he couldn't wait.

If only he weren't such a stickler for well-thought-out plans, he'd ditch the next few steps so that he could let the cat out of the bag now. But what he still had planned was far too good to push to the side. Sloane deserved the guilt and pain that his plan would bring. So did Grace. He would make them both sorry they'd ignored him for so long.

He would prove to them both that he was superior to them in every way. Then he would go on to create his own legacy. To hell with both of them and what they represented.

The sound of an incoming message on his phone had him returning to the task at hand. He didn't have time to daydream or think about the future. He had to stay focused on the next steps, not the ones fifteen or twenty beyond where he was.

You couldn't rush perfection.

Smiling, he pulled up the chat app attached to the website he frequented deep down in the dirty recesses of the dark web. It's where he met his contact within the FBI. Maybe he should've been wary of the person that went by *DiSantoisaKiller*, but there was something about them that called to him, like a kindred spirit of sorts. They hated Sloane almost more than he did and were willing to do whatever they could to help him take her out. He didn't even have to work hard to cultivate a relationship with whoever was on the other end of the screen name.

Of course, he'd wondered how they knew about him in the first place, but in the long run, it didn't matter. If they posed a threat, he'd take care of them after they served their purpose. Once Sloane was out of the way, he wouldn't need to keep them alive.

DiSantoisaKiller: *They've left Port Townsend. I can see they've checked out of the hotel, but I don't know where they've gone. There's nothing in the file. I think they know I've been helping you.*

DLegacy76: *Well, that doesn't bode well for you, does it?*

"Fuck," he growled as he slammed a palm against the steering wheel.

He couldn't let on how much the news pissed him off. Could he continue with his plan even though his FBI insider was compromised? Of course. He would adapt if need be. The problem was he liked having the inside scoop. He liked knowing just how much she was affected by what he was doing. He liked knowing his contact was making her life a living hell through official channels while he was out in the world doing the work he was meant to do.

DiSantoisaKiller: *Don't worry about me. I'll move the heat onto someone else while getting everything you need.*

He scoffed. How fucking full of himself was this guy to think he'd be worried about their neck. He didn't give a shit what happened to his little insider. If he was compromised, someone else would take his place to give him what he needed. He always had a backup plan in place.

DLegacy76: *I'm not worried about you at all. I just need to know if I need to replace you with someone better.*

DiSantoisaKiller: *There is no one better. I've got clearance you won't be able to find anywhere else. Stick with me, and you'll have no problem taking her down. I'll get you what you need.*

DLegacy76: *I'll be waiting.*

He signed off quickly, not wanting to see what annoying groveling his contact would try next. Either they could make it happen, or they couldn't. He didn't need their false promises. He needed action.

He sighed, checking the time again, then looked around the rest stop. Waiting was driving him crazy, but he knew it would be worth it in the end. He rubbed his hands together, then stopped when he realized how absurd he probably looked, like a mediocre TV villain without the maniacal cackle.

Maybe once his task was complete, he'd be able to laugh, but until then, he needed to stay laser-focused on finding the next part of his plan. He knew Grace would appreciate what he left behind for Sloane next, even if she would never admit it.

She would see he was a chip off the old block after all, which was all she'd ever wanted. And exactly what Sloane could never give her.

CHAPTER TWENTY-TWO

The loud bang against the wall by her head woke her up. The shriek that followed kept her from quickly falling back to sleep. A bang or a crash coming from the room next door was nothing new. Isabelle was used to the weird noises and could almost always sleep through them. But the shriek made her heart race and had her eyes popping open to check the room around her.

As silence surrounded her, she realized she probably imagined the noise. Maybe it was part of the dream she couldn't remember. It wouldn't be the first time. They always felt so vivid while she was sleeping, but everything faded away the second she opened her eyes.

The hotel room was so quiet she could hear the buzz of the ice machine that was just outside of her room, and the faint familiar sounds of the TV in her parent's room next door. Everything was as it should be. Her eyes tried to flutter closed once her heartbeat slowed back to normal, but as soon her eyes were closed all she could see was blood. But that didn't make any sense.

A muffled scream punctuated the silence, sending Isabelle shooting upright, her hand resting over her heart. She knew she didn't imagine it this time. Someone was screaming. Something wasn't right. Where was it coming from? Was the screamer outside or in one of the rooms around her? Could it have come from her parent's room? Was something happening to them?

Isabelle's hands shook as she contemplated what she should do. Did she stay hidden in her room, or did she check on her parents? If they were in trouble, she'd be putting herself in danger by going next door. If they weren't in trouble and she interrupted whatever they were doing, they wouldn't be happy with her. She would regret the decision either way, but she had to know they were okay.

Didn't she?

Slowly, she crawled out of bed, hoping the squeaky springs weren't loud enough that they could hear her moving around. She put her ear against the inside door that connected her room to theirs and listened closely. For a long moment, there wasn't anything for her to hear, then one whisper followed another, then another. One voice sounded angrier than the other, though she couldn't make out what they were saying, it was the tone that gave them away.

A whimper and a gruff 'no' had her jumping back away from the door, her heart pounding against her chest. She had no idea what she should do. Her parent's room was where the noises were coming from, but maybe whatever was *happening in there was okay. Maybe they weren't being hurt by someone else. Maybe they were having fun.*

But did people usually scream when they were having fun?

Uncertainty made her stomach hurt. What if something terrible was happening to them and she sat in her room and did nothing? What would she do if her parents were hurt and she'd let it happen?

Still unsure, she reached for the handle to the connecting door. The cold metal bit into her skin. She pulled her hand away quickly, shocked when blood dripped from her palm onto the floor. Tears filled her eyes...

"No...no... don't."

A hand on her thigh broke through the memory, but just barely. She could feel herself sinking back into the night everything changed, the door slowly opening as she made the worst decision of her life.

"Sloane, hey, Sloane, wake up..."

The hand on her thigh and the voice begging her to wake up helped drag her out of the nightmare. Her eyes flew open, tears filling them instantly as she looked up at Cade. He was turned around in his seat, his concern for her clear as day.

"I'm sorry," she said, her voice shaky and rough. "I didn't mean to fall asleep."

Just past Cade's head, she could see Reid's eyes in the rearview mirror. He looked just as concerned as Cade. How bad had her reaction to the memory been that both men were worried about her? It wasn't the first time Reid had witnessed her having a bad dream, though it had been a while. But the look on his face made it clear this was a new experience for him.

"Are you okay?" Cade asked, his hand still on her leg even though the way he was sitting couldn't be comfortable.

It was like he didn't want to lose contact with her, afraid she might fall back into whatever had been hurting her, and he'd lose her. The hand was just as much for him as it was for her. Whether she wanted to admit it or not, she needed the comforting weight. The heat of his palm through her jeans grounded her in a way she couldn't explain.

"I'm fine. I guess all this talk about my family has my subconscious setting free all the things I've worked hard to forget over the last two decades."

"It's probably going to get worse before it gets better, but you already know how potentially helpful your memories can be."

"I know. Even though I'd much rather they all stay hidden under the pile of rocks they've been buried under all these years, I know remembering could help. Maybe I'm missing something because I've intentionally blocked it all out."

She could tell Cade wasn't entirely happy about her reliving her past, but he couldn't argue against it potentially being helpful. The smile he gave her was weak at best, but she knew he'd support her in whatever she decided to do. But it wasn't like she could force her brain to remember the things it had purposely forgotten out of self-preservation. If it came down to it, maybe a hypnotist could help. It was something she'd never tried before, but if it meant catching her mother and her unknown partner, Sloane would give it a try. She'd do anything to end this.

Cade gave her leg another soft squeeze before turning back around in his seat. She watched as he checked his phone, then set it back down in the console between him and Reid.

"We should be reaching the hotel shortly. Diane said one of the Portland agents is hanging around to hand off everything they have from the newscaster's envelope. Once we get settled, Sloane can go through what was in both envelopes and see what she can make of it."

She'd planned on going through the pictures on her phone during the drive to Portland but had barely started reading the note when her stomach started to roll, and saliva filled her mouth. So much for best-laid plans.

"Who knew reading in the car made me nauseous?" Sloane asked with a laugh.

"It's probably being in the backseat that did it. I get a little carsick when I sit in the back with Tally. I like spending the extra time with her, but man, does it make me queasy. Especially when Tal wants me to look at something she's doing on her tablet or the book she's flipping through."

"I didn't take you for a backseat kind of guy," Sloane joked. "You like being in control too much."

Reid laughed. "You're not wrong, but Tally, is a whole different story. That little girl has me wrapped around her finger. Just like you and I'm guessing just like she's getting Cade. All she has to do is smile and we're putty in her hands."

"Sounds about right."

Sloane loved that Cade didn't hesitate to admit Tally had pulled him under her spell the way she had the rest of them. Even with that, it was Reid's admission that made her feel better. Not being able to hold up her end of the bargain was bothering her more than she would say out loud, though she didn't need to. Both men knew her well enough to know she would add the time she'd wasted to her growing pile of things to feel guilty about. She was supposed to be ready to go over everything once they reached their final destination, but now they'd have to wait for her. It would set them back a little, which was time they didn't have. Not when there was a killer out there that was unpredictable and always a few steps ahead of them.

She had no idea what he'd released to the press. Had he told them about her, about her true identity? Did he talk about her mom? Rosalie wouldn't be happy about that. It was bad enough the FBI was now aware that she was alive but alerting the public? That wouldn't go well for him.

Sloane felt like they were going round and round while he had all the time in the world to kill someone else. She needed to get her shit together and fast. Of the three of them, she was the one with the insight that could help them the most. She just had to figure out how the hell to access it before it was too late.

CHAPTER TWENTY-THREE

Cade felt like he was teetering on the edge of a cliff, and no matter what direction he stepped in, he was going over. Everywhere he looked was a shitty situation that was in all likelihood going to end badly. He couldn't protect any of them from what was coming.

Especially not Sloane.

She was the eye of the storm. Everything that was happening revolved around her, and eventually, it would pull them all under. All he could do was hope they could tread water long enough to make it out the other side.

In the meantime, he'd do everything he could to help Sloane shoulder the responsibility she was carrying. He knew she was feeling the weight of what her mother had started with their unsub. Guilt over what happened to Richard and the other victims ate at her. It showed in the haunted look in her eyes and the dark circles beneath them.

She was exhausted. They all were. Emotionally, mentally, physically. They were drained beyond their normal capacity, but they had to keep going. There was no end in sight. Which only made Cade worry about Sloane and her well-being more. After the memory turned nightmare on the drive to Portland, he had a feeling she was going to fight falling asleep moving forward. She'd do anything to avoid reliving what her parents put her through, even the good times. But she also knew those memories were important. She was in a no-win situation, and there was nothing he could do to help her get through it.

Cade glanced over at the couch to check on Sloane before looking down at the time on his laptop. They'd been at the hotel for nearly half an hour. While he and Reid brought up their bags and got everything settled, Sloane commandeered the couch so she could go through the items sent to her by the killer. She hadn't moved in thirty minutes, hadn't made a single sound as she scrolled through the pictures on her phone.

He couldn't imagine what it would be like to be blamed for every life someone else took, which was essentially what the unsub was doing. Sloane was his driving force, and now the world knew it. What surprised him the most was that the killer hadn't outed Sloane by telling the world who she was. The true identity of the missing Isabelle DiSanto was highly sought after in the deepest recesses of the dark web and amongst the serial killer fanboys. The only thing Cade could think of was that outing Sloane as Isabelle would take the spotlight off of him, something a psychotic narcissist would never want to happen.

"I don't get it."

The sound of Sloane's voice drew his eyes back to the couch. Her gaze rested on him instead of her phone this time. She looked like she was on the edge of losing it and all he wanted to do was tell her it was all going to be okay. But it wasn't, at least not anytime soon, and he couldn't lie to her. There was no room for false hope in what they were doing.

There was no doubt in Cade's mind that things were going to get infinitely shittier before they ever got better, and there was nothing any of them could do to stop it. Not even Sloane, though he would never admit that to her. She needed to feel like she was going to make a difference, and maybe she was, but it wasn't going to be today or even tomorrow, no matter how hard she worked to figure things out.

"I don't understand why he's calling me out but not telling the world who I am. Wouldn't that get more eyes on what he's doing?"

Cade nodded. "I was just wondering the same thing. My only guess is he'd get eyes on him, but not in the way he wants. He doesn't want the focus to shift from him to you too much. Just enough to know that you're to blame for what he does, but if the world found out you were Isabelle DiSanto, the story would be about you and not him. He thinks he's better than everyone else, including your mother, and this is his opportunity to prove it."

Sloane scoffed and shook her head. "That line of thinking is going to get him killed. If not by one of us, then by Rosalie. She will not take too kindly to her authority being challenged. If she didn't hesitate to kill the love of her life, she's not going to blink an eye at taking out whoever her protégé is."

Standing up, he grabbed his laptop off the table then walked over to the couch to join Sloane. He'd given her space while she was going through the evidence, but now it was time to get down to business. Before he could call out for Reid, the other man was walking out of the bedroom and into the living area of their suite.

"Emily and Tally, say hi," he told them as he pulled a chair from the dining table closer to the couch. "They're enjoying the new plan, which I guess is just one long road trip to see the sights. Jennings has them on the move, never staying in one place for too long, which is a pretty solid plan if you ask me. There is no way for this guy to pinpoint them and use them in whatever his fucked up plan is. Especially not if he wants to stay focused on Sloane."

Sloane gave her ex a weak smile. "That's good. At least they're safe and enjoying themselves, and that's much better than being locked in a stuffy safe house where he could easily find them."

"We have to catch this guy, Sloane. We can't let him get to them."

"We won't. I promise."

Though her voice sounded strong and sure, Cade could tell by the way her hands shook in her lap that she was terrified she wouldn't be able to live up to that promise. Emily and Tally were the most important people in her life, and if something happened to them, she'd never forgive herself. And Cade had no doubt she'd give up her life trying to avenge them.

Cade couldn't let that happen.

"So let's work on that promise. Does any of the new evidence seem familiar or tell you anything we didn't already know?" he asked, bringing the conversation back to Sloane's feelings about their unsub.

"He wants attention. The fact that he wasn't getting any forced him to go to the news himself, which I'm sure had to piss him off. He's not only looking for attention from me, for reasons we still haven't figured out, but he wants my mom and the world to know how great he is at what he does. He assumed everything he left behind, including the Roman numeral, would do the trick."

The carving of a Roman numeral into the feet of his victims was their unsubs signature, one that made his kills easier to track as long as they were made aware of them. Sometimes it took local law enforcement agencies a while to enter their case information into the system, which in turn delayed the process for the FBI and, in this particular situation, led the unsub into taking matters into his own hands. Cade's biggest problem with the situation was that a bulletin was sent out to all agencies, letting them know about the carvings. The second they saw them, they should have notified the FBI.

"Why aren't we getting notifications anytime someone is found with the carving?" Reid asked, nearly echoing the thought in Cade's head.

"That's one of the things we need to ask Diane as soon as we can get a meeting with her. We should've known the second those numbers were found."

"I have a feeling we're not going to like the answer," Reid muttered.

Cade had the same feeling.

Sloane scrolled through the pictures on her phone until she landed on one in particular. The one that added even more questions to their already overflowing pile of "whys." Why was the unsub suddenly using her book as his source material?

153

She whimpered beneath him. Blood from her dead husband dotted her face and the right side of her body. She struggled against his hold, but she was no match for him. He made quick work of tying her arms to the headboard above her. He tightened the knot until she cried out in pain. He wanted it to hurt.

She deserved the pain after what she did to him. Well, maybe not her exactly, but the woman she represented. Though women were all the same. Taking what they wanted without considering who they hurt in the process.

Whores.

Every single one of them needed to pay.

Trailing his knife along the side of her face, she tried to pull away, but it only made him dig the knife in deeper. Blood welled up along the path, trickling down into her hair in places. Tears mixed with the blood, turning the vibrant red into a duller pinkish hue.

Sloane read the passage from her book like she would have if she were giving a reading at a book signing or performing the book for the audio version. Hearing the chilling words falling from her lips was a bit unnerving though he didn't know why.

"First, he uses your parents' methodology, and now he's using your books as a blueprint? It seems this guy doesn't have a story of his own, except the stupid numbers, which works more in our favor than his. This way, we don't have to keep count cause he's doing it for us."

Cade could hear the disdain in Reid's voice and knew just how the other man was feeling. Their killer was deadly, to be sure, and intelligent, but he was also a copycat. He was only formidable because he'd spent some time at the Rosalie DiSanto school for serial killers. Without her, he'd be nothing more than a run-of-the-mill scumbag. He wouldn't have delusions of grandeur, and he wouldn't have the balls to go to the press when he wasn't getting the attention he wanted.

If he were capable of doing what he was doing now before he hooked up with Rosalie, he would've been on the FBI's radar long before he started taunting Sloane. The fact that he had only been killing for a few years told them a lot about the guy they were chasing. The fact that he was inexperienced and had no creativity of his own didn't make him any easier to catch, though, which was disappointing.

"He's not as smart as he thinks he is, which isn't quite working in our favor as much as I wish it would. I think what we need to do is fuck with his plans. He's clearly very organized and has this whole thing planned out as meticulously as he possibly can. If we can mess with that, maybe we can get him to do something stupid," Sloane suggested as she set her phone down on the couch next to her. "He wants me, but first, he wants to toy with me. Taunting me, then killing my friend, now he's using one of my books to continue his killing spree. Everything he's doing is an attempt to weaken me until he's ready for the final showdown."

"You make him sound like some lame villain from a bad cable TV movie. I don't think he's going to be that easy," Cade told her, though he was reluctant to say that truth out loud.

"I don't either," she admitted. "But I'm his motivation. So much so he went out of his way to deliver a package to me, one that included a rather large butcher knife for reasons he only knows. He's fixated on me and wants me to know it. Let's use that knowledge to mess up his plans."

Cade shook his head, but before he could speak, Reid took the words out of his mouth.

"We already said we're not using you as bait."

Sloane huffed and rolled her eyes. "I'm not saying I want to be bait, and I'm not going to stand out in the open and wait for him to sneak up on me. But, what if, instead of following him on his killing spree back down to San Francisco, we skip ahead."

"So instead of waiting to see where he goes next, we head to San Francisco first?" Cade asked; then, when Sloane nodded, he asked follow-up questions. "Do you think that would work? Would he give up whatever the rest of his plans are to skip to the end of the book?"

Shrugging, Sloane picked up her phone and dropped it into her lap. "I don't know, but it's worth a shot, isn't it? What's the worst that happens? He keeps on killing and meets us in San Francisco a couple of days from now. How would that be any different than us chasing after him like a bunch of dipshits?"

Nobody said anything for a few minutes, and the silence was unsettling. Cade looked at Reid, who was looking between him and Sloane. The uncertainty he saw in his expression was probably mirrored on Cade's face. Jumping ahead of the unsub was a risk, but Sloane wasn't wrong. What would the difference be? Either they followed him while he went on his merry way killing, or they jumped ahead of him and hoped like hell he'd skip ahead to join them.

"What if we jump ahead and he keeps killing? What if us not being close behind means we don't catch him when he fucks up?" Reid's questions were solid concerns. Ones he had but didn't voice.

"There's no guarantee we'd catch him even if we were right up his ass. All we know right now is that he was in Portland this morning, and he's headed south...we think. We don't know if he's following I-Five all the way down or if he plans on zigging and zagging his way along Oregon and Northern California. What if he decides to get on a plane at some point instead of driving? We have no way of knowing what he's planning next, but what we can do is take a chance that he'll follow us if we get to San Francisco first. If we're right and he does, we'll save a couple of lives."

"And if we're wrong and it just pisses him off?" Reid asked.

Silence engulfed them again as Sloane picked up her phone and scrolled through the pictures. This time she stopped on the letter the killer left with the package he sent to the news anchor.

"The FBI seems to think I'm a joke, or maybe they don't think I'm a threat, but they're dead wrong. Two lovely couples have paid the price, and more will follow until the FBI pays attention to me. They know what I want, but just in case it isn't clear, the gifts I've left behind should help. Isabelle knows what she needs to do. Maybe this time she'll be strong enough to make the right choice. If not, innocent people will continue to pay for her sins. Until next time, the Roman Numeral Killer."

Sloane paused while the words sunk in. Not that he or Reid needed it. They'd read the note more than once on the drive while she slept, and he suspected they could both recite the words by heart at this point. And he knew for a fact that neither of them was comfortable with what the unsub wanted, which was Sloane.

"Look, I'm just as uncomfortable with the thought of offering myself up to this guy as you both are, but I can't just sit around and do nothing. Can we at least run this by Diane and see what she thinks?"

Cade sighed, then nodded. "Fine. We'll see what Diane thinks about your plan, but in the meantime, we continue going through everything we have, and then you get some rest."

She opened her mouth to protest but was stopped by Reid. "We all know you'll run yourself into the ground before you admit to being exhausted, but we can see it in your eyes. What good will you be to anyone if you can barely function? Sleep isn't going to hurt you."

She scowled at him, obviously not a fan of being ganged up on. Cade couldn't blame her, but she had to know it was for her own good. Hell, they all needed some rest, and maybe if she'd settle down, he and Reid could too.

"No, but what pops up while I'm sleeping might," she admitted. "I know it could be important, but I don't know if I'm ready to go down that road yet, maybe after we find this guy. Then I can focus on my mom."

"Okay, then we get you some sleeping pills or something. We'll do whatever we need to do to make sure you get some rest. Your body is still healing from your face-off with Kyle Atwood. Not to mention the emotional toll finding your friend has taken on you," Cade pointed out, though it pained him to do so. "Reid and I will take turns keeping an eye on things while you get some sleep. Then in the morning, if Diane gives the okay, we'll get on a plane to San Francisco and let Anderson, or whoever the leak is, let the killer know where you are."

Sloane's shoulders slumped forward in defeat. She knew she wasn't going to win the argument, not when it was two against one, and most definitely not when it was about her well-being. Cade and Reid cared about her too much to let her run herself ragged, and they needed her too much to let her become a liability.

"Fine, but I want to talk to Diane tonight. I'll sleep better if I know what the plan is."

This time Reid nodded, then pulled his phone out of his back pocket. "I'll give her a call now and see what we can do."

Cade watched as the other man got up and left the room, leaving him alone with Sloane. At some point, while they talked, the distance between them had lessened. He wasn't sure which of them had moved or if it had been both of them that seemed to gravitate toward each other. He just knew that being close to her was a balm to his frayed nerves. What was on the horizon terrified him. His desire to protect Sloane at all costs was so high it made his body vibrate with the need to do something. At the moment, what he wanted to do was pull her into his arms and never let her go.

As if she could read his mind, she leaned into him, her head resting against his shoulder.

"I'm scared, Cade. I don't know what the right call is. I don't know if we're going to be able to stop this guy. And if we do, will my mom pop out of the woodwork or another one of her students? What will we have to face before things go back to normal? Will we ever get there?"

He could lie to her and tell her they would, that eventually, everything would be okay again, but that wasn't what she wanted to hear. She wanted to know that he understood how she was feeling because he was feeling it too. She wanted to know that they were in this fucked up story together.

"I'm not even sure I know what normal is anymore, but whatever happens next, I'll be with you one hundred percent. I'm not going anywhere."

"Thank you."

"I'd do anything for you, Sloane. I hope you know that."

He hoped she could hear the truth in his statement and knew he wasn't just saying them to make her feel better. He meant it. Whatever she needed. Whatever he could do to help her, he would do it in a heartbeat. He no longer cared about his job. If the FBI wanted to fire him for siding with Sloane or for protecting her, then so be it. She'd done nothing wrong. She was as much a victim as any of the people the unsub had killed. Except she had to live with what the guy was doing in her name.

It didn't matter what the consequences were. Cade would do whatever it took to keep Sloane safe and make sure no one could hurt her, herself included.

He'd put it all on the line for her—even their future. Nothing else mattered if she didn't survive.

CHAPTER TWENTY-FOUR

There was nothing sophisticated about dismembering a human body. If you asked him, butchering a person like they were some kind of animal was barbaric and ruined the beauty of the kill.

But a plan was a plan. And there was always a method to his madness. Removing the head of Sloane's neighbor was about the effect it would have on her, and so was using scenes from Sloane's books.

He couldn't pick and choose what he wanted to do. Not at this point in the game anyway. He'd known what he was in for, and even though he found it disgusting to do what the text told him to do, he would do it anyway.

Sloane was definitely fucked in the head. Despite her attempt to ignore her roots, all it took was one read-through of her novels to see she wasn't as removed from her family as she liked to pretend she was. Whether she wanted to admit it or not, she was a killer, just like everyone else with the DiSanto name. Not that killing on paper was good enough for such a famous family.

As he sliced through the woman's skin, his saw hitting bone, he cringed. What he was forcing himself to do was distasteful and abhorrent, but, in the end, the shock factor would be worth it, which was what he had to keep reminding himself as he worked. Now that Sloane and her FBI friends knew what he was doing, would they expect him to take it this far? Dismemberment was way outside of his usual methods and a far cry from what he'd been taught and perfected.

The fun he had before he slit the woman's throat was where he felt the most like himself. That was where his passion was fed. It had nothing to do with Grace and nothing to do with Sloane. It was all him. The woman beneath him was just his type. Slitting her throat brought him more pleasure than the last few kills put together. Even though the aftermath was for Sloane, the beginning was for him.

When he spotted her across the rest stop parking lot, he knew she was the one. He knew the hours he'd spent waiting weren't a waste of his precious time. She was perfect with her long dark hair and big, brown eyes. Beautiful and probably a hell of a lot of fun on a typical night, he knew she was exactly what he needed to execute the next part of his plan.

Usually, he'd walk up to a beautiful woman and ask her if she wanted to have some fun. The direct approach never failed him. A little flirting and a smile made them putty in his hands. But tonight, he wasn't at a bar or the supermarket. The direct approach probably wasn't the best bet at a dark yet not deserted enough rest stop. He needed another method that would get her right where he wanted her.

That was where a well-placed nail and his trusty signal jammer came into play. An hour later, he was on the side of the road offering a damsel in distress his assistance. When she let her guard down, he knocked her out and shoved her in the back of his van. He played with her for hours while he waited for the steady stream of cars to slow to a more manageable trickle. She fought like any beautiful, strong-willed woman would, which only made him enjoy his work more. Her tears mixed with her blood as his cock pulsed inside of her.

It was a beautiful sight.

Once they were alone and he was sated, he dragged her limp body into the nearest bathroom. He propped a 'closed for maintenance' sign outside the door so that they wouldn't be disturbed during the unsavory part of their evening. Sawing through the human body was a messy business, even when blood no longer pumped through the veins. An ax would've been easier, but that wasn't the killer's weapon of choice in Sloane's book, so he had to suffer through the teeth of the saw getting caught in bone or tendon, and then the tearing of muscle and flesh as he ripped it free. Messy and tedious. The things he did for his true calling.

When she was in as many pieces as he cared to get her into, he carefully placed her body parts in random places around the rest stop. He left her head sitting on a shelf inside the room the volunteers used to pass out the gross free coffee. Knowing that would be the show-stopper, he stapled the note for Sloane to the woman's forehead. He made sure to leave her right foot somewhere it would be easily found, his signature Roman numeral carved into her fleshy heel.

He smiled as he walked back to the van, stripping off the coveralls he'd bought at a home improvement store in Portland as he went. Pleasure coursed through him knowing just how much the scene he'd set would disturb the people who found the body, and Sloane, when she got wind of what he'd done.

Everything was exactly as it should be. Nothing could kill his good mood. Maybe once he got cleaned up, he'd go out and have a bit of fun that didn't end up with anyone lying in a pool of blood. It was something he enjoyed on occasion, and now seemed like as good a time as any to find someone to enjoy for the sake of carnal pleasure only.

He knew better than to get too excited about the way everything was working out so flawlessly. All good things had to come to an end eventually. He just kind of hoped he'd get to enjoy it longer than thirty minutes. Of course, he should've guessed it would be her that ruined everything. Even though it was nearly four in the morning, he knew the devil didn't sleep. She liked to make him squirm. She liked to call when he least expected it. That was how she showed her dominance.

Too bad for her. He didn't give a shit about her anymore, and she didn't scare him the way she used to. He was stronger than her now, better than her. Before too long, Grace would be the one cowering whenever her phone rang. She'd be the one looking over her shoulder, wondering when he was going to make her life a living hell.

That moment was coming a hell of a lot sooner than she realized. All he needed to do was get rid of Sloane first, and then Grace would get her turn.

"What do you want?" he growled as he climbed into the back of the van and finished stripping off the bloody coverall.

"Is that any way to answer the phone?"

The tone of her voice was sickeningly sweet, but he knew it was just an act. She was trying to disarm him before she reamed him for what he'd done. It wouldn't work, of course, but he wasn't going to let her know that. At least not yet.

"I'm busy, and in case you didn't notice, it's four in the bloody morning; it's too damn early for you to call. So either something's wrong, or you're calling to yell at me, and I'm guessing it's the latter. Excuse me for not being excited to get scolded like a child right now."

While he waited for her to say what she had to say, he went about cleaning up. He couldn't afford to linger in the parking lot too long, so he put her on speakerphone, allowing him to have both hands to wipe the blood from his body. The bleach was harsh against his skin, but he was used to it. He reveled in the feel of the burn, the slight tinge of pain it brought. It reminded him that he was alive and in charge of his destiny. A weird thing to feel, but he loved it just the same.

"Fine, you want to get right to it, then here we go. What the fuck do you think you're doing?" she snarled. "Do you know what you've done? Do you realize how fucking stupid you're being?"

"Am I? Maybe I'm the smart one, and you're the idiot. I'm doing what you never could."

She scoffed, and he could almost picture her face. "Did you ever stop to think about how I've gotten away with what I do for as long as I have? It's because I don't flaunt my kills to the public. You're going to get caught, and I won't be there to help you out of the mess you've created for yourself."

"You were caught once," he pointed out but regretted it the second the words were out of his mouth.

"Was I?" she asked. "In case you forgot, I'm free to roam around the country killing whenever I feel like it. My one brush with the law had nothing to do with me and everything to do with Isabelle being too young to realize what she was missing out on."

"If you believe that, then you really are an idiot. She knew what she was doing when she turned you in. She knew what she was missing out on. I would've never done that to you."

She scoffed again. "You say that, yet here you are telling the world about yourself and what you're out there doing. You've basically told Isabelle and the FBI that I'm still alive. You've told them that I took you under my wing and taught you what I know. Instead of going undetected and living the perfect life doing whatever the hell you want, you've turned into an attention-seeking whore."

"I am not."

He realized a second too late that he sounded like a whiny baby when he spit out the words. He might as well have stomped his foot and thrown a little tantrum for all the good the words did. He could not let her turn him into something he wasn't.

"You need to end this nonsense now. You don't want me to come find you, dear boy. If I have to stop you from continuing this quest you're on, you'll regret it."

"Why don't you mind your own business."

"She is my business," she reminded him. "I told you not to fuck with her. Yet you did it anyway. Don't forget that you need me, boy."

"I don't need you. I have my own contacts. I have people who are willing to do anything I ask of them. Face it. I've replaced you in more ways than one."

Her laugh filtered through the phone, the sound sending a chill up his spine. Had he made a mistake crossing her? He didn't think so, but only time would tell. If she hadn't killed her precious Isabelle after all these years, she wouldn't kill him. He was sure of it.

"You're going to regret this."

It was his turn to laugh.

"I don't think so. I'm having the most fun I've ever had in my entire life, and I feel freer than I've ever felt before. Do whatever you want, but it's my show now. Just wait and see what I have in store for you and your dear Isabelle. You're going to wish you'd stayed on my side."

He disconnected the call before she could respond and threw his phone onto the passenger seat. With a satisfied smile on his face, he climbed into the front seat and started the van. She'd call back sometime soon, and when she did, he'd be ready for it. In the meantime, there was still a lot of fun to be had, and no one, not even Grace, would ruin it for him.

CHAPTER TWENTY-FIVE

As an FBI agent, Cade was used to many things no one should ever have to get used to, like feeling helpless to stop terrible things from happening. He was used to the atrocities that humans were capable of, the depths of which gave him nightmares more often than he'd ever admit. And he was used to being tired. So very, very tired.

But nothing could have prepared him for the bone-deep weariness he currently felt. The weight of Sloane's case was squarely on his shoulders, and he knew without a doubt he was going to fail. He just wasn't quite sure how. Would he catch whoever was after her but lose her in the process? Or would he be able to keep Sloane alive but fail to bring in her tormentor and her mom? Would Sloane lose another person she loved because he couldn't protect them?

He hoped like hell he was wrong, but dread coursed through him, thick like blood. He couldn't let on that he was worried. Sloane was already scared and angry, hanging on by a thread that could snap at any moment. She had enough on her plate. And Reid...well, he was Reid. Plus, having his ex-wife's crazy family affect his loved ones was enough. He didn't need to deal with Cade's insecurity issues on top of everything else.

He tried focusing on the computer in front of him, but his eyes were starting to cross. The clock in the corner said it was nearly two in the morning, which meant it was almost time for Reid to take over the night watch so Cade could get some sleep. Unlike his reluctant partner, who tossed and turned on the pull-out couch in their suite until he couldn't take it anymore and headed out for a run, Cade was too tired not to fall asleep the second his head hit the pillow, even if he was forced to sleep on an old, lumpy mattress that had seen better days.

They'd hoped for a room with two beds, but the closest they could get was a one-bedroom suite with a sofa bed. They'd given Sloane the bedroom so she'd not only have privacy, but so she could hopefully get some rest. She was running on fumes despite the nap she took on the way to Portland. If they weren't careful, she would run herself into the ground trying to catch the person that killed her friend, and then she'd do it again, trying to find her mom. She'd sacrifice herself in a heartbeat to bring them both to justice, a fact Cade was far more aware of than he wanted to be. Keeping an eye on her well-being was a distraction he didn't need, but one he couldn't ignore.

Knowing he wouldn't get any more work done for the night, Cade logged out of the computer, then stifled a yawn behind his hand. It had been a long day, or was it two? He wasn't quite sure when he'd last had the chance to sleep for more than a couple of hours at a time. And it didn't look like he'd get the opportunity any time soon. Not as long as someone was after Sloane.

In the morning they'd hop on an FBI-issued plane and head to San Francisco in the hopes that they'd get their unsub to give up his plan and skip ahead with them. Since they didn't need to stay off of anyone's radar anymore, flying was once again an option. It would be easier and a hell of a lot quicker than driving the 600 plus mile distance between Portland and San Francisco. At least on the plane he would feel like he was doing something. Sitting in the car for another ten hours or so would've felt like a giant waste of time. Which was something they didn't have in abundance.

Glancing over at the bedroom door, Cade sighed. If he had his way, he'd hide her somewhere no one would be able to find her. He checked his phone for the time, then started toward the couch. With any luck, Reid would walk through the door any minute. Then Cade could stop worrying about Sloane and get some rest himself.

A muffled sob drew his attention back to the bedroom door. He waited a moment, unsure if he'd imagined the noise or not. Was she awake or crying in her sleep? Should he check on her? Cade had no idea how to react.

Maybe he'd be better off waiting for Reid to come back so the other man could make sure his ex was okay. She was always mad at him anyway, so it wouldn't matter if she was pissed at him for checking on her.

"No...stop...please don't."

The pleading, though still slightly muffled, had him moving. The last thing he wanted was for her to be traumatized by a memory she didn't want to have. Even if he believed her memories might be the key to unlocking a few of their mysteries.

Cade pushed the door open and quietly stepped inside. His eyes adjusted to the darkness quicker than he expected, allowing him to see Sloane in the middle of the king-sized bed, the blankets wrapped around her waist. Her head moved from side to side as she continually murmured 'no' at whoever she was seeing in her dream.

"Sloane."

He spoke softly as he approached, not wanting to startle her or make things worse. Sitting on the edge of the bed, he placed a hand on her shoulder. She screamed 'no' again, but this time her arm flew out, her hand connecting with his cheek.

"Sloane, stop," he said as he leaned over her and put pressure on both of her shoulders to hopefully stop her flailing. "Wake up, Sloane. It's not real. None of it is real."

Her body bucked beneath him as she tried to fight him off. "Please...no..."

Panic filled his chest. He wasn't sure what he would do if he couldn't get her to wake up. Where the hell was Reid when he needed the man most?

"Sloane. Damn it, Sloane, wake up."

He shook her lightly, hoping the movement would break the dream's hold. Her breathing slowed, a whimper escaping her as she tried to curl in on herself. Cade brushed the hair off of her face as he said her name over and over, hoping the sound of his voice would continue to help pull her out. It took longer than he expected to coax her awake, but when her eyes finally fluttered open, relief flowed through him.

"Cade?" she asked, her voice shaky.

"Hey, are you okay?" he asked as he leaned back to give her some space. "That sounded like a really bad one."

Tears filled her eyes as she shook her head. She was visibly terrified for the first time since he'd known her. She'd faced off with two serial killers in the last month and had seemed sure of herself and her ability to take them down. Now, the mere memory of her mom had her shaking like a leaf. Before he could prepare himself, she was launching herself up off of the bed and into him, her arms wrapping around him to pull him close, like she was trying to soak up his strength.

"It's going to be okay," he promised her, though he had no idea how he was going to keep it. There were too many variables, and too many things were coming at them at once. Even Sloane herself was a variable he couldn't control, and she'd do whatever she wanted, whatever she had to, in order to end things.

But for now, all she needed from him was comfort, and he was more than willing to give her that.

"I don't know how it can be," she sniffled. "It's all falling apart. Nobody is safe because of me and my messed-up family."

Cade shook his head. "You aren't responsible for any of this. You didn't ask to be born into a family of killers, and you didn't ask for your mom's psycho protégé to seek you out. None of this is your fault."

"I've spent so much time fighting to forget everything that happened. I'd gotten so good at compartmentalizing, nothing fazed me. But now, the walls are crumbling down faster than I can handle. I don't know how much more of this I can take. I don't know if I can keep going back there even if it helps the case."

"You're not alone, Sloane. Don't forget that. You don't have to do any of this by yourself. I've got you."

Her hot tears soaked through the shoulder of his t-shirt, but Cade didn't care. He tightened his hold on her and just sat there while she cried in his arms. Eventually, her breathing evened out, and the tears stopped. She pulled away, her gaze lifting up to meet his.

"Stay with me," she said softly, half plea, half demand.

"Of course."

It didn't matter to Cade if Reid was back or not. Nothing short of the killer storming their hotel room could drag him away from Sloane. Not when she needed him. Hell, not when he needed her just as much. For one night, for only a few hours, they could be vulnerable together. In the morning, they'd go back to bottling it all up as best they could.

She smiled at him as she laid back down on the bed and patted the spot next to her. He kicked off his shoes, then climbed under the covers, scooting over on the mattress until his body was touching hers. Sloane sighed, then rolled over, so her front was pressed against his side, her arm draped over his waist. Cade fought back a sigh of his own as he worked his arm under her head, then wrapped it around her. She snuggled in closer, her head resting against his chest.

The moment felt oddly normal, despite being anything but. He'd revel in the ordinariness of the moment as long as he could. Their demons would always be there when they woke up.

CHAPTER TWENTY-SIX

The gentle chime of the alarm on her phone drew Sloane from the most peaceful night of sleep she'd had in far too long. For a second, she felt guilty for getting the rest she needed when she knew people were suffering because of her. She felt guilty for falling asleep in Cade's arms when they both should have been burning the midnight oil trying to figure out who killed her friend. Why should she get to have a moment of contentment when so many others were in pain?

Rolling over, she grabbed her phone then swiped a finger over the screen before flopping down on her back. She didn't want to get up and face the day. More than that, Sloane didn't want to get up and face the fear she'd finally recognized in the middle of the night. She hadn't felt that kind of terror since she was thirteen, and even after all of the things she'd seen since, that fear was debilitating.

It was too bad she couldn't hide away and let someone else fight her battle for her. She could beg Cade to run away with her, and they could wait it out. Maybe Rosalie and her little helper would get bored and move on, leaving her friends alone. Maybe they'd stop killing people just to torment Sloane, and she could finally live the normal life everyone talked about.

And maybe pigs would sprout wings and fly.

A crash from the living area reminded her that she couldn't waste any more time thinking about the maybes. There was a killer out there that she needed to stop. Sitting up, Sloane didn't bother looking at the other side of the bed. She knew Cade was gone and had been for a while. She could only imagine the grief he'd gotten from Reid about staying with her. Well, Reid could go ahead and fuck himself with his opinion. She'd needed Cade last night, and he'd come through for her. That was all that mattered.

"It's about time you got up," Reid grumbled as soon as she walked out of the bedroom.

He looked like he hadn't slept a wink the night before or any night in the last few months, for that matter. The dark circles that had been present when he showed up at her cabin were more pronounced, and she was pretty sure he'd lost some weight since then, making his cheekbones stick out more than they used to.

"Good morning, Reid. It's so great to see you too. Did you have a great night? I did."

"Why are you such a smart ass?"

Sloane laughed. "Is that the question you want to ask? You've known me a long time, and I'm still the same person. Nothing's changed over the years."

He glared at her, then looked down at his phone. "I must have blocked out how frustrating you are to be around."

"No, you didn't. What's got your panties in a twist this morning? Did something happen while I was asleep? Where's Cade?"

Reid shook his head, then scraped a hand over his face. "Nothing happened. It's been radio silence all night, which is both good and unnerving. I hate feeling like we're struggling to catch up with this guy."

"I get it. Try adding that to feeling like the whole mess is your fault. It's been frustrating, to say the least," Sloane admitted before plopping herself down next to a pile of pillows and blankets on the couch. "We need to finish this."

"I agree. I'd like to go home and see Sara, and this little adventure we're on is interfering with my plans."

Looking over at her ex, Sloane smiled. "Oh, and what plans are those? Actually, maybe I don't want to know."

She laughed as she raised her hands in the air, only to be smacked in the stomach by one of the decorative throw pillows. She stared at Reid for a second, unsure of what was happening, then laughed even harder when she realized they were joking around with each other. How long had it been since they enjoyed an ordinary moment like they were currently sharing? Far too long. But maybe, just maybe, there was hope for them to rekindle a friendship of sorts once everything was over. It would be easier for Emily and Tally if she and Reid could find peace.

"Don't worry. I definitely wouldn't be sharing those kinds of plans with you. It's bad enough knowing what you and Cade were up to the other night."

"Hey, no one asked you to show up in the middle of the night and ruin things," she reminded him. "I would've been a lot happier to hear all about this shit show in the morning. At least then I would have another orgasm or two under my belt."

"Jeezus, Sloane. I didn't need to know that," Reid groaned, making Sloane laugh so hard she snorted.

"I know. I just like making you uncomfortable. It's one of my favorite pastimes. Now, tell me about these plans of yours. Do they include a ring?"

Reid sighed as he joined her on the couch. "Shouldn't it be weird to talk about this?"

Shrugging, Sloane pulled her legs in so she sat cross-legged on the couch, her body angled toward Reid. This was the most civil conversation they'd had in years, and she wanted to enjoy it.

"I don't see why. We're both adults, and we both want the other one to be happy. Just because I've chosen to spend my life alone doesn't mean I want you to. I think Sara's great. A little more Disney princess than I'm used to. I mean, who is genuinely that freaking nice all the time? I half expect woodland creatures and birds to follow her around."

"I wondered the same thing at first. Is she a psycho waiting to slit my throat in the middle of the night? Does she have the faces of her past boyfriends hanging on a wall in her basement?" Reid laughed. "It was hard for a jaded cynic like me to realize that's just who she is and that there are actual people out there who haven't faced off with the worst the world has to offer."

"I don't know if I'd have anything in common with someone like that," Sloane admitted.

"You'd be surprised. Plus, it's refreshing to have someone in my life, besides Tally, of course, that is full of optimism. Sara saw the good in me when I didn't see it in myself. She reminded me that we all make mistakes, and even if they haunt us, we still deserve to be happy. One or two moments don't, and shouldn't, define us."

Reid's statement slammed into Sloane with a force she wasn't prepared for. One thing her ex-husband never lacked was confidence. Sometimes he even bordered on cocky, and as far as she had seen since reuniting with him, he hadn't changed all that much. To hear that even for a moment, he didn't believe in himself was shocking. She didn't know for sure, and she wasn't about to ask, but she had a feeling his doubt surfaced after the demise of their marriage.

Knowing she might have had a hand in making him feel unworthy of happiness sucked. Did he hurt her? Yeah, probably more than she'd ever admit. Was she angry with him for a long time? Yes, but she never once wished him ill-will, not even when she thought he deserved it.

"I'm glad you found her. I never meant for you to doubt yourself, Reid. You deserve to be happy."

Reid stared at her for a moment, then dropped his gaze to rest on his shoes. "I hurt you, Sloane. I was a bastard back then, only thinking of myself, foolishly believing you'd be fine if I threw you to the wolves. Hell, I was dumb enough to believe we'd be fine, even though I betrayed you. I was an idiot."

"You were, but even idiots deserve love and happiness."

"I'm going to propose."

"Holy shit. That's huge. Do you know when? Do you have a plan? I hope it's better than the way you proposed to me."

Laughing, Reid looked back up at her. "I'm just waiting for the perfect moment, though we'll be wearing clothes when I do it."

"Probably a good call," Sloan laughed. "Do you already have a ring?"

"I've had it for months. Cooper kind of stole my thunder, then this case came up, and now everything's a bit chaotic. But as soon as things calm down, I'm going to do it. I don't want to wait anymore. I think maybe a part of me has been holding back because I felt like I owed you an explanation."

Shaking her head, Sloane smacked him with the pillow he'd hit her with earlier. "You don't owe me anything. Don't wait. When we get back to San Francisco, go see her. Give her the ring and tell her you can't wait to spend the rest of your life with her. There's always going to be a case. There's always going to be chaos. Don't let this stand in the way of your future."

Reid seemed to think about her words for a moment, then smiled at her. "If I can get away for a moment, I'll do it."

"I'll make sure you have time," she promised him. "Cade and I can work on things until you get back. It's not like we have any leads, and we'll probably end up sitting around waiting for another body to drop."

"Well, that's comforting."

"Sorry, but you know what I mean. Just don't think about that. Think about Sara and your happily ever after. Every princess deserves a prince."

"Ha," Reid snorted. "Definitely not much of a prince, but hopefully, Sara will say yes anyway."

"She will," Sloane assured him as she stood and tossed the pillow onto the couch. "Now, I need to get my ass in gear and take a shower. We've got a long day ahead of us, and I'm sure Cade will want to get going as soon as he gets back."

"Is everything okay with you two?" Reid asked before she could walk away. "I didn't mean to fuck things up."

"Yeah you did, but I get it. I needed to know what was going on. I also get why no one told me sooner," she admitted. "As for Cade and me, well, we'll see. I don't even know if that's something I'd want to pursue. We live completely different lives, on different sides of the country, and I enjoy my solitude. But it doesn't matter. Not until we catch Richard's killer and Rosalie. Until then, I don't have time to worry about my personal life."

"And I do?" Reid scoffed. "You really should listen to your own advice."

"It's not your mom out there taking killers under her wing and teaching them how to be the best. I know all the reasons I shouldn't, but I feel guilty every time someone dies because of her, whether she's the one that held the knife or her little helper did. I should've done more to make sure she was captured."

"You were a kid."

"Not the entire time. I knew deep down she wasn't dead, but I lived the lie just like everyone else did. Logically, I know there was nothing I could have done, but logic doesn't keep the guilt away."

Before Reid could respond, she turned and walked toward the bedroom, closing the door to shield herself from Reid's gaze once she was inside. Her eyes drifted over the bed, the sheets and bedspread a crumpled mess. She wouldn't forget the few hours she'd spent wrapped in Cade's arms while he comforted her. She'd use the strength he'd given her to continue on. Then, once Richard's killer and Rosalie were in FBI custody, maybe she'd give herself the chance to revisit what she shared with Cade before her world was blown apart.

Of course, first, they'd have to survive the fight, and Sloane didn't need a Magic 8 Ball to see that the outlook wasn't so good.

CHAPTER
TWENTY-SEVEN

She was gorgeous. Tall, blonde, legs for days, and lips that he couldn't help but picture wrapped around his dick. He liked what he saw, and if the sly smile on her face was any indication, she was a fan of what she saw too. He took another slow perusal of her body; from her beautiful blue eyes down to her toes which were painted a sexy as sin red, then back up until his eyes met hers.

If only he had time to partake in her, he could tell she'd be a ton of fun. Maybe even someone he could talk into a repeat performance whenever he was in town and felt the need for sexual release, but not the need to kill.

Unfortunately, he didn't have time for distractions. He needed to stay focused on the task at hand, not what it would feel like to ease the tension in his shoulders by fucking the pretty girl out for lunch with her friends. It didn't matter that he couldn't do anything until he heard back from his contact.

He couldn't make a move until he knew Sloane was right where he wanted her.

Checking his phone for an update, he fought back the urge to scream when he saw the screen was still blank. He punched in an angry demand for news, smiling when the bubbles appeared underneath his message.

DiSantoisaKiller: *You need to calm down. I'm trying to get you what you want, but I'm also being forced to do damage control. If I don't do my job, people will get suspicious. If I'm caught, you'll never get what you want.*

DLegacy76: *You need to try harder. I don't respond well to incompetence.*

DiSantoisaKiller: *Fuck.*

DLegacy76: *You knew what you got into when you agreed to help me. Get me what I want or pay the price.*

DiSantoisaKiller: *Fine. But I'll need an hour or two. I should have some information by then.*

He smiled, his gaze moving from his phone over to the blonde who was still watching him. An hour or two was just what he needed to take what he wanted from her, then be on his way. He winked at her, then looked back down at his phone.

DLecacy76: *You've got it, now don't disappoint me.*

Closing out of the app, he placed his phone on the table just in time to find the blonde approaching him. He loved it when he didn't have to do any work.

"Mind if I join you?" she asked, her voice sexier than he imagined.

"I would be an idiot to say no."

He waited fifteen minutes before he asked if she'd like to go somewhere else. It was longer than he'd planned, but he didn't want to risk her saying no. In no time, they were fumbling blindly into her apartment, clothes, and shoes flying everywhere. When she dropped to her knees in front of him, he realized his imagination hadn't done her lips around his cock any justice. The real thing was a sight to behold.

For an hour and forty-five minutes, he fucked her all over her apartment. Against the door, on the floor, in her bed, and then the shower. As he sprawled out in her bed, he congratulated himself on taking a much-needed break. It had been well worth pausing his plans to take the blonde for a spin. Now, he was sated and clear-minded and ready to move on.

Getting up, he did his best not to disturb her, then moved around the apartment quietly, gathering his discarded clothes. He pulled his pants on, then removed his phone from his pocket so he could check his messages. It had been long enough that his contact should have what he wanted. He needed to know what Sloane was up to, and he needed to know now.

DiSantoisaKiller: *They're headed to San Francisco. They've got a room at the Xavier.*

"Fuck," he yelled before slamming his fist against the wall by the door.

When he realized what he'd done, he stilled, listening to see if his friend had heard his outburst. He wondered how he would explain things if she did. Did he even really care? No. He didn't. If she noticed his outburst and asked questions, he'd just do what he did best and silence her.

DLegacy76: *What the fuck. That's not the way it's supposed to work.*

DiSantoisaKiller: *I don't know what to tell you. She's boarding a plane now. You better figure out your plan.*

DLegacy76: *You better watch yourself.*

He didn't bother to say anything else. Instead, he threw his phone down on the table, an angry roar escaping him. This wasn't how things were supposed to go. She was supposed to follow him. She was supposed to stay one step behind him the whole time, never able to catch up while he toyed with her. Why would she skip ahead? Was she hoping to keep him from continuing his killing spree?

Well, if that's what she wanted, she had another thing coming.

Stripping his pants back off, he walked into the kitchen, searching each drawer until he found what he was looking for. With the butcher knife wrapped in a kitchen towel and hidden just slightly behind his bare leg, he stalked back into the blonde's room. He'd already forgotten her name. Sasha, Ashley, Rachel, something like that. Not that it mattered. Before long, she'd be nothing but another notch on his belt.

"Hey," she murmured, her voice a husky sound that sent a shot straight to his dick.

He climbed onto the bed, her brows furrowed in confusion as he pulled the sheet off of her, then straddled her body. Within seconds, the sleep-induced haze lifted, and she smiled up at him, the same sultry smile she'd given him back at the restaurant. The poor delusional girl thought he was coming back for another round. Maybe if he hadn't checked his messages, that would be precisely what he'd be doing, but instead, she was going to be the unlucky recipient of his anger. He needed to get rid of the rage coursing through him before he did something that ruined his plans.

"Mmmm...is that for me?" she asked, reaching down to grab at his dick. "I can't wait for more..."

Before she could finish, he shoved the kitchen towel between her lips, muffling the sound of her voice. Her eyebrow raised in question, but she wasn't worried. Her eyes shimmered with lust as she arched her back, putting her naked breasts on display. She thought they were playing. Just his luck, he was about to kill a woman who could have easily become one of his favorite playthings.

He used the bra they'd haphazardly tossed onto her bedpost to secure her hands over her head. She moaned against the towel, and he could smell her arousal. The dummy was getting off on what he was doing, yet she'd never find release. Fear would replace everything she felt as soon as she saw the knife. And that's when he'd be the one needing release.

Leaning into her, he brought his lips down to her ear like he was going to whisper something sexy into it. She sighed against the towel as his body pressed down against hers.

"I'm sorry it has to be this way," he told her before sitting back up and pulling the knife out from where he'd tucked it under his leg.

Her eyes widened as he traced the blade along her cheek. He could see the fight in her eyes, but she was too smart to move. Even just a centimeter would mean bad things for her, though it didn't matter what she did since he would kill her either way.

Then once he was done with her, he would make everyone pay for forcing him to ruin such a good thing. He'd start with Sloane, then move on to the jackass who was feeding him information. Then once they were both taken care of, he'd move on to his mother. Depending on who you asked, Grace Baldwin or Rosalie DiSanto was the catalyst behind everything. She was the reason he was slicing through the skin of the blonde that fucked like a dream.

And someday soon, she would learn that he was better than her. Scarier than her. And he wouldn't hesitate to kill her, even though she'd given birth to him. He wouldn't be Isabelle's replacement. He was everything she couldn't be and more.

He was the true DiSanto heir, and he was going to prove to everyone he deserved the name more than his parents and sister ever did.

CHAPTER
TWENTY-EIGHT

"I just wish I knew why he was obsessed with me."

She'd been wracking her brain for days, trying to figure out why the killer was so focused on her. Was it just because he was a student of Rosalie? Or was there something else fueling his fire?

None of it made any sense.

Especially the fact that he was suddenly using her books as inspiration for his kills. Was this turn of events supposed to be another slap in the face? He'd already told the world he was the killer, so it wasn't as if he was trying to pin the murders on her. Unless he wanted people to think he had a partner, but that didn't seem right either.

There were too many damn questions and not enough answers regarding his motivation. And then there was the biggest question of all.

Who the fuck was this guy?

"His obsession could stem from anything. He's got a crush, or he's trying to eliminate the competition. Who knows. We just need to figure out who he is. With any luck, you'll be right and jumping ahead will get him so pissed off he'll make a mistake."

Sloane wanted to be right, but she had a feeling the unsub was going to take his anger out on someone that didn't deserve it. And to make matters worse, he'd leave nothing behind to help them figure out his identity. Did they make a mistake going along with Sloane's plan? Maybe they should've continued following him instead of trying to one-up him.

"Hey guys, Diane's got some news," Cade said as he joined them.

He set his laptop on the table between her and Reid, then slid into the chair next to her. He didn't have to do anything, just being nearby helped her feel more in control. When she was alone, she felt like she was spiraling. Memories flickered in her brain whether she was awake or asleep now, and even the ones that most people would consider good were bad for her well-being.

"I know you guys are about to start your descent into San Francisco, but we just got word that a woman was found dead in her apartment just outside of Roseburg, Oregon. She was stabbed multiple times, her throat slit, and the Roman number for forty-one was carved into the bottom of her foot."

"Shit," Reid muttered. "Was there a note?"

Diane shook her head. "He didn't leave anything behind this time."

Sloane's brows furrowed as she waited for Diane to say more about the scene, but the other woman remained silent, waiting instead for one of them to say something.

"This doesn't make any sense."

"What do you mean?" Diane asked, her voice crackling over the wireless connection.

"Well, first off, she doesn't fit the pattern. Where's number forty? Second, why would he kill someone and not leave a note? His whole thing right now is to taunt me, right? Our game isn't over, so why would he go back to murders that don't move the game along? We would expect him to continue using passages from my books or pictures from my childhood. Leaving nothing doesn't fit."

"Shit," Reid muttered again.

"We missed something, both at the current scene and somewhere in between. There has to be a victim somewhere between Portland and Roseburg. And if it's just one, then maybe he's moved on to the next book. Instead of killing couples, he's moved on to...fuck," Cade paused as realization hit him. "We need to have all of the southbound rest stops secured, and we need to get ERT teams out to each of them now."

"I'll get the troops moving," Diane assured him as she turned away from the screen and yelled for her assistant.

She gave him instructions before turning her attention back on the three of them. The look on her face told Sloane whatever she had to say wasn't going to be good.

"Michael just got word that they found a note on the woman's bathroom mirror. It appears to be written in blood, but they won't know for sure until they test it."

"What does it say?" Sloane asked though she didn't want to know.

"You did this."

Sloane closed her eyes and wiped her sweaty palms on her jeans. She took a deep breath and then another, hoping the slow inhale and exhale of the recycled airplane air would help calm her stomach.

It didn't.

"She wasn't planned then."

She could feel Cade's eyes on her. Hell, she could feel all three sets of eyes on her, and she understood the skepticism she knew they were feeling because of her statement. She sounded so sure of what she was saying because she was. Whoever this woman was, she was not part of the unsub's plans. What she wasn't sure of was why he acted out. What happened to make him alter his carefully crafted plot? Was it the fact that she was skipping ahead?

Or was it simply because the guy was a psychopath?

Either way, Sloane knew without a doubt that he'd deviated from his course for one reason or another, and this poor woman, whoever she was, paid the price. Now she just had to convince the others that she was right.

"He's been meticulous about everything so far. He brings what he plans to leave behind with him. The notes are always carefully crafted, not hastily scrawled in the victim's blood or on something he found in their house. He brings his weapon of choice with him, except for the couples, but that was because the storyline called for it. I bet in this instance they'll find a knife is missing," she surmised. "I'd also hazard a guess that the file has been accessed recently. He got word we were skipping ahead, and that's why this woman is dead."

"Isn't that a bit of a stretch?" Diane asked.

Before Sloane could respond, Cade shook his head. "I don't think so. He could've easily snapped if he found out that Sloane wasn't falling in line. Maybe he was enjoying a non-murderous version of an afternoon hook-up, and when he got word from his contact that Sloane wasn't playing the game right, he took it out on this woman."

"Did he finally make a mistake? If the news set him off, he might not have been thinking straight when he punished the victim for Sloane's disobedience. Maybe he left behind handprints or DNA from their consensual romp, then forgot to wipe the place or her down before he left," Reid pointed out. "We need to get ERT to comb over her place and her. Check her fingernails. If he's any good, she probably has skin under her nails."

Diane yelled for Michael again so he could pass along the new instructions. She asked him to have the local police trace the victim's last known whereabouts too. If they could figure out where she'd been, they might be able to find their unsub. They had to have met somewhere before they ended up back at the woman's apartment.

"I've got one more piece of news. Before we found out about the most recent victim, we got word back on the evidence taken from Sloane's place and the Briggs cabin. None of the blood on the dog belonged to the unsub. Also, the only skin under Briggs's fingernails was his own. Unfortunately, we came up empty regarding the physical evidence. We're still working on the camera, they're trying to track the signal down, but they need Anderson to sign off on some things, but no one can get ahold of him. The fucker's probably taking a nap while the rest of us are out here trying to find a killer."

Sloane snorted at Diane's choice of words. The other woman hated Tom Anderson almost as much as Sloane did, but she usually tried to pretend to be polite about her hatred. Apparently, those days were over.

"He doesn't want the killer caught. Not if he's been helping him this whole time. He's probably off hiding somewhere, hoping Sloane and this guy take each other out, and no one will ever be able to prove he's been the leak this entire time," Cade said, his jaw flexing as he ground his teeth together.

She could tell he wanted to say so much more but was trying to keep his anger at bay. An announcement over the intercom reminded them that they were near their final destination. Sloane was eager to touch down in San Francisco. For some reason, she felt like they were that much closer to ending things now that they would be exactly where the unsub wanted them. She was also nervous as hell. What if they couldn't predict what he was going to do next? What if they couldn't stop him from killing over and over again?

Would he do what she hoped and divert from his plan now that they skipped ahead, or would he prolong the inevitable and take even more lives on his way to the bay area?

"Let me know when you've checked into the hotel. I'll try to get you more information by then," Diane promised before her gaze landed on Sloane. "This isn't your fault. This guy is a sick fuck, and there's nothing you could have done to stop him before now. Focus on what's coming, not what's already happened. Dwelling on that shit won't do you any good."

Before Sloane could respond, Diane's face was replaced by the FBI wallpaper on Cade's computer. Her parting words hung in the air, making Sloane wonder how the hell the other woman seemed to know her so well after such a short period of time.

It wasn't easy trying to stay focused on the here and now. She could see the faces of the dead when she closed her eyes. The guilt she felt threatened to take her down, but she knew she couldn't let it. She had to keep slogging forward so she could finally face off with the man who was using her to fuel his killing spree. He's the one who opened Pandora's box. He was the one that was going to wish he'd never heard of Sloane Matthews, let alone poked her.

When she finally got the chance to look him in the eye, he was going to realize she was a lot more like her mother than anyone knew. Yet, she wouldn't kill him. No, she'd make sure he got what he deserved, and then some. She'd just have a little fun toying with him first.

CHAPTER TWENTY-NINE

He'd lost control.

After everything he'd done, after all of his careful preparation, he allowed one tiny thing to send him over the edge. He couldn't believe he'd made such a monumental mistake. Nothing about what happened with the blonde was okay.

His one hope was that the shower they'd taken together had washed away most of what he could have possibly left behind on her body. He'd done his best to wipe down the surfaces he remembered touching, but he'd done a lot in that apartment in such a short amount of time. And without the luxury of being able to wipe the place spotless, he just had to live with what he'd done.

This time everything really was Sloane's fault. How could he have been stupid enough to let her get to him? He may have just given her the ability to figure out his identity, which was the one thing he wasn't ready to give her just yet.

Not his name, but who he was. He knew they wouldn't find anything at any of the other scenes. He'd walked away from those without a scratch. With the blonde, the odds were against him. If he hadn't left a piece of himself behind, he'd be shocked.

He needed to stop dwelling on what had happened. What was done was done. Instead of spiraling into his feelings, he needed to decide what he wanted to do next. Did he continue on his path like nothing happened? Or did he give Sloane what she obviously wanted and skip to the end, where he'd really make his presence known?

Both options had the potential for big things. People would remember the Roman Numeral Killer no matter which way he went. He would go down in history with the likes of Bundy, Gacy, and the Cutthroat Couple. He would leave his mark.

Everyone would know his name.

His phone rang, knocking away the thoughts of what it would be like to be one of the greats. Glancing over at his phone, he groaned when he saw the name on the screen. The last thing he wanted to do was deal with Grace, but he knew if he didn't answer, it would only piss her off more. Since he was in no position to take her on just yet, he needed to keep her off his ass. If he didn't, she would likely do something that would ruin his plans. He'd come too damn far to let her fuck things up now.

"What."

"Is that any way to talk to your mother?"

She sounded far calmer than she had the last time he talked to her, but he knew it was an act. He was making waves, something she'd strictly forbidden more than once. She'd gone unnoticed for twenty years, and now the FBI knew she was alive. Her precious Isabelle knew she was alive too. Which meant for him everything was going according to plan, but for her, life was falling apart.

"It's not like you're calling to have a friendly mother/son chat. There's a lecture coming, or an attempt at one anyway, so just say what you want to say so I can ignore it and do what I want."

"You ungrateful little shit."

He scoffed. "What the hell do I have to be grateful for? I grew up thinking there was something wrong with me, that I was an abomination. Instead of keeping my desires bottled up, I could've been finding my real calling all of these years. I could've grown up with parents that understood me. But no, I was abandoned at a fire station and forced to grow up in a family that sucked the joy out of me," he said harshly.

He could barely mask his pain with the anger he felt in equal measure. Finding out he was adopted answered every question he ever had about himself. It made everything make sense. Which was something he'd been lacking most of his life. Everything was suddenly clearer the second he found out about his true parentage.

"We..."

"I don't want to hear it. We both know you only came looking for me because your precious little girl wants nothing to do with you. She's the ungrateful one. She had all of the opportunities I didn't have. You missed out on years of molding me into the killer you wanted by your side. Instead, you get what you get, and that's me doing what I want when I want. Thanks for showing me the ropes, mom, but it's my turn to show you a thing or two."

"Your arrogance is going to be the end of you."

"I guess we'll see," he laughed, knowing the sound would grate on her nerves.

"Don't come crying to me when your sister takes you down.

She was delusional, thinking his baby sister could even touch him. Isabelle or Sloane didn't have the balls to take him on, no matter what name she went by. She was too damn soft. Something she'd proven over and over. The world, his world, would be so much better off when she was gone. Whether or not mommy dearest joined her would all depend on Grace.

Once everything was done, he hoped she'd come around, realizing he did them both a favor getting rid of that piece of trash. But if she didn't, well, he had no problem dispatching his mother as well. Maybe he'd be better off without her. If she was gone, she couldn't interfere with his plans or second guess everything he did. Mommy didn't always know best. Sometimes the student outplayed the master.

"Like that could happen. Don't come running to me when I take her out for good, and you're down to just the kid you threw away. I'm going to make you regret pushing me away again for the sake of your precious Isabelle."

"You don't..."

"Goodbye, Mother. I hope you're happy."

"You're going to..."

He didn't let her finish, though he didn't have to in order to know what she was going to say next. She'd become a broken record ever since he told her about his plan. It made him wonder why the fuck she'd sought him out in the first place if she didn't plan on supporting him. Shouldn't a mother encourage her kids to chase their dreams? Shouldn't they be impartial and not play favorites when there is more than one? Didn't she owe him for throwing him away as a baby?

He'd spent 35 of his 44 years wondering why he didn't fit in. She owed him.

"I know, I know, I'm going to rue the day, yadda yadda. I guess we'll see. Until then, leave me alone. I've got things to do, and you're just delaying the inevitable with your bullshit."

This time he didn't bother giving her a chance at a rebuttal. He didn't want to hear any more of her nonsense. Taking his eyes off the road for a second, he swiped his finger across the phone's screen ending a conversation he knew would only make him angrier. He needed to show her exactly what he was capable of when he was pushed too far.

First, he'd tell the world everything she begged him not to.

Then, he'd see about getting rid of the competition.

CHAPTER THIRTY

He still wasn't sure they'd made the right decision to come back to San Francisco, but Cade had to admit he liked knowing there were other people close by that they could trust to keep Sloane safe. They were up to their eyeballs in the unknown at the moment. Was Anderson really the leak? Was he acting alone, or were there other agents working with him? Was Rosalie something they had to worry about at the moment, or would she stay in hiding while they dealt with the Roman Numeral Killer?

Cade didn't like not knowing where the danger was coming from. Usually, he'd circle the wagons and hide out until they knew more about what they were facing. Unfortunately, that wasn't an option in this case. Not when there was a fox in the hen house. And not when Sloane would do whatever it took to take care of the threat against her.

If Cade or Reid tried to stash her in a safe house somewhere, she'd find a way to run. It didn't matter that she knew she needed their help. If she felt like they were holding her back, then she'd go out on her own, which was the last thing any of them wanted.

When they got to their room at the Xavier, Reid went about stashing their bags in the bedroom while Sloane made her way to the TV. They hadn't been in the air very long, but from Diane's phone call, it was obvious things were unfolding quickly on the ground. Who knew how much of it had made its way to the media. If their unsub was as pissed as they thought he was, there was always the chance he'd gone to the press himself with another note, or worse.

The sound of the TV filled the room just as his phone rang. He saw Diane's name on the screen, and his stomach bottomed out. Something else had happened.

"Our unsub has a name," she said before he could even say hello.

"Did we get a print or something?" he asked loud enough that Sloane and Reid turned his way, though Sloane's attention on him was short-lived.

Cade pressed the speakerphone on his phone, so the others could hear what their boss had to say. Reid joined him by the door, but Sloane stayed on the couch staring at the television. He couldn't tell if she was paying attention to the call or what was on the screen. Either way, whatever she was hearing had her brows furrowed, and her jaw clenched tight.

"Nope. The asshole went to the press again. He found another reporter looking to make a name for herself. He gave her the scoop, and she went live about thirty minutes after I talked to you last."

"So, who are we dealing with?"

Before Diane could answer Reid's question, Sloane did. "He says his name is Connor DiSanto, and he's my brother."

"What the fuck?" Reid muttered, looking from Sloane to Cade, then back to Sloane.

Cade watched her intently, wondering what was going through her head. No one had ever mentioned a brother before, and it wasn't in any of the reports or files on her family. And Sloane had never once even hinted that there was another kid of the Cutthroat Couple.

Diane's voice brought their attention back to the conversation. This time Sloane joined them after turning off the TV. She looked lost but determined. There was confusion in her gaze, which led him to believe she was just as baffled by the announcement as they were.

"This guy says he's here to finally claim his legacy. As the lost DiSanto heir, he's going to take over the mantle as the most feared serial killer in the country because the rest of his family has been a huge disappointment."

"Well, he sure is cocky," Reid pointed out. "Is he going after both of them then? I find it hard to believe that Rosalie would appreciate being called out like that."

"He wants them both to know they've disgraced the DiSanto name. Rosalie stayed in hiding for all of these years, and Sloane gave up everything, including the family name. He plans on reminding everyone what the family is capable of," Diane said, disgust filling her voice.

"But I don't understand what he's trying to pull here. I don't have a brother."

Cade thought about that for a moment. It was obvious she hadn't grown up with a sibling, so maybe this guy wasn't a blood relative but a delusional student of Rosalie who'd gone so far off the deep end he believed he was her son. Maybe he felt like she'd adopted him, not officially, but spiritually, when she took him under her wing. As he learned everything he could from her, he became an honorary member of the DiSanto family.

His misguided outlook on his relationship with Rosalie would also explain why he hated Sloane so much. She'd been born into the family he'd always wanted, and she took it for granted. She had everything he wanted and could have been the heir he now claimed to be. If he got her out of the way, he could take up the role he already believed to be his.

What he didn't understand was why he cared about Sloane at all. She'd done everything she could to separate herself from her family and the devastation they'd dealt out across the country. Overall, a very small number of people knew her true identity. Aside from the FBI, Sloane only told a few people about her past. It wasn't something she was proud of, and it wasn't something she wanted to remember.

"Hopefully, we've got some of his DNA from the Roseburg scene, then we can run a comparison against yours and your parents. When it comes back that he's not related to you, we can dispute his claims publicly. That will take some of the wind out of his sails."

Cade shook his head even though Diane couldn't see him. "Do you think that's a good idea? What if calling him out like that sets him off more than we already have? We want to catch this guy, not send him on a killing frenzy."

Diane sighed. "That's a good point. Fuck. I don't know what to do with this guy. He's unpredictable and clearly unstable."

"We need to figure out what makes him different from any other unsub we've faced, besides the fact that he's obsessed with Sloane," Cade offered.

"I still think I'm our best bet. He wants me, and he wants to take me out of the picture for some reason. Maybe we let him think he's got a shot."

"No," Cade said at the same time as Reid.

"We can't risk it," Reid continued. "I know you think offering to do exactly what he wants you to is the right call, but it's not, outing yourself as Isabelle DiSanto isn't going to make him stop. All it will do is ruin your future. And you'd be doing it without the guarantee that we'll even catch the guy."

"I hate that you know me so well," Sloane grumbled. "Look, do I want to tell everyone who I am? Of course not, but I'm willing to do whatever it takes to end this. I reinvented myself once. I can do it again."

"Let's save that for the worst-case then," Diane suggested. "In the meantime, maybe we can make it look like he's got a chance to get what he wants. Anderson is still in play, so maybe we let it leak that Sloane plans to go to the press to denounce this guy's claims. He definitely won't like that very much. Maybe his anger will push him to make a mistake, and we can grab him."

Cade watched Sloane as she contemplated Diane's idea. If this Connor guy was spiraling like they thought he was, pushing his buttons, even in a passive-aggressive way, could send him scrambling to regain control. While he wasn't a fan of putting Sloane further in his crosshairs than she already was, he wasn't sure they had much of a choice. They needed to make a move sooner rather than later. It was the only way they would be able to end things before they got any worse.

If they decided to go through with it, the question would become whether or not he would risk facing Sloane when she was with the FBI. More than likely, his big plan was to lure her into his web like a spider would a fly. He wanted her alone. Not with backup. They had to hope they'd pushed him close enough to his breaking point that Sloane merely saying she was going to the press would be enough for him to come after her. Otherwise, she might have to go through with the threat, which none of them wanted.

A smile spread across Sloane's face, one that would have been chilling if he was Connor DiSanto.

"Let's do it. I'll write something up that you can put in the file. I think I know just the right way to word things to really piss him off."

"I like your style, Sloane. You get me something, and I'll make sure Anderson gets his hands on it. Do you think you can have that for me tonight?" Diane asked, amusement tinting her usually professional tone. "I'd love to take both of these bastards out as soon as we can."

"I'll start working on it now," Sloane said before heading back to the couch to grab her backpack.

She pulled a notebook and pen out from the largest pocket. Within seconds she was in the zone, and her hand was flying across the page. He watched her while she worked, her lower lip tucked between her teeth, her brows furrowed in concentration.

"What do you need from us?" Reid asked, bringing Cade's attention back to the phone call.

"You just keep her safe. And each other. I don't think this guy will hesitate to take one or both of you out to get to her. We also can't underestimate Rosalie. She hasn't reared her ugly head just yet, but it's only a matter of time. There's no way she'll sit on the sidelines while her children go at it, even if this Connor guy isn't really her kid. I don't think she's going to want anything to happen to either of them."

"Jeezus, this is a fucking mess," Reid grumbled.

Glancing over at the other man, Cade watched Reid scrub a hand over his face, his shoulders slumped in defeat. Unfortunately, he knew exactly how he felt. Well, maybe not exactly, since none of his family members were in danger, and he hadn't known Sloane nearly as long, but he was still more than mildly invested in keeping her safe. He also wanted to make sure Emily and Tally could go home.

There were too many variables. Too many unknowns. But that just meant he had to stay focused if he was going to help Sloane and Reid defeat Connor and Rosalie. He couldn't let his personal feelings and fears get in the way. He couldn't let Sloane's stubbornness get in his way. There'd be plenty of time to dwell on things once everything was over.

Assuming they all survived anyway.

CHAPTER THIRTY-ONE

As the night wore on, a numbness settled over Sloane. After writing the fake script, she spent the rest of the night pretending like the unsub's latest announcement didn't completely freak her out. If she had a sibling, she'd know about it, right? This wasn't a soap opera or some nighttime cable drama. Long-lost siblings didn't just climb out of the woodwork in real life.

Or did they?

The possibility was fucking with her head.

As much as she wanted to, she couldn't discount that there was a chance this guy was telling the truth. If he was, then everything she thought she knew would be thrown into question. She'd really have to dig deep and try to remember more of her childhood. Was he older or younger? Had her parents ever mentioned him? Where the hell did he live, and why not with them?

Every little piece of the puzzle revealed to them pointed in the direction of her past. It might be the key to everything, including taking down this Connor guy, finding Rosalie, and ending the whole fucked up DiSanto family. Sloane needed to step up her game if she was going to figure it out.

Even if Connor wasn't related to her by blood, he wanted the DiSanto legacy to be his, which wasn't good for any of them. The plan to make him so mad he made a mistake had to work. If it didn't, Sloane wasn't sure they had any other options. He would go on killing, making the FBI and Sloane look like amateurs as he danced around them. Just like her parents had.

"Are you okay?" Cade asked, poking his head into the bedroom she'd wandered into nearly an hour before.

She'd done nothing but sit down on one of the queen-sized beds and stare off into space. Part of her hoped a miracle would pop into her head if she gave herself some peace and quiet. Of course, that didn't happen. She was even more confused and scared now than she had been before she sat down.

"Honestly? I have no idea," she admitted, shocking them both.

Cade had a way of pulling the truth out of her even when he did nothing but ask a completely innocent question. Thankfully for her, he didn't seem to realize the power he held. At least not yet, though she had no doubt it would only be a matter of time before he realized how much he could get out of her without even trying.

"I wouldn't be either," he said as he took a tentative step into the room. "Do you mind if I join you?"

"Did something happen?"

The eagerness in her voice annoyed her. She hadn't been out of the room long enough for something to change. Nor had she heard anyone's phone ring, which would have been a sure sign there was news. She just wanted so badly for everything to end. She wanted Tally, Emily, and Cooper to be safe so they could go home. She wanted to have a chance to find a new normal now that her life had been upended. She wanted Reid to have a chance to have a happy life with Sara. She wanted Cade to...well, she wasn't quite sure what she wanted for Cade just yet.

Was he the answer to the questions she had about her future? She had no idea, nor did she have the time to contemplate what she truly desired. Not while there were two killers focused on her and her true family. Not while the people she loved were forced to be constantly on the move.

"I wish I had better news, but nothing's changed so far. Diane sent a text a bit ago applauding your work and letting us know it's been put in your file. She also baited the trap a bit and sent an email to Anderson letting him know what you're planning."

"So we're back to sitting around and waiting then," Sloane sighed.

"I know it sucks, but we don't have a choice."

Sloane looked down at the hand Cade placed on her leg in an attempt to soothe her emotions. The heat from his palm did precisely what he'd intended it to do, soaking into her body and chasing away the chill the numbness had brought with it. It also set her nerves on edge in a completely different way. They still hadn't talked about what happened between them, and she knew they needed to. It just didn't feel like the right time. She hated leaving both of them confused, but their time would come. She had to believe that.

"I know. I just wish there was more I could do. I feel completely helpless here. I..."

Before she could continue, her phone rang, the catchy tune of her ringtone drawing her attention to the bedside table where it was charging. The screen lit up with the word unknown, and since there wasn't a number underneath it, she figured it was yet another stupid robocall. She turned back to Cade, annoyed at having been interrupted.

"Aren't you going to answer it?"

Cade leaned over her and picked up her phone when she shook her head.

"It's probably a telemarketer or something," she told him. "I don't answer unknown numbers."

"It could also be your long-lost brother or your back-from-the-grave mother. Do you want them to have to leave a message?"

Sloane hated that she hadn't thought of the possibility herself. Given the leak in the FBI, it wasn't a stretch to think they'd be able to get her private number. Would either of them take the time to call her, though?

"Fine," she relented, then swiped her finger over the screen. She immediately put it on speakerphone before saying hello.

"Isabelle...Sloane...is that you?" the feminine voice on the other side asked.

"Who's asking?"

"Is this Sloane Matthews?" the voice asked again.

"Fine. It is. Now, who's this?"

Sloane nearly growled out the question. She wasn't interested in playing games.

"My name is Grace. Grace Baldwin and I'm a friend of your mothers."

Sloane scoffed. "You're a friend of a known serial killer?"

"That's not the woman I know, but yes, for all intents and purposes, I guess you would say I'm a friend of a known serial killer."

"What do you want, Grace? How did you get this number?"

Sloane could feel the anger simmering in her gut. Who the fuck was this woman, and why the hell did she think it was okay to call her? She glanced over at Cade, who had his phone in his hands. He was furiously texting with someone, probably Reid and Diane letting them know what was happening. She didn't think they'd be able to trace the call. If she had to guess, the phone Grace Baldwin was using was likely a burner.

"Your mom gave it to me in case of an emergency. She wanted me to tell you that he's telling the truth."

In this scenario, Sloane didn't have to ask who the 'he' was.

"Bullshit. I don't have a brother."

"You do. I promise you he's exactly who he says he is."

"How? How can I believe you? How could I not know about him?"

A sigh filled the phone line, which meant Sloane wasn't going to get the answers to her questions.

"It's her story to tell, and she promises someday she'll tell you the truth. For now, just know he's not delusional, but he is very, very dangerous."

"Fuck," Sloane muttered. "How can I stop him?"

"I don't think you can. Just be careful. That's all I can say."

Before Sloane could ask anything else, the phone line went dead. Grace Baldwin had hung up on her.

"What the fuck was that?" Reid asked from the doorway.

She hadn't even noticed him come into the room, so his presence startled her. Not that she needed much help with being on edge. Her heart felt like she'd just run a four-minute mile. She was surprised she hadn't dropped her phone, given how sweaty her palms were.

"She said her name was Grace Baldwin, but I don't know. Could that have been Rosalie?" Cade asked her, drawing her attention from Reid back to him.

She shrugged. "I honestly don't know. I haven't heard her voice in twenty years. I don't know if I'd be able to recognize it."

"Do you think she'd be ballsy enough to call you? Wait, that's a dumbass question. Of course, she would," Reid admitted. "But it seems weird that she only called you to tell you this guy is the real deal. Why would she think that would matter to you?"

"Maybe she hopes you'll be nicer to him now that you know he's truly a member of your family? I bet in her perfect, crazy world her two children join forces and become the killing duo to beat all killing duos."

Sloane shuddered at the thought. Could Cade be right? Is that what Rosalie was after? Even all these years later, did she think that Sloane would join the family business? That all it would take to get her to change her mind was a sibling she could join hands with. If that was the case, the woman was crazier than Sloane realized.

"That's it. My life is finally complete, and I can get out there and start my life's work of murder and mayhem."

"Sloane," Reid warned, using just her name and the tone he knew she hated.

"Whatever. You know sarcasm is my way of coping. Do you think Anderson knows he's been helping a DiSanto this whole time?" she asked, barely holding back a chuckle.

Reid shook his head though he gave her a pointed look. "Honestly, I don't know if he'd even care. He hates you so much. He'd make a deal with the devil at this point."

"Sounds like he did," she pointed out. "Hopefully, he doesn't care because we need him to continue feeding Connor information. We can't have him suddenly grow a conscience or anything like that. Let's hope his hate for me is as strong as you think it is."

Sloane looked back down at her phone, wondering if the woman she just talked to was a friend of Rosalie's or the woman herself. Her gut leaned toward the latter, but she had nothing concrete to explain her feelings. Nothing she could use to prove she was right. With any luck, the woman would call her again, even if Sloane didn't want to talk to her. There were so many questions she wanted to ask, not just about Connor, but about all of it.

Where had Rosalie been all these years?

Why was she just now reaching out to Sloane?

Why didn't she know she had a brother sooner?

The last one was the most important one at the moment. How the hell had a secret that big been kept from her all of these years? And not just from Sloane, but from the FBI. How had no one known a second DiSanto heir existed? As far as

Sloane knew, there'd never even been a whisper of it on the dark web. And this was what all of them had hoped for—the heir to evil.

Connor was everything Sloane had been afraid she'd turn into and then some. Knowing she'd made it 37 years without becoming her parents while this other kid hadn't made her feel somewhat better about herself. She didn't want to face the fact that she might have to turn into the one thing she hated in order to protect the people she loved.

But she would do it in a heartbeat.

She would turn into her mother if she had to. She would cut down her brother in the same way her mother tried to teach her all those years ago. And she would do it all with a smile plastered on her face.

Sloane would do whatever it took to make sure she won the war.

CHAPTER THIRTY-TWO

Staying awake was harder than she thought it would be, but she didn't want to miss out on spending time with her parents. It had been so long since she'd gotten the chance to watch a movie with both of them, stuffing themselves with popcorn the entire time. Now that she was getting older, her parents were getting busier. She hated it, but she understood. Most of the time, she liked being in her room anyway, but she still missed the time she used to spend with both her mom and her dad.

Her eyes fluttered shut as her momma ran a finger from the bridge of her nose over her forehead, then through her hair. She repeated the motion over and over while Isabelle fought against the sleep the move always brought over her. She didn't want to fall asleep, at least not until the movie was over. Then her daddy would carry her up to her room, tuck her into bed, and give her a kiss on her forehead while her momma told her to have sweet dreams. Tonight would be just like the old days.

The days Isabelle desperately missed.

She couldn't quite figure out when things had changed. Maybe it was when she turned double digits and was no longer a little kid. Maybe now that she was a big kid, they didn't think they should do all the fun stuff they used to do. Now they wanted her to focus on school, though that wasn't hard for her. Especially with her momma as her teacher. She made learning fun. It probably also helped that Isabelle loved school. She loved books and learning and discovering new things.

Someday she'd go to college and do something amazing, even if her daddy wanted her to join the family business. She wasn't sure what the family business was, but she knew she didn't want to drive a smelly truck around the country her whole life. It had been fun to go with her dad sometimes when she was little. She got to see so many cool places, but the driving part was boring, even with her spending most of her time reading. If she was the one driving, she couldn't read, which would make the entire thing super boring.

Isabelle struggled to open her eyes now that she'd left them closed for so long. Ugh. She was going to fall asleep and ruin a great night.

"Do you ever think about him?"

Her momma's voice made her stir, but she still felt sleep working hard to pull her under. She wanted to ask her momma who she was talking about and why she would ever think about him. Boys were icky. Even though her momma said she wouldn't always think that Isabelle wasn't a fan.

Boys her age were stupid, and they smelled. They teased her too, which she didn't understand. She'd never done anything to them. Her momma said it was because they thought she was cute, and that was how they let her know. But their stupid mouths just made her want to push them down.

"Sometimes. *I wonder if he's okay. I wonder if he's mine.*"

Who was her daddy talking about? Who was okay? Who was his? Isabelle was so confused, but it was probably just the sleep making things hazy. In the morning, she'd ask them who they were talking about. When she woke up, she'd ask the questions swirling around in her head.

In the morning, she would...

"What the hell?" Sloane muttered, her eyes still closed tight.

She wasn't sure if she hoped the dream would disappear or if it would continue if she just didn't open her eyes. She knew it wasn't a dream, though. It was a memory of a time before her family fell apart. She was more sure of that than anything else. Sloane remembered being so happy she got to spend time with both of her parents. The movie they watched wasn't that great, but that wasn't what the night was about.

That night was about quality time. Something they'd sorely lacked as Sloane got older and her parents got bolder with their killing, though she didn't know that was the reason at the time. They'd realized that once she turned ten, taking her with them was a lot riskier. She never found out what made that the turning point, but it was when they stopped traveling as much as a family.

It wasn't until she was thirteen that they tried again. A night that went from disaster to tragedy really fucking quickly.

Now that she was starting to remember the night nearly three decades earlier, Sloane wondered how she could have forgotten the conversation she'd overheard. She never did ask them about it. The next morning her dad was gone by the time she woke up, and her mom was all business. Then suddenly, her mom was gone too, and their neighbor was watching her while her mom was at a business conference. By the time they were all together again the conversation she overheard was buried deep in her subconscious, destined to be forgotten.

Until now.

Knowing sleep wasn't likely an option, Sloane decided against wasting time even trying. Work was a far better way to spend her time. She needed to tell the guys about her memory, and then she needed to try to look into Connor's past. What had her dad meant by 'I wonder if he's mine?' The words didn't make sense to her, but her gut told her they were important.

She sat up in bed, the covers falling from her shoulders to pool at her waist. A chill crept over her skin, so she grabbed her discarded hoody and pulled it on. Quietly, she climbed out of bed, not wanting to wake whoever was in the second bed. Glancing over at the clock on the table, she saw it was a little after two in the morning, which meant Reid was on duty and Cade was in the other bed getting some shut-eye.

A shiver ran up her spine as she wondered what would have happened if her dream had been a nightmare. Would he have crawled into bed to hold her in his arms the way he had the other night?

For a moment, she wondered if she should wake him up so he could hear about her dream now, but in the end, she decided to deal with him later so he could get some sleep. Cade had been sleeping as well as she had, which meant not well at all. Reid would do for now. After all of their ups and downs, Reid wasn't her first choice for a late-night companion, but she felt slightly better about their relationship after their heart-to-heart the day before. He could still be a complete ass, that was who he was, but she didn't take it personally. It was his nature, not something that was specific to her.

Though she did bring out the worst in him more often than not, usually it was by accident, but sometimes she did it on purpose mainly because he was driving her crazy and deserved it.

"What are you doing awake?" Reid asked as soon as she walked into the suite's living area and quietly closed the door behind her.

"I had a dream...or rather more like a memory, I guess. It was a flashback to a night I spent with my parents. I think I was about eleven or so."

Sloane sat down on the couch next to Reid, his attention on her slightly unsettling.

"I remembered them talking about 'him' while I fell asleep. My head was in my mom's lap, and my feet were in my dad's while we watched a movie together. I don't know who 'he' was or what they were talking about exactly, but I remember wanting to ask them about it the next morning when I woke up, but I never did."

"And you think what? That they were talking about this guy that's claiming to be your brother?" Reid asked.

She was surprised to hear the uncertainty in his voice instead of his usual skepticism. Usually, he brushed off her hunches and gut feelings.

"I don't know, really," she admitted. "My mom asked my dad if he ever thought about him, and my dad said he wondered if he was okay, then said 'I wonder if he's mine.'"

"What does that mean?"

Sloane shrugged then adjusted her position on the couch, so her legs were curled underneath her. Even though she was still jacked up from the dream, the longer she sat still, the more her lack of sleep started to weigh on her.

"I wish I knew. Maybe my mom was with someone else before she got together with my dad. Or she had an affair while he was off working and ended up pregnant. They always acted like they were each other's first and only true loves, but life can be lonely sometimes."

"Your mom could have been hooking up with someone before she even met your dad," Reid pointed out.

"True, though from what I'd been told, my grandpa was as strict as they come. If she'd gotten pregnant before my grandparents were killed, she would've gotten a beat down for it. As it was, she got smacked around after she got caught talking to my dad in his truck. The whole town knew my grandpa hit my mom and my grandma, yet no one did anything about it."

Reid scrubbed a hand over his head, then glanced over at her. "At least that's the story your mom told you. Maybe it wasn't as bad as she made it out to be."

There was the Reid she was used to. Always playing devil's advocate. Always trying to poke holes in whatever anyone said. She knew he wasn't doing it to be a jerk but to find the truth of the matter. Sometimes he was spot on, and other times he dug deep only to find out he'd wasted his time. Either way, his determination to get to the heart of the situation was one of the things that made him a damn good agent.

"You're right. She could've made it all up for all I know. But that doesn't change things. There are now two people saying I have a long-lost brother, and now I have a memory that seems to confirm it. If nothing else, he's a half-brother, which would explain why Rosalie took him under her wing and why he's so obsessed with the family legacy."

"Well, that's great. Your fucked up family tree has gotten bigger. What the hell are we supposed to do with that?" Reid grumbled.

"I always wanted a sibling when I was little, someone to play with while my parents were busy. Instead, I had my stuffed animals as my companions, which wasn't all bad. At least they didn't talk back, steal my toys, or hit me," she joked, poking fun at things she knew Reid had done to Emily when they were growing up.

"Hey, that's what brothers are supposed to do," Reid argued. "Emily loved having me around when we were kids."

"Sure she did," Sloane laughed before changing the subject back to her new family member. "I don't know where we go with this information. They spent their entire lives knowing there was a kid out there, but it doesn't sound like Rosalie looked for him until somewhat recently."

"So, we need to figure out where the hell he's been this whole time and how they found each other."

Sloane nodded but didn't say anything as her curiosity took over. Did her brother grow up in a loving household? Did he have two parents who showered him with the love and affection all kids deserved? Or did he grow up in an abusive, untenable situation? Had he developed homicidal tendencies when he found his birth mom, or was he the perfect example of the evil gene theory, killing innocent animals throughout his childhood? Who the hell was Connor DiSanto?

"Do you think he was like them before he met Rosalie?" she asked Reid, her voice wavering a little.

Her parents had hoped for a child who'd follow in their footsteps, and now they had one. Yet when they were kids, they threw him away and kept her instead, the black sheep of her murderous family. The only one not willing to take a human life for shits and giggles. The only one who didn't seem to feel the need to kill.

"It doesn't matter. You know that whole evil gene thing is bullshit."

"But if he was like them even when they didn't raise him, doesn't that prove the theory? At least a little."

"No. All it proves is that he has a screw loose somewhere, and that doesn't mean it's genetic. Come on, Lo, if anything, you are proof that the evil gene isn't a thing. If it was, you'd be out there murdering people for fun."

Sloane sighed, trying not to let Reid's use of the old nickname bother her. "Don't I kinda do that with my books? Maybe I've figured out a way to channel the gene into my writing instead of actually killing people."

Reid scrubbed a hand over his head again, then looked at her with the stern dad look he liked to throw at her and Emily on occasion. She tried not to laugh since he knew it didn't work, but hell, at least he was getting practice for when he and Sara had kids.

"I'm trying to keep my voice down, so we don't wake Cade, but I really, really want to scold you right now," he admitted. "Do you really think I'd have fallen in love with you if you had it in you to be like your parents? Do you really think I'd let you near my family if you had it in you to be a cold-blooded killer? Emily, Tally, and my mom are the most important people in the world to me, and I brought you into their lives and made you their family. So much so that you still stayed a part of their world when we ended. Do you think I'd let that happen if you were capable of continuing the DiSanto legacy?"

Sloane let Reid's words sink in until she started to feel better. If she was a danger to his family, he never would have allowed her to be near them. Even after the incident with the pedophile that ended her FBI career, she remained close to Emily. At that point in time, he could've easily told her to get lost, yet he let their relationship continue. He let her be an aunt to Tally even though they were no longer married or even talking to each other when the little girl was born.

Reid saw the good in her, and he always had. Even after everything that happened between them and the things she'd done, he still believed she was more than the blood that coursed through her veins and the family she was born into. She was more than the last name she threw away as soon as she had the chance.

Suddenly she wanted to reach over and pull her ex into a hug so she could let him know how much his faith in her meant to her. Instead, she opted to pat his knee as tears filled her eyes. She'd save the awkward moment for when they could all go back to their regular lives.

"Thank you, Reid. I know saying that couldn't have been easy for you, but it means a lot to me that you still believe in me after all this time. We don't always get along, and sometimes we might not like each other very much, but you're a part of my family, whether we like it or not."

"Great. Another pain in the ass I can't get rid of."

Sloane snorted. "Nope. Sorry to break it to you, but you're stuck with me buddy. As long as I make it through this alive anyway. Though even if I don't, I plan on coming back to haunt you because it sounds like fun."

"Jeezus, Sloane. Can we not talk about that shit? You're making it through this. We all are. We're going to kick this guy's ass, and then we're going to find your mom and make her pay for everything she's ever done."

"Then you'll marry Sara and have lots of babies, and I'll...well, I'm not sure what I'm going to do next since I can't go back to Hope's End. That bastard ruined it for me."

Reid smiled over at her, a dreamy look on his face. "I like the way that started, but the ending was a bit depressing. You know you could always move back here. You'd be close to Emily and Tally and any other nieces or nephews Emily and Cooper bring into the world. I know they'd love to have you around, and honestly, it wouldn't completely suck to see you more often."

"That's a great way to put it."

"You know what I mean," he laughed. "Or maybe your future is Cade. I don't like how things went down, but that's not entirely his fault. He's not a bad guy when work isn't getting in the way."

Laughing, Sloane shook her head. "That's high praise coming from you, but I don't think that would work out. I can't be here and dating Cade at the same time. Not when he lives in Virginia. I'm also not sure how I feel about dating an agent again. But I'm not sure what I'll do after this, and frankly, I don't have the energy to think about it. My life is in shambles at the moment, and I need every ounce of brainpower I have to focus on finding my mom and brother. Which is something I never, ever thought I'd say."

Reaching over, Reid grabbed her hand, a gesture that caught Sloane off guard almost as much as his words had earlier. The man was full of surprises.

"You're not alone in this. Cade and I have your back. Jennings has your back. We'll figure this out, keep you safe, and then you'll finally get to put your fucked up family behind you."

"If only it were that easy," she murmured. "We need to talk to Diane tomorrow."

"We will, but hopefully, this guy will take the bait we set up, and by tomorrow afternoon, this part of the story will be over."

Sloane hoped Reid was right, and they could wrap up the Connor DiSanto chronicles before anyone else got hurt. Then it would be on to her mother, which she knew would be an even more difficult task. Rosalie had stayed unnoticed for two decades, and she'd been living her best life with no one the wiser until now.

If they took down this brother of hers, Sloane knew Rosalie would want to avenge her son, no matter how mad she might be at him for outing her. It was only a matter of time until she came after her daughter to get revenge. Her daughter, the betrayer of the family.

And when that time came, Sloane was going to be ready for her. She wasn't a little girl anymore. She didn't worship her mom. She didn't seek her approval, not on purpose anyway.

Sloane would take her mother down, even if it meant she went down with her. She wasn't afraid of the dark or of ghosts, and she wasn't scared to do whatever it took to rid the world of the DiSanto family once and for all.

CHAPTER THIRTY-THREE

His blood boiled in his veins, sending heat coursing through him. That stupid bitch thought she could disparage him? She thought she could stop him? His sister was even dumber than he thought.

Connor knew she wouldn't be able to help herself, though. It was part of the reason he went public with who he was. He wanted her to out herself. He wanted her to tell the world who Sloane Matthews was. If he did it, she could easily deny it, though the crazies that worshiped the DiSanto family wouldn't let it rest until they figured out which of them was telling the truth. The rest of the world would write him off as a liar, something he couldn't afford at this stage in his game.

Telling the world who he was would bring ridicule upon him, but he knew it would also bring his dear sister out of the closet. She wouldn't let him get away with what he was saying.

And, of course, she fell for his trap. The one problem was that instead of just outing herself, she planned on trying to turn the public against him. He wasn't delusional like she said, and he wasn't deranged. He was merely doing what he was born to do.

Sloane or Isabelle or whatever the hell she wanted to be called was a pain in his ass that he needed to deal with, which was why he was in San Francisco sooner than he planned instead of following through with the rest of the kills. He needed to stop her before she opened her stupid mouth. As much as he wanted the world to know who she was, he couldn't let her say the rest, which was why he was also on his way to her hotel.

He'd had so many things he wanted to do before the inevitable confrontation with his sister. Still, she'd accelerated the timeline with her actions, which meant he had to follow suit. They would have it out. And she would get what was coming to her. Then when he was finished with her, he'd finish out his original plan before paying Grace a visit.

She would either get on board, or he'd make her sorry. At this point, he wasn't quite sure which one he preferred.

With a smile on his face, he pulled up just outside of the loading zone in front of Sloane's hotel. He'd gotten lucky that there was an open spot so close to the front door; a fortunate turn of events that gave him a good feeling for what was to come.

He knew it was risky going after her in broad daylight on a crowded street, but no risk, no reward. It didn't matter if anyone saw him. He'd gone through the motions of putting on a wig and hat, and dark sunglasses covered his eyes. He had lifts in his shoes, making him slightly taller than he was, and the clothing he wore was bulky and ill-fitting.

Even if there were witnesses and cameras, they'd have a difficult time matching his face to anything in the system. And the name he went by now, Connor DiSanto, wasn't the name on his birth certificate or his driver's license. Those were still under the name his adopted parents had given him way back when. They'd figure him out eventually, he had no doubt about that, but he didn't plan on making it easy for them.

He pressed a button on his phone, so the computerized voice read the message he got from his inside man. It didn't matter that he'd already listened to it five times. His sister's words fueled the fire burning within him. He could never let her say them out loud. She couldn't go in front of a room full of the press at the FBI office. Even though he wanted her to tell the world who she was, he couldn't let it happen yet. He still had so much to do to prove himself first. Then she could ruin her life once the world believed he was truly the only one who could fulfill his parents' mission.

He could nearly repeat her stupid planned speech by heart; he'd listened to it enough. He let the app continue to read the rest of his exchange with the idiot he'd been using to help him. The man had no idea who he was working with. He had no idea he'd been working with a member of the family he despised so much. It made the situation even more enjoyable for Connor.

DiSantoisaKiller: *What are you going to do?*

DLegacy76: *I'm going to stop her. I planned on dealing with her later, but she's upped my timeline. The dumb bitch will ruin everything if she goes in front of the press and says that bullshit.*

DiSantosiaKiller: *Maybe they won't believe her. She's lied about who she is for years; maybe you can spin her as the liar instead of you.*

DLegacy76: *That can be plan b. What I'd really like to do is get her out of the way altogether. Doesn't matter what she has to say if she's dead.*

DiSantoisaKiller: *I still can't believe I've been helping a DiSanto this entire time. I should've seen it, but I was too blinded by my hatred for your sister. I sold my soul to take out someone much worse, and I don't even care.*

DLegacy76: *Don't fool yourself. You knew exactly what you were dealing with, if not who. You wanted blood as much as I did and would do anything to get it.*

DiSantoisaKiller: *Once this is over, I might set my sights on you.*

DLegacy76: *You won't.*

DiSantoisaKiller: *How can you be so sure?*

DLegacy76: *How can you be so sure you'll make it any further than my sister?*

DiSantoisaKiller has logged out.

Connor laughed, remembering how quickly the man removed himself from the conversation. There was so much more the pawn didn't realize about what he'd done over the last few years. His hatred for Sloane made him an easy mark. Connor didn't believe that the man would ignore his existence for a second, which meant tying up loose ends once he was done with his sister. He'd probably enjoy taking care of the pompous asshole far more than he should, but why shouldn't he enjoy his work?

Leaning back against the headrest, he watched the hotel entrance in his rearview mirror. Connor had no idea how long he'd have to wait. He'd put people in position to help his plan along, he just had to hope they did their job, and he could get her alone. He wouldn't hesitate to take either of the shitheads she was with down if he had to. They meant nothing to him but everything to her.

He pulled his phone off of the holder attached to the dash and pulled up the app he'd used to hack into the hotel's cameras. He had the perfect view of the lobby elevators, so he'd know the second they came down. There was a slight chance they'd try to go out the back, but Connor had a contingency plan in place for that possibility.

He'd tried to be patient. He'd wanted to draw it all out, but now that his plans had been derailed he wanted things to happen quickly so he could get what he came for. Even so, he knew everything he'd done, all the planning, all the disgusting things he'd been forced to do, would all be worth it when he finally got his hands on his little sister. He'd have to make it extra painful for her to pay her back for the lengths he'd gone to, like dismembering a body. It was her fault his brilliant plan included using her stories as a blueprint. It was her fucked up brain that made him do it, so she'd have to pay for it. He'd just add that to the laundry list of things she'd pay for. Getting their father killed, getting their mother killed, betraying the family name. And the worst offense of them all...taking his rightful spot in their family.

If it weren't for her, he'd have lived a happy life with their parents. They'd both still be around, doing what they did best. Connor might have spent the last few years looking for his soulmate, a kindred spirit to help carry on the DiSanto name. Instead, he spent most of his life looking for his purpose.

Sloane had ruined it all, and it was time for her to see just what she'd done. Then, once she realized how wrong she was, she'd get what was coming to her.

And then some.

CHAPTER THIRTY-FOUR

Sloane's palms were sweaty, and no amount of wiping them on her pants seemed to do any good. The elevator ride down to the lobby seemed to take forever, though she wasn't sure if that was a good thing or a bad thing. Part of her wanted to get the show on the road. The rest of her was scared of what might happen when they did.

Was Connor going to take the bait as they hoped? Or would he have a plan of his own? As far as she could tell, he was intelligent and cunning. He was like her parents, which did not bode well for them. But he was also cocky, and arrogance could easily be his downfall. At least that's what Sloane was hoping for.

If he didn't show up, would she have to go through with the plan and out herself as the long-lost Isabelle DiSanto? And if she didn't, what would the consequences be? How would he react to her not going through with her threat? She knew there was already chatter on the internet about this guy being the real deal. The DiSanto fanboys and girls were going apeshit over there being another child to worship.

The fact that there were serial killer fans out there was sick enough, but to know they were fawning all over the psychopath that was her brother, was a whole new level of gross. It also meant the search for her would start anew. People had always wanted to know where she'd gone.

Whatever happened to Isabelle, that traitorous little bitch?

The serial killer fans wouldn't be the only ones wondering either. All of the people who believed Isabelle was just as evil as her parents would also chime in. Especially now that her brother had proven the evil gene was a real thing, at least in their eyes.

The blog posts would pose the question, then delve into the many theories about her whereabouts. Witness protection, death, serial killer, but better than her parents ever were. Housewife raising little serial killer babies. Not one of them would guess she'd gone on to become a law enforcement officer, though if they were as bright as they thought they were, that should've been their first guess. What better way to kill under the radar then become someone who hunts killers for a living?

"I'm going to get the car. You two wait in the lobby until I pull up out front," Reid instructed them as soon as the elevator doors opened.

They stepped into the lobby, Cade and Sloane heading toward the sitting area next to the front door, while Reid hurried through the door and to the left. She watched until he was out of sight, then joined Cade on the plush couch that gave them a great view of the front desk as well as the sidewalk in front of the hotel.

"How are you feeling?" Cade asked though she had a feeling he already knew the answer.

She'd still been awake, sitting on the couch, when Cade got up for the day. He'd joined her on the sofa then waited for her to tell him what was going on instead of peppering her with questions like she knew he wanted. He silently listened to her as she recounted the dream/memory and then what she wanted to try to figure out. She conveniently left out all of the other stuff she'd mentioned to Reid, not wanting to delve too deeply into her feelings about her new brother and her family as a whole. Or how she might be just like them.

"I keep having these moments of 'what if,' and I don't like it. I hate not knowing what this guy is going to do. He's so much like my parents that you'd think he'd be predictable, but he isn't. We have no way to know for sure that Anderson told him what I planned on saying or that he reacted the way we wanted him to."

"At least we know Anderson accessed the file. We just have to move forward like things will go according to plan. If they don't, then we pivot."

Sloane laughed, though it was almost involuntary. "Sorry. Anytime someone says pivot, I hear it in Ross's voice. You know from Friends. Pivot!"

"Great, now I'm never going to be able to say that again without thinking the same thing."

"You're welcome."

Cade nudged her shoulder with his. "This is all going to work out, you know. Whether this particular part of the plan works or not, we're going to get this guy, and then we'll go after Rosalie. I won't rest until you aren't looking over your shoulder anymore."

"Cade..."

"Doesn't matter what you're going to say, Sloane. This is my fight now as much as it is yours. I'm going to help you whether you want me to or not, so you might as well just let it happen."

Before Sloane could respond, a well-dressed man was running up to them, a handheld radio squawking in his hand.

"Agent Cade, one of the housekeepers just radioed down that someone tried to break into your room. One of the security guys is in pursuit down the back staircase."

"Stay here," he ordered her. "Don't leave this spot until Reid gets back. Do you hear me?"

Cade's stern FBI voice shouldn't have been a turn-on, but it kind of was. It was also kind of annoying. Who did he think she was, a child?

"Just stay put, okay?" he said again. This time his tone was softer, with a touch of pleading.

"I'll stay out of trouble," she told him but left the words 'I promise' out just in case.

Cade nodded, then followed the other man through the lobby and down the hall by the elevators. Sloane had a sickening feeling Cade was running after a diversion. Something set up by Connor to get her alone. The question was, did she fall for it, or did she do what she said and stay out of trouble.

Sloane looked out the window toward the bustling San Francisco street and found a man standing just to the right of the door, staring at her through the floor-to-ceiling window.

He wore a hat, dark sunglasses, and baggy clothes. She knew instantly who he was and that he was there for her. Did he want to talk, or did he plan on trying to get her to go with him? What was his endgame? And did she want to give him what he came for?

Looking back toward the hallway, she sighed. She wanted this over with more than anyone else. What harm could a conversation do? He wouldn't be dumb enough to try to take her in broad daylight. He had to know there were plainclothes cops in the vicinity, and Reid would be back any second. She needed to get answers more than she needed to be a good girl. As she started walking toward the door, someone called out to her, but she didn't turn to see who it was.

"I'm just going right outside the door to get some fresh air. I'll be fine," she told them though she wasn't sure if they were close enough to hear her.

It was likely a security guard or the person who reported the break-in to Cade. He'd probably told them to keep an eye on her knowing she would do something he deemed stupid despite her saying otherwise. She couldn't blame him. For the short time that he'd known her, she'd most definitely proved that she would step out into traffic if it meant making sure no one else got hurt.

Once outside, she stayed close to the door, ready to run back inside if she needed to. She took a deep breath, then held it, even though it tasted like exhaust.

"I'm not sure if you're stupid or brave."

She recognized the voice, though she didn't know how. Letting the air she was holding out in a loud whoosh, she turned her head just enough to see that he'd moved closer to her, his back to the door of the hotel like hers was. He wasn't looking at her but was instead intently watching the cars as they drove by.

"I could say the same thing about you. Pretty fucking ballsy to show up here. Especially when I have the FBI watching my every move."

He shrugged, then turned to look at her. "I don't see anyone watching you now."

Sloane shuddered. The way he said the words made it sound like he'd done something to make sure he got her alone. It did seem to be taking Reid too long to get back with the car. And she knew the attempted break-in was a setup. She also didn't see anyone nearby that could remotely be of help if Connor tried something stupid.

How many people did he have doing his bidding?

"What do you want, Connor?"

"I want you out of the way, dear sister. I want to be the sole heir to the DiSanto legacy. I want mom, and all of the DiSanto fans out there to forget Isabelle ever existed. You ruined everything. You don't deserve to be a part of this family. I can't let you go to that press conference and tell them who you are."

"I would love for everyone to forget about me."

"They won't. Not until you're dead and gone. Then they'll have to forget, and I'll be the one they worship."

Sloane shook her head. "You're a nut job. You know that, right? Did you ever stop to think that maybe I'll be even more popular after I'm dead? Or that your precious mother won't be happy with you for killing her daughter? It doesn't matter. You aren't going to kill me and when it's all said and done, you'll pay for what you've done. I won't stop until you're rotting away in prison for the rest of your life."

His laughter rang out around her. The sound sent shivers down her spine. The only other time she'd heard a laugh that sadistic was the night her father tried to kill her. As she begged him to leave her alone, he laughed and laughed, mocking her pleas while he waved his knife around. According to him, she'd ruined everything, and now her brother was saying the same thing.

"I think it's time we have a real brother/sister chat. Don't you?" Connor asked as he slid a little closer to her.

She felt something poke her in the side; the tip of a knife slipped through the fabric of her coat and shirt and pierced her skin ever so slightly. Fuck. She was in serious trouble. Why had she been so stupid? When Reid and Cade found out what she'd done, she'd never hear the end of it. If she ever saw them again. All she'd wanted to do was talk to the man ruining her life, and now she was going to pay for underestimating him.

"See the green sedan over there? Walk over there slowly. We're going for a ride."

"And if I don't want to go for a ride with you?"

"It's cute you think you have a choice, Isabelle. Get in the damn car."

Sloane shuddered again. The way her birth name rolled off of his lips had fear filling her chest. He was crazy, and he didn't have a single care in the world. He would end her right there on the sidewalk if she didn't cooperate, even if it didn't fit into his plans. His plan no longer mattered.

Was that the way she wanted to go out? Gutted like a fish in front of the hotel for the guys to find.

"Fine," she muttered as she started to walk toward the car.

She moved slowly, mostly so she didn't draw attention to them, but also because the knife he held against her had broken through the skin already. She could feel blood slipping down her side. Did she dare make a move? Or did she hope like hell Reid or Cade showed up before Connor shoved her into his car? There was no doubt in her mind Connor planned on killing her. Whether he did it here or somewhere else didn't matter to him. The only difference was whether it was over fast or he got to draw it out.

She stopped walking halfway to the car and turned her head to look at him, careful not to move her body at all.

"You're going to kill me either way, right?" she asked, though she didn't expect him to answer. "I'm guessing going with you means a horrible, torturous death. Making a move here means I die much quicker, without giving you the satisfaction of drawing me to the brink of death over and over. Am I right? That's okay. You don't have to answer. I already know how you work. You're mommy's little toy after all."

"I'm nobody's toy," he growled. "She may have taught me a thing or two, but I am better than her. I'm better than both of them. You don't know me, bitch."

Oh, but she did. And he was giving her exactly the reaction she'd been expecting.

"Uh oh, he's resorted to calling me names. Whatever will I do?"

She knew taunting him probably wasn't the best idea, but she also knew it would make him mad. Angry people often made mistakes. They let their guard down, too blinded by their anger to focus on the person making them mad, which was precisely what Sloane wanted.

"I know what you're trying to do, and it won't work. I won't let you bait me."

She laughed. "Seems like I already have. You're here, aren't you? Did you really think I would tell the world who I am? I might be stupid enough to come out here and face you, but I'm not stupid enough to ruin my life."

"Bitch."

"Sticks and stones..."

He growled, the knife inching further into her side. She needed to get away from him.

"You're going to pay."

"Sloane..." someone yelled her name from her left, giving her the opportunity she needed to slide out of his grasp.

Once the knife was gone, she whirled on Connor, her left-hand coming up to rake across his face. Her nails left scratch marks along his cheek while his sunglasses flew to the ground. His fist came at her face at nearly the same time, though it only connected with her bottom lip as he staggered to the side. Once he recovered, her gaze met his, and she nearly recoiled at the hatred she saw there. He was seething, his breath coming faster as he raised the knife over his head.

"Stop. Put the knife down, or I'll shoot."

Sloane recognized the voice this time. Reid had finally returned with the car. As always, his timing was impeccable.

Connor looked over her shoulder at her ex, then back at her. He growled again, then with a final whispered promise, he grabbed her by the shoulders and threw her to the ground. She tried to brace herself for the fall but landed on her injured wrist, a yelp escaping her.

"Shit, Sloane, are you okay?" Reid asked as he stopped at her side and crouched down to look at her.

"Don't stop here, go after him," she insisted even though she knew she was hurt.

Blood still trickled down her side from the wound he'd given her, and now she could feel blood running down her chin. And to top it off, she'd made her wrist worse by landing on it again. Just when she thought she'd finally get the damn brace off.

"I'm not leaving you alone. Where the fuck is Cade?" he yelled as he checked her over. "You were supposed to stay inside."

"I don't need a lecture right now, Reid. Can we just go back inside if you aren't going after him? I need some ice and band-aids and probably another fucking X-ray. I think I might have bruises on top of my bruises. Son of a bitch that hurts," she said through clenched teeth as she tried to move her wrist a little.

Before Reid could help her up, she heard Cade calling her name, then he was at her side, and both men were picking her up off of the ground. Cade tried to look her over, his eyes roaming from her head to her feet and back up. His thumb brushed over her chin, wiping away the blood, but didn't get too close to her lip when she hissed and tried to back away.

"Where the fuck were you?" Reid asked as he pushed Cade away from her. "She could've been killed. He was here waiting for her. Connor almost got her."

"I told her..."

"Hey," Sloane yelled at the two men. "Not now and not here. Can we please go back up to the room before the pissing match starts? I need one of you to check my side and see if I'm going to need stitches."

"What the fuck, Sloane?" Reid yelled the question even though she was standing right next to him.

"I said not now," she yelled back. "If you can't get your shit together and get me back upstairs, I'm going to call Diane and have her send someone to come get me. I know you two want to keep me in a fucking bubble, but that's not going to work for me. And I will not stand here and wait for you two to duke it out before we talk. So what's it going to be?"

"Let's go upstairs," Cade said, which didn't surprise her since he was usually the more sensible one of the two men.

"Fine," Reid agreed, though the throbbing vein in his temple and his red cheeks told her he wasn't happy about it.

Sloane didn't give a fuck about what either of them wanted at the moment. Her body was throbbing in multiple places and not in a good way. She needed some pain killers, some booze, and some ice, stat. Then once she was settled, Reid could have his moment. At least as long as his yelling didn't make her headache worse. Otherwise, there'd be hell to pay.

CHAPTER THIRTY-FIVE

Cade knew the minute they were in the room and the door closed behind them, Reid was going to let loose. Maybe the elevator could get stuck before they reached their floor, and he and Sloane could get a break before their lecture. Though he knew that wouldn't work for Sloane. He could tell the adrenaline was wearing off, and she was really starting to feel whatever her attacker had done to her.

The cut on her lip wasn't too bad, but it was still bleeding and would need to be cleaned. The way she held her arm against her body wasn't good, though he didn't know if it was because of her wrist or the injury she'd mentioned outside. Her skin was pale, and she looked like she was at risk of passing out if she didn't sit down soon.

She wasn't wrong when she said they wanted to keep her in a bubble. The injuries she'd sustained over the last couple of months had been difficult for him to process, especially the fading bruises around her neck from Kyle Atwood. And now, she'd been nearly taken out again, and he wasn't there to protect her. As much as he wanted to lay into her for not listening to him, he'd never do it. He wanted to take care of her, not yell at her for being disobedient.

Reid didn't care how she felt; all he wanted to do was remind her of her stupidity. He wanted to blame Cade for being incompetent. Remind him that it would have been Cade's fault if Sloane had been killed or, worse, taken. Cade didn't need the other man to say a word. He was well aware of his failure. He was to blame for Sloane's injuries even though he didn't inflict them himself. He was to blame for her trauma. It didn't matter that no one could stop Sloane when she had her mind set on something.

To Cade's surprise, Reid didn't start in on them as soon as they walked in. Instead, he guided Sloane to the couch then grabbed a couple of tablets from the bottle of Ibuprofen sitting on the coffee table. Cade left them there so he could grab the first-aid kit from his bag in the bedroom, then rejoined them. He set the kit on the table then sat down on the couch next to Sloane's right side.

"Alright, let's see it," Cade said while Reid opened up the kit and grabbed an alcohol wipe.

Reid sat down on the couch on her left side, then used her chin to guide her face toward him so he could look at her lip. She hissed as Reid dabbed the wipe against the cut. Cade could see the tears filling her eyes before she blinked a few times, sending the tears back where they came from. She grimaced as she shrugged out of her jacket and again when she tried to use her right hand to lift her shirt up.

"Here, I've got it," Cade told her before pulling the fabric away from her body.

Once the shirt was free from her skin, he lifted it up so he could see what Connor had done to her. Reid handed him a new unwrapped wipe that he used to clean the skin around the wound, then he grabbed another one to clean the wound itself. It didn't look as bad as he'd initially thought it would when she mentioned stitches. He didn't think it would need any, though they would need to apply some pressure to it so it would stop bleeding.

"It's not too bad. I don't think they'll need to sew you up, but you might as well have them check it out while you're at the hospital. It doesn't look that deep, just long."

He pulled the needed items out of the first-aid kit and went about bandaging the wound. The bleeding had nearly subsided by the time he was done, which Cade was thankful for. Aside from her wrist, Sloane's injuries were relatively minor and would heal quickly. She'd gotten lucky. They all had.

"He pushed the knife in, then slid up. I thought the whole thing would be as deep as the initial spot. I'm pissed I need to go to the emergency room and get my wrist looked at. I used it to brace myself when he pushed me down."

"We'll head there after we talk to Jennings if that's okay with you. But before that, I want to know what the fuck happened. Where were you, Cade? You were supposed to be protecting her."

Cade sighed. "I know. This is all on me."

"Like hell, it is," Sloane growled. "You told me to stay put, and I didn't. That's on me. I knew the break-in was a ruse to get me alone, yet I walked right outside to talk to him. I didn't want to stand around waiting. I wanted answers even if chances were he wouldn't give them to me. I figured cops were watching, and you'd be back soon with the car. What happened there. Why did it take you so long to get back? And where the heck were the local cops that were supposed to be watching out for us?"

Reid raked a hand through his short hair, his shoulders dropping. Cade knew the other man felt just as guilty for not being there for Sloane. And if he was a betting man, he'd put money on Connor having something to do with Reid's delay.

"When I got to the car, it was blocked in. Someone had parked behind it, then left their car there. I called the cops and a tow truck company, then decided to come back here to see if we should just call someone to come get us. That's when I saw Sloane out front looking uncomfortable with a guy far too tall and bulky to be you. It didn't even dawn on me that the car was there to slow me down until everything was over."

"Sloane's got a point, though. Where was our backup? Why hadn't anyone moved in when they saw her walking away with the guy? Or even after he pushed her down and took off?" Cade asked.

"We'll have to ask Diane about that. I'm sorry I was so pissed off at you guys. We all made mistakes."

"The whole point of this was to get Connor to come out of hiding. I don't know if he'd been as ballsy if you were both right at my side. He had to get me alone, and I had to take the risk. I'd do it again even though it could have cost me my life."

"It was a risk for him too. I'm sure the security cameras got good footage of him."

"I think he believes the disguise, and I use the word loosely, he was wearing will keep us from figuring him out, but as soon as I knocked the glasses off of his face, I recognized him. I've seen him before at the coffee shop in San Anselmo. He was sitting next to me and Emily the day she told me about the Atwood case. I ran into him the day I met with you, Cade. I actually talked to him a little. I think he enjoyed being that close to me, and I had no clue who he was. He was familiar, though, and now I know why. He looks like my dad."

"Jeezus. I knew he could've hurt you all at any time because of the pictures, but fuck, he was right there. Fuck."

"I know. I'm so sorry, Reid."

"It's not your fault. You didn't ask for this any more than the rest of us."

By the look on her face, Cade could tell that Sloane was just as surprised as he was by Reid's understanding. That wasn't his usual MO. They both had expected him to be snarky and hurtful. Maybe the man was growing up a bit as the case progressed.

"So what do we do now? He's not going to be happy his plan was foiled. Will he try again, or do you think he's off licking his metaphorical wounds?" Sloane asked.

Cade shook his head. "I honestly don't know. Most unsubs would back off, go into hiding and regroup. I don't think that's Connor's style. He's going to do something big. Maybe go to the press again. Or maybe try grabbing you again. Right now, he's pretty much a ghost, so we need to figure out a way to find him. Maybe we use Anderson to our advantage and get him to give up Connor and how they've been communicating."

"I think you're right. Anderson is our only chance at finding this guy. Other than throwing Sloane out there to give him another shot at her."

"That's not an option," Cade said harshly.

"Now, hold on a second. Shouldn't that be my decision?" Sloane asked, anger deepening her voice.

"And on that note, I'm going to go call Jennings and give her an update. I'll have her check the footage from the coffee shop for signs of our guy. They should still have it all on hand from the Atwood case. What can I tell her to look for?" Reid asked as he stood.

"He's about your height, has a brownish-red goatee, brown hair, and eyes. He was wearing a brown leather jacket both times I saw him."

"Got it. Now don't yell at him too loudly. We don't want the SAC to hear you."

Reid laughed though his joke fell flat for Cade and Sloane. As soon as the other man closed the door to the bedroom, Cade braced himself for Sloane's anger to hit him full force. When he turned to look at her, though, her shoulders were slumped, and tears had gathered in her eyes. She looked like the fight had left her entirely. He wanted to pull her into his arms so she could soak up some of his strength. But unfortunately, it didn't work like that, and he was pretty sure she wasn't ready for his comfort just yet.

But when she was, he'd be there for her.

He'd already promised her this was his fight too. What he hadn't told her was that he cared about her. Probably more than he should, and because he cared about her, he would do everything he could to make sure she not only came out of this in one piece, but she'd thrive in the aftermath. They'd take care of her brother and her mom, and then when the dust settled, he'd help her figure out what she was going to do next.

With any luck, he'd be part of her plans. A huge part.

CHAPTER THIRTY-SIX

Sloane had been acutely aware of Cade's fingers as he bandaged up her wound. Then again, when he placed his hand on her knee, the weight and heat of it calmed her shredded nerves. His hand still rested there while she tried to decide if she should yell at him or not. She didn't think she had it in her. Now that her adrenaline had finally crashed, every last ounce of energy she had at the beginning of the fight with her brother was gone.

She was a fucking mess.

But they didn't have time for her to break down. She could do all of that after they found Connor. Until then, he was a loose cannon. There was no telling what he was going to do next, though she had a feeling he was going to make them pay for messing up his plan. How, she wasn't sure. But it probably meant another body or two.

"We need to make sure everyone is safe and accounted for. He won't hesitate to punish us for what happened, and he'll want to make it hurt."

Cade nodded. "As soon as Reid is done with Diane, we'll make some calls. Since he's here, I think we'll be okay. No one's in town right now."

"Unless he has minions who will do more than just his errands for him," Sloane pointed out.

"We can't think like that."

Sloane sighed, her head falling back against the couch. "I know, I'm just worried and scared. He terrifies me, Cade. I can't explain it, but he's like both of my parents wrapped up in one crazy ball. He doesn't give a shit about anything other than getting me out of the way. And killing, of course. He wants to make a name for himself."

"We'll catch him, I promise. He'll make another mistake, just like he did today."

"I don't think he will. Not before someone else pays for being associated with me. God, I've got this terrible feeling in the pit of my stomach. I should've just gone with him today."

She could feel Cade stiffen next to her, his body going rigid as soon as the words left her mouth. She wasn't entirely sure if she meant them or not, but it was how she was feeling at the moment. And if someone else died because of her, she'd feel it forever.

Cade's hand gripped her chin, gently using it to turn her head, so she was looking at him. She rolled her eyes but didn't jerk her head away. The sincerity in his eyes had her wanting to hear what he had to say even if she couldn't bring herself to believe a word of it.

"Look, I know you've taken all of this onto yourself, assumed responsibility for everything that Connor's done, but none of it's on you. None of this is your fault. You didn't bring this on anyone. Richard didn't die because he was your friend. None of these other victims died because you were born. Going with Connor today wouldn't have stopped him. All it would have done was give him what he needed so he could keep going."

"But..."

"No. I don't care how strong or how capable you are. Going one-on-one with him while he was armed and crazy would've ended in your death, and you know it. You wouldn't have gotten the upper hand no matter how hard you tried. He would have tortured you until he had his fill and then probably a little more for good measure. Then he would have slit your throat just like mommy taught him."

She closed her eyes for a moment, fighting off the nausea that swarmed her stomach. Cade was right. Nothing would've changed if she'd gone with Connor. The only difference was she'd be dead. He wouldn't stop doing what he was doing. He'd keep on killing; there was no doubt about that. But would he at least lay off her loved ones once she was gone? Or would he try to take out Cade and Reid and the others just to tie up loose ends?

"I'm sorry," she whispered as she opened her eyes.

Her gaze met his, and she instantly felt better. In a very short period of time, James Cade had become her rock. She just needed to look at him, and she knew she'd never be alone again. He would be there for her through everything, no matter how hard it got. When she had moments where she thought she couldn't go on, he'd get her to see she could. And when she had moments where she thought going off half-cocked was a good game plan, he'd show her it wasn't. Whether or not he could stop her was up for debate, but she appreciated his determination nonetheless.

"You have nothing to be sorry about. This is an impossible situation. No one would condemn you for cowering in a corner, but no one's surprised you aren't either. You're the strongest person I've ever met. I know you've got this, even when you start to doubt yourself. You just need to remember what I said. None of this is on you, so stop letting the guilt weigh you down. Instead, use that energy to make Connor regret ever messing with you."

She smiled, then winced as the movement pulled at the cut on her lip. "Shit."

"I guess none of that for a while," Cade laughed as he grabbed a tissue from the table and started dabbing at the fresh blood on her lip.

"Not a big deal. I tend to have resting bitch face anyway," she joked, wincing again as she spoke. "Damn. Guess this thing is going to bleed forever if just talking is going to be a problem."

"It'll heal quickly. Put some of this on; it should help."

Cade handed her a yellow canister with a blue lid. She flipped it open and dipped her finger inside, then spread the jelly across her bottom lip. It felt oddly sensual doing so in front of Cade, even though it was anything but. The intimate feeling intensified when his gaze dropped to her lips. Would it be a terrible idea to drown herself in Cade for a little while?

"Holy shit," Reid yelled, his voice carrying through the closed bedroom door causing Sloane and Cade to jump.

The door banged open as Reid joined them, his phone in his hand. "Anderson's dead."

"What?"

"Jennings had been trying to reach him all morning, but he never showed up to the office. She had someone go out to his place, and they found him there, naked in bed, his throat slit."

"Holy shit," Sloane murmured Reid's earlier exclamation.

Anderson was dead. And it wasn't Connor that killed him, given the other man was in Richmond, Virginia, and Connor was in San Francisco. Did that mean her brother had minions willing to kill for him? If not, then who killed him, and why?

"They think he'd been dead for a while. Maybe four or five hours," Reid told them as he sat down in one of the dining chairs at the small two-person table. He pulled open his laptop and started typing away.

"So Connor couldn't have done it," Sloane said out loud so she could get validation for her theory. "Which means he could have a partner willing to kill for him."

"Shit, maybe. I hadn't thought of that," Reid answered. "It definitely couldn't have been Connor. There's no way he could've gone from Virginia to California in time to attack you."

"Then there's someone else in play. We need to get the details on Anderson's case as soon as we can. In the meantime, we need to take Sloane to get her wrist X-rayed. Do you want to stay here or go with us?" Cade asked Reid.

The other man looked over at them, then back at his computer. "You go. Jennings is sending someone to pick you up, so you'll have backup in case he comes back. I'll meet you guys at the office once you're done."

"That works for me. Sloane?"

"Ummmm...sure. That works, I guess," she said, surprised that Cade even bothered to ask her opinion. "I doubt he'd be stupid enough to come back now, though."

"Doesn't matter," Reid said. We don't know for sure what he'll do, so we can't be too careful with you."

"I get it. Can you please make sure everyone else is safe too? I'm worried he'll send one of his minions after someone close to me again. And now that we know he has people who will kill for him, we can't assume the people outside of California are automatically safe."

Reid nodded. "Got it. I'll figure things out with Jennings."

A ping sounded from next to her, and Cade picked his phone up off of the table. "Looks like Gardner's here. We should get going."

Cade closed the lid of the first-aid kit before standing up. He offered her a hand so he could help her off of the couch. Usually, she'd wave it off, but today she just didn't have it in her. All she wanted to do was crawl into bed and sleep the rest of the day away, but that wasn't an option. After the hospital, they'd head to the FBI office, and there was no telling how long that would take. Maybe while she was waiting to see someone in the ER, Cade could find her some coffee. She had a feeling she was going to need it.

Once they reached the lobby, Cade was overly cautious, not that Sloane could blame him. She knew he felt guilty for leaving her alone earlier, and it didn't matter that she was okay. In his mind, he should've been there to protect her, just like she should've been there to keep Richard from being killed.

Guilt was a bitch that she and Cade were all too familiar with. Not really what she had in mind when she wondered what they had in common, but at least they'd be able to understand each other.

Sloane waited inside the lobby while Cade made sure no one was lying in wait for her outside. Once he was finished, she stepped outside so she could make her way to the loading zone where Silas Gardner was idling, waiting for them. The older man was probably thrilled to be acting as their chauffeur. However, she didn't take it personally like she would have when they first met. No one was a fan of chauffeur duty.

As she and Cade walked out to the car, his hand rested on his gun, ready in case Connor jumped out at them. It was good he was prepared, but Sloane knew they didn't have anything to worry about. Connor wouldn't return just yet. He'd do something to cripple her and her team emotionally. Then he'd be back to kill her. She didn't know how she knew that was his plan. It just felt right.

Cade opened the back door of Gardner's FBI-issued sedan and helped her inside. He didn't even give her a chance to try to put the seatbelt on herself. Instead, he grabbed the buckle and pulled it across her body. He leaned into the car, his body pressed against hers in a slightly awkward way. She bit back a laugh as she wondered just what Silas Gardner thought as he watched the embarrassing situation unfold.

Once she was safe and sound, Cade closed the door then climbed into the front seat. Sloane let out the breath she'd been holding and worked on getting comfortable, which wasn't easy when she didn't want to move her wrist or risk opening the cut on her side. Before she could do much, her phone rang, the sound obnoxiously loud in the small car.

She could feel Cade look over the seat at her, but she just shrugged as she tried to pull the phone out of her pocket. As soon as it was free, she glanced at the screen and shook her head.

"Unknown number again," she said before swiping her finger over the screen. "Hello."

"Sloane, it's Grace. I wanted to check in on you and see if your brother is behaving himself. Your mother tried talking to him."

"Hello, Grace," Sloane said so she could get Cade's attention. "I'm sorry to say that mommy's chat didn't do any good. My darling brother isn't being the good little boy she hoped. I'm actually on the way to the hospital because of him. The bastard attacked me this morning."

"Son of a bitch," the woman growled, the sound scarier than it should have been through the phone. "That little shit. Your mother isn't going to be happy to hear this."

"Or maybe she will. She probably wants me out of the way just as much as he does."

"I can guarantee that's not the case. In a perfect world, she'd love to have both of her children by her side."

Sloane scoffed. "One big happy murderous family, huh? Sounds like a dream come true."

She could feel Cade and Gardner both looking at her. Of course, Grace had to call while she had a captive audience. Though she would've let Cade listen in, she wasn't too keen on having the older agent be a part of the conversation.

"Look, I promise you, your mother isn't going to stand by and let Connor do this. She's already pissed at him for this game he's playing. She told him to leave you alone, and he went against her wishes and will be punished for that."

"How can I believe anything you say?" Sloane asked.

She had no idea what to believe when it came to this woman. It all seemed suspicious and a bit coincidental, and Sloane didn't believe in coincidences. Plus, there was something about the woman this time that bothered her, but she wasn't sure what it was.

"You either do, or you don't. There's very little I'm keeping from you and whatever I'm not telling you is for your own good."

"So you say."

"You always were a stubborn girl," Grace said, a laugh punctuating her statement.

The way she spoke made it sound like she actually knew Sloane, though maybe it was something Rosalie had told her once upon a time. Before she could ask Grace what she meant, the other woman started speaking again.

"I didn't just call to check on you, sweetheart. I also wanted to let you know that you don't have to worry about the one that was feeding information to Connor. He's been taken care of. Hopefully, that will help you get ahead of your brother."

"What?"

"I've got to go, Sloane. Please be careful."

Sloane started to speak, but the call was disconnected before she could get a word out. She dropped her phone in her lap and stared down at it. What the hell had just happened? Did Grace just admit she killed Anderson? Or was she saying

Rosalie did? And what the hell was it that bothered her so much about Grace now that hadn't when they talked the first time.

"You always were a stubborn girl."

"I didn't just call to check on you, sweetheart."

"Do you ever think about him?"

"Holy shit."

Cade turned again to look at her; concern etched into his gorgeous face. "What? What did she say?"

How did she tell Cade something she couldn't prove, but knew deep down was the absolute truth? The second the thought occurred to her, Sloane knew no other explanation made sense.

"She wanted to check on me. And she wanted to tell me that the leak wasn't going to be an issue anymore."

"So either she or Rosalie killed Anderson?" he asked though it felt more like a rhetorical question.

"That's the thing," she paused, closing her eyes so she could check her gut one last time before she dropped a bomb on him.

"Sloane..."

Her eyes opened, her gaze meeting his.

"Cade...I think that was my mom."

CHAPTER THIRTY-SEVEN

Glass shattered as soon as his fist hit the mirror. He wasn't usually one for hysterics, but he had to admit punching the mirror felt oddly therapeutic. Maybe it had something to do with the fact that he was envisioning his sister as he swung. It was her handiwork he'd been checking on anyway. The gouges her nails left along his cheek had stopped bleeding before he got back to the house he was using, but his irritation with her and her stupid ex-husband was still very, very raw.

It didn't help matters that Grace called while he was on his way back to the house. He couldn't stop to take the call, and even if he could, he didn't want to deal with her. If he had to guess, his little sister had probably tattled on him, and now he was in big trouble. Insert big, fat eye roll here. They weren't little kids anymore. Tattling wouldn't do anyone any good. Well, not Sloane anyway.

Knowing he was in trouble fueled Connor's fire, which wouldn't be good for her or their mother.

He was beyond pissed, and there was nothing Grace could say that would stop him from continuing on with what he had planned. He got damn near giddy thinking about it. She wasn't on his initial list, but he had to admit there was a beauty to what he was going to do. They would be sorry they ever fucked with him.

Not bothering to clean up his mess since it wasn't his house anyway, he made his way down the hall to the other bathroom to make sure he looked presentable. The blood welling on his knuckles combined with the scratches on his face were already going to be difficult to overlook. The rest of him had to make up for his injuries so he could get in the door. After that, none of it would matter.

Twenty minutes later, he was looking pretty good. He would have no problem charming his way inside of his intended destination, even with the cut on his face. Grabbing the vase of roses he'd picked up earlier and the car keys off of the kitchen counter, he went through the side door to the garage. He had two cars to choose from, though the black SUV was the only one that gave off the vibe he was going for. The minivan was a little too 'soccer mom' for his liking.

The drive took another twenty-five minutes because traffic was so bad, but Connor didn't mind the wait. In the long run, anticipation would make the experience even better for him. He could imagine everything from their introduction to his explanation of what would happen and then the big finale. God, it was beyond perfect.

If only he could be there when Sloane found what he'd left for her this time. It would be the cherry on top of a very fucked-up sundae. She'd know instantly she was to blame for what happened, which meant she'd do exactly what he wanted her to do.

Once at his destination, he flashed a badge at the doorman, thankful when he didn't stop him to ask questions or inspect the badge too closely. Not that Connor didn't have all of the answers he'd need to get through twenty questions asked by an old man who'd rather be reading the newspaper in his underwear than opening doors for moderately rich assholes. The elevator doors opened as he approached. He smiled at the older woman that got off before getting on and pressing the button for the 15th floor. She smiled back, then let her eyes drift down over his body.

Maybe he should've been worried that the woman was taking such an interest in him, but he honestly didn't care if she could be used as a witness later. The building probably had cameras mounted all over the place, yet he hadn't bothered to try to disguise himself or avoid them. It didn't matter anymore if Sloane or the FBI could identify him. They'd never find him. Especially not after he was finished with his business in San Francisco.

The apartment he needed was just down the hall from the elevator, far enough away from most of the foot traffic, giving them plenty of privacy. It was perfect for what he had planned. He knocked on the door, the roses held in front of his face in case she looked out the peephole. She threw it open with a gasp.

"Oh Reid, they're beautiful."

Connor fought back the smirk that wanted to take up residence on his face and worked on holding a neutral expression as he lowered the vase.

"I'm sorry for the confusion, Dr. Larson. My name's Connor. I work with your boyfriend," he said before flashing his badge at the woman. "He asked me to come over to keep watch until he can get home. Not sure if you were told, but Sloane was attacked outside of their hotel this morning, and they're worried it's not safe for you to be alone."

He always found using parts of the truth to be a good idea. The less you lied, the less you had to remember. Connor assumed Sara was a brilliant woman; she was a trauma surgeon after all. She wouldn't easily fall for a ruse or his charm.

"Oh no, poor Sloane. Maybe I should give them a call, make sure she's alright."

Connor nodded. "They were headed to the hospital to get her checked out when I got the call to pick up these flowers and come over here."

Her brows furrowed as she decided what to do. "Well, maybe I should wait for a little while. Do you want to come in?"

"Well, I'm supposed to stay outside, but maybe I could use your bathroom real quick. I don't want to impose, but the extra-large soda I had with my lunch seems to be hitting me now."

"Oh, sure," she said as she stepped back. "Head down the hall; it's the first door on the right."

"Thank you so much, Dr. Larson. I really appreciate it."

"It's Sara, please, and it's no problem whatsoever. It's the least I can do since you delivered these beautiful roses and are going to hang out here to protect me. Can I get you anything, some water, or tea?"

He stepped inside the apartment and waited for her to shut the door behind him. A teeny tiny part of him regretted what had to happen next. She seemed like a lovely woman, and she was a helper. There weren't very many of those left in the world. Unfortunately, none of that mattered. Sara Larson had to die because her boyfriend got in his way. It was as simple as that.

"A glass of water would be great."

"I'll grab that for you while you're in the bathroom."

She turned her back on him to make her way to the kitchen, and he knew that was his cue. He followed behind her, pulling his knife out of his jacket pocket. The scent of the roses and her shampoo assaulted him as he got closer to her. Before she could react to his presence, he put his left hand over her mouth, then shoved the knife into her back.

The vase crashed to the floor. Glass and water spread around their feet as the roses fluttered to the ground to meet them. Sara screamed against his palm, pain and fear laced the sound, but it was too muffled for anyone but him to hear it. Her knees buckled, so he lowered her to the ground. As soon as he uncovered her mouth, she tried to scream, but he held the bloody knife up to deter her.

"I am sorry I have to do this, Sara. I didn't want to hurt you, but your boyfriend and his bitch of an ex made me do it. They forced my hand, and now you have to pay for their interference."

She whimpered and tried to curl into a ball, but the glass on the floor made moving dangerous. Blood pooled beneath her, then spread out around her. It turned a muted shade of pink as it mixed with the water from the vase. Connor found himself mesmerized by the river of pale pink blood that wormed its way toward him. Even in these pricey buildings, the floors weren't as level as they should be.

Shaking his head, he pulled a roll of duct tape out of his pocket and ripped a piece off to put over Sara's mouth. He could do whatever he wanted without worrying about covering her mouth with his hand or threatening her. No one would be able to hear her now, and she wouldn't even try to scream with the tape covering her lips, which meant his fun could truly begin.

Connor smiled down at her, enjoying the picture she created as she squirmed on the floor, trying to push herself away from him. It seemed she no longer cared about the shattered glass. She was going to be a ton of fun. He shoved the knife back in his pocket, then bent down and put his hands under her armpits so he could lift her. While he didn't care if the glass hurt her, he didn't want to kneel in the vase fragments. He'd already lost enough blood for the day.

Picking her up, he carried her like a soiled baby until he reached the hallway that led to the bathroom and the bedroom she shared with Agent Dickhead. He dropped her there, a muffled cry escaping her as her body hit the floor with a thud. Her eyes rolled into the back of her head, then fluttered shut. Oh, he couldn't have that. She needed to be awake for everything he had planned for her.

"Come on, beautiful. Open your eyes. I need to see those gorgeous blues of yours. If I can't see them, then this all gets a hell of a lot worse for you."

She whimpered but did as she was told. Pain and fear warred with anger turning her eyes a darker shade than they usually were. He'd done some research on the beautiful Dr. Larson each time he was in town, but he'd never had the chance to get up close and personal with her. Even though he hadn't planned on making her one of his taunts for Sloane, he still liked to be prepared. Now that he was enjoying some time with the gorgeous woman, he hated that he'd missed out on getting to spend time with her like he had the others.

Lowering himself to the ground, he straddled her prone body and removed her clothes. He started with the blouse first. The fabric was soaked with blood and water and stuck to her skin, which annoyed him more than it should. He was impatient to see what he was working with.

The knife helped him rid her of her bra and underwear after he pulled her wet, sticky jeans down her legs. Tiny pieces of glass were embedded in her feet and calves; a few were also in her side and stomach. He picked them out of the places he might come in contact with, being careful not to knick himself.

Once she was naked, he took his time looking her over. She was damn near perfect. Reid Morgan had upgraded when he kicked Sloane to the curb and shacked up with Sara. He bent over her, his lower lip between his teeth as he traced her jaw with the tip of the bloody knife he'd retrieved from his pocket. She stayed perfectly still, not even taking a breath as he moved the blade down her neck to the valley between her perky breasts.

"You are a vision, aren't you, Sara. Does Reid know how lucky he is to have you? How lucky he is to be the one that gets to part these creamy thighs and shove up into you whenever he wants. Does he worship your body every night like a good man should?"

Connor continued moving the knife all over her body, her skin growing paler by the second, which meant he didn't have a whole lot of time left to play. He placed shallow cuts all over her breasts, stomach, and thighs and licked his lips as she squirmed. Blood welled in almost thirty different places, and each of them made his dick harder than the one before.

He throbbed against the zipper of his jeans, begging for release. Who was he to deny it? He stood, ready to pull off his jacket, when a knock on the door stopped him in his tracks.

"Were you expecting someone? Shouldn't you have mentioned that to the nice FBI man who was here to protect you?" he asked. "Don't worry. I'll take care of them."

He set the knife down on the counter and straightened out his jacket. Hopefully, the fabric was dark enough whoever was at the door wouldn't notice the specs of blood. His hands were another matter, so he grabbed a towel off the counter then made his way to the door. He looked out the peephole and sighed. There was no one there, though he could make out the top of a plastic bag sitting on the doorstep. She'd ordered take-out. Of course.

Dropping the towel on the floor, he turned back toward the hallway and smiled when he saw she was no longer lying where he'd left her. Oh, the poor dear girl was trying to make a getaway. It was cute and a bit hot that she thought she was strong enough and smart enough to get away from him. There was nothing she could do to put off the inevitable. But maybe they could have a different sort of fun in the meantime.

He slowly made his way through the decimated vase and flowers to the pile of clothes she'd left behind. A pool of blood marked where she'd been, while a trail of blood marked where she was going. He could see her legs disappear into the bedroom as she dragged herself down the hall. Damn, she was something else.

Instead of following her immediately, he grabbed the bag of food from in front of the door. The scent of Chinese food filled his nostrils, making his stomach rumble. He might as well curb his actual hunger since he wouldn't be able to take care of any other hunger he might have. He grabbed a carton of food, some chopsticks from the bag, and a beer from the refrigerator, then made his way down the hall.

He couldn't see her right away, so he bent down and peeked under the bed where she curled in on herself, blood seeping from her back. Smiling, he climbed on top of the bed, shoes and all, and popped open the beer and the food. For a long time, the only sounds in the room were the ones of him chewing and occasionally washing the food down with an IPA he wasn't a big fan of.

When he was finished, he tossed the empty carton on the white comforter already stained from his shoes and clothes. Not that he gave a shit about ruining Agent Morgan's bedspread. The man would have much bigger problems to deal with when he got home than a damn blanket.

Sara hadn't made a sound in a long time, at least not one loud enough for Connor to hear over himself. Climbing off of the bed, he laid down on the floor so he could see her. It was too dark to tell if her chest was moving with each breath she took, so instead, he held his breath so that he could listen for sounds of life.

As soon as he heard it, he laughed. "I can still hear you breathing."

She whimpered in response.

"I'm not going anywhere, Sara. Not until you breathe your last breath. So you can either come out from under the bed and let me finish you off quickly, or we wait. I've got plenty of time. No one is going to save you. So what will it be?"

It didn't matter what the poor girl decided. Connor was going to watch her die. He could tell by the sound of her ragged breathing that there was blood in her lungs. If she was smart, she'd crawl out from under the bed and let him finish her off. She'd be gone a hell of a lot quicker than if she waited for her wounds to take her.

"I promise I won't fuck you. Does that help? I don't fuck corpses, well, not usually anyway. But I promise I won't do anything other than put you out of your misery. Otherwise, you're going to drown in your own blood. You know all about that, don't you? How painful it is. Do you really want to do that to yourself?"

The whites of her eyes were all he could make out. Maybe he should've turned the lights on when he came in. There'd been plenty of light streaming in the bedroom window for him to eat the food she generously bought for him, but it didn't cover the space under the bed very well.

"Come on, Sara. Let's end this."

She whimpered again, then started to crawl toward him. He moved out of her way then helped pull her out from under the bed when her strength gave out. Despite the blood matted in her curly brown hair and her deathly pale skin, she was still a gorgeous woman. Her strength and determination added to her beauty. The world would be worse off without her, but that was Sloane's fault, not his.

"Good job, Sara. I've got you," he told her as he rolled her onto her back, then straddled her again. "I'm sorry it has to be this way. You deserve so much better."

Her eyes fluttered closed as a tear slid down her cheek. The poor girl had been through enough, and Connor knew he was a little too close to overstaying his welcome. With one last look at her beautiful face, he slid the knife across her throat, watching as the blood welled to the surface and rolled down the sides of her neck to the hardwood floor beneath her. While she choked and struggled to breathe, he carved his signature just below her collarbone instead of her foot. He'd thought about leaving without marking her, but he wanted the bitch and her ex to see the proof of what they did. He wanted them to know without a doubt that he wasn't someone they could fuck with without consequences.

Connor stayed with Sara until she drew her last breath, then rolled her back under the bed so it would be a little harder for her boyfriend to check on her. The amount of blood on the floor would give things away, but that didn't matter. He couldn't just leave her lying there for Reid to see as soon as he came into the room. He had to work for it.

With a smirk on his face that wouldn't go away no matter how hard he tried, Connor made a quick stop in the bathroom to check himself out before he dared leave the apartment. Was it obvious he'd just killed a woman? If so, he couldn't have that. He had to make it down the hall, down the elevator, through the lobby, then around the corner before he was Scott free. He couldn't have someone stop him because he was covered in blood.

He washed his hands, getting rid of as much blood as he could, then wiped droplets from his face. The blood on his jacket and pants were just dark splotches against the fabric, nothing he couldn't explain away.

Once he was away from the scene of the crime, he had one more stop he had to make before he could go back to the house he was borrowing and change into something a little less bloodstained. He needed to make sure he was ready for what came next.

He had plans with his darling little sister in a few hours; she just didn't know it yet.

CHAPTER THIRTY-EIGHT

It wasn't even seven yet, but as far as Sloane was concerned, it was well past her bedtime. The day had been unbelievably long and emotionally charged. Between the attack that morning, the trip to the hospital, then spending hours at the FBI field office, she was drained. There was nothing left in the tank. It would be a miracle if she didn't fall asleep the second her head hit the pillow.

"Sara must have gotten called into the hospital or something. She still isn't answering her phone."

Sloane glanced toward the driver's seat and watched concern dance over Reid's face. It didn't sit well with her that he hadn't been able to reach Sara most of the day. He brushed it off as not a big deal since she went long periods without answering her phone when she was in surgery. He was used to her not always answering right away. What set Sloane's radar off was that Sara wasn't supposed to work that day.

"Do you want to swing by your apartment?" Cade asked from the backseat.

Cade had insisted she take the front seat despite their height difference since it would be more comfortable for her. She'd tried to argue with him, but he wouldn't back down. Stubborn man. Not wanting to waste more time and too damn tired to put up much of a fight, she'd climbed into the front seat, then he leaned in to help her with the seatbelt. If she'd sat in the back behind Reid, she could have done it herself, but she had a feeling that was exactly why Cade offered to switch with her.

"No. I'll drop you guys off first, then head over there. Sloane looks like she's about to keel over, and since she won't take anything more than over-the-counter pain meds, I'm betting she's ready for a stiff drink by now."

Sloane laughed. "Hopefully, it'll help dull the ache so I can fall asleep. Although, I'm not sure I'm going to need much help. I'm exhausted."

"It's been a crazy day," Reid agreed. "How's the hot pink treating you?"

"I'm pissed I had to get a real cast this time and that Gardner got to the doctor first," she grumbled though it was half-hearted at best.

While hot pink wouldn't have been her first choice, she had to admit the color made her smile. Although, that could be more because Silas Gardner, the man who was not happy to have her around a month ago, played a joke on her. It was the one bright spot in the middle of a shitty day.

"The look on your face was pretty priceless," Reid laughed. "You know who would love that, Tally. She's gonna be jealous you have a pink cast, and she doesn't. It would match her tutu collection."

A smile tugged at Sloane's lips as she envisioned her niece twirling around in one of her many tutus while showing off her new pink accessory. God, she needed this bullshit to be over, so she knew Tally and Emily were safe. She missed them both terribly and hated that they had to constantly be on the move because Sloane had a psychotic brother who wanted to take away everything she held dear.

Before the guilt could overcome her, Sloane looked over her shoulder at Cade. "Do you think we'll be able to find Connor and Rosalie? Do you think we'll be able to stop them?"

It was the one thing she wanted to ask back when they were at the office meeting with SAC Diane Jennings but didn't because she didn't want the older woman to realize how uncertain she was. Sloane wanted everything to be over, but she had no illusion they would be able to end anything anytime soon. Rosalie or Grace or whatever name she was going by had been in hiding for twenty years. She might be out of hiding for the moment, but that didn't mean she'd be easy to find.

Then there was Connor.

He'd taken the bait once, but could they get him to do it again? Would he be that stupid?

From what little Sloane knew about the man, she didn't think they'd get that lucky. If they couldn't get him to come to them, how would they stop him, and how many people would they lose in the meantime? Even just one more person was one too many for her, but she had no idea how to stop the inevitable.

"I don't know."

"Well, shit, I was hoping you'd have some grand plan that would magically fix everything. I want this shit to be over," Sloane admitted.

Cade's honesty shocked her. Not because she expected him to say what she wanted to hear, but because she did think he'd have some kind of plan to catch Connor. He was the level-headed one of the group, after all. If anyone was going to come up with what they needed to do next, it was going to be him.

"We all do. I don't know what it will take to get Connor to show himself again, especially with Anderson out of the picture. Hopefully, just knowing how close you are will be enough. He won't be able to help himself."

Sloane scoffed. "I'm not going to hold my breath on that one."

"I don't know, Sloane. He seems pretty obsessed with you," Reid pointed out, not that any of them needed him to. "If he was willing to take the risk today to try to grab you, there's a good chance he'll try again. We just have to be ready for him next time."

"How do we do that now that Anderson's dead?"

Sloane's question hung in the air for a couple of blocks. Now that they needed to use Anderson to their advantage, they couldn't. Of course, the asshole was screwing them over even after death. It's what she'd expect from the man who'd made her life a living hell for so many years.

"I don't know yet, but I'm working on it. Do you think your mystery caller would help us?" Cade asked.

"You think she'd turn on her son?" Reid wondered as he threw the blinker on.

Thankfully, traffic was pretty light, allowing him to turn before either she or Cade could answer his question. Did she think Rosalie would help them take Connor down? Anything was possible. What they had to do was figure out what Rosalie wanted. How would assisting the FBI benefit her? She'd do a lot of things if it helped her in some way. Money. Freedom. Face time with her wayward daughter. Sloane had no idea what she'd ask for, but she knew she'd ask for something.

"If she calls again, we can ask her what it'll take to get her to betray Connor, but I can almost guarantee you the bureau won't be willing to give up whatever it is she wants."

As they contemplated her statement, Reid parked the car in a reserved spot outside the hotel. They would no longer have to worry about their vehicle getting messed with, and it would also be much better and safer to have the car right out front.

They all moved a hell of a lot slower than usual as they got out of the car and headed toward the hotel lobby. She wasn't the only one running on fumes, it seemed. They'd barely walked through the door when the night manager stopped them and handed them a note that was left for her.

"This can't be good," Reid muttered, stating the obvious.

Sloane stared at the envelope in her hand, recognizing the handwriting immediately. She'd seen it enough times over the last week to know Connor had left the note for her. Not that she had any doubt before seeing her birth name scrawled across the envelope. Whatever the message said was important enough to risk going back to the hotel where a swarm of FBI agents could have been waiting for him. Her stomach rolled. She had a sinking feeling the note was going to answer a question Reid had been asking most of the day.

With Cade and Reid both standing behind her, she took a deep breath, then pulled the piece of paper out and unfolded it. Her stomach flipped as she let her breath out, and her eyes focused on the short text written on a piece of hotel stationery. Had Connor walked right up to the front desk, with no cares in the world, just so he could leave her a note. The man was crazy and ballsy, just like her parents.

"Fuck...no...Sara."

Reid's frantic tone told her he finished reading the note before she did. And it also told her that the sinking feeling she had was right. Sara hadn't gotten called into work.

Dearest Isabelle,

You stupid bitch. You should've just come with me. It's your fault she had to suffer. You and that stupid ex of yours. He shouldn't have interrupted my plan, and you shouldn't have fought me. I made him pay first, but you'll get yours next. I promise.

Your Big Brother,

Connor

A sob escaped her lips as she finished reading the note. She turned to look at Cade and Reid and realized that she needed to get her shit together for Reid's sake. Cade was already on the phone with Diane getting backup sent to Reid's apartment. Reid, on the other hand, looked like he didn't know what to do. His skin had paled considerably, his eyes wide from shock. He looked like a statue.

Sloane reached out and pulled the car keys out of his hand, then grabbed his hand to lead him outside. Cade followed behind them, his voice low as he talked to his boss.

"We should let the FBI handle this," he said to Sloane, though there was no conviction behind his words.

He knew just as well as Sloane did that they needed to get to that apartment. Whether or not it was a good idea to take Reid with them was another story altogether. But she knew if they left him at the hotel, he'd be hot on their heels the second the shock wore off.

"She might be alive," Sloane said quietly, hoping Reid couldn't hear her.

Cade looked at her like she'd lost her mind, but didn't put a voice to his thoughts, probably for Reid's sake. When they got to the car, Sloane helped Reid into the backseat then climbed into the driver's seat despite Cade's protest. She waved him off, started the car, and put on her seatbelt before he could say anything else. Thankfully, he made the wise decision to shut up and get in the car himself before she left without him.

It turned out to be a good thing that Sloane was stubborn since Cade ended up taking calls from various people throughout the short drive from the hotel to Reid's apartment. She'd barely had a chance to come to a stop before Reid was jumping out of the car and running into the building.

Sloane removed her seatbelt before she even turned the car off. She needed to keep Reid from doing something stupid. The local police and the FBI weren't there yet, which meant they were on their own for the time being. Reid couldn't go up there alone. Nothing good would come from him being the first one to his apartment.

"Reid. Wait," Sloane yelled as she ran after him.

She squeezed through the closing elevator doors, barely making it in time. Reid didn't even notice her presence. Grief, anger, disbelief, and every emotion in between played over his features on the short ride to his floor. He barreled past her into the hallway, running down the long hall at a sprint that would make the trainers at Quantico proud.

"Reid, stop. You can't go in there."

She hurried after him, hoping to catch him before he entered the apartment. He stopped at the door, but not because she told him to, but because he didn't want to go any further. Reid Morgan was hesitating to enter a crime scene for the first time in his career.

"I have to."

"Reid..."

"Sloane, I know what you're trying to say, but I have to go in there. I have to see her."

Sloane sighed. "I get it, but let me go first at least. Let me check things out."

"He could be in there."

She shook her head even though Reid wasn't looking at her. "He's not. He wouldn't leave the note then come back here to ambush us. Connor's too smart for that, he'd know we would have backup. Let me go in there. I'll come back to get you, I promise."

When Reid didn't move or say anything, she figured that was her sign he was onboard with her plan. Either that or he just couldn't bring himself to go inside. Unsurprisingly, the door wasn't locked. Most killers didn't bother to lock up once they were done, and her brother was no different. Sloane looked over her shoulder at Reid, tears streaming down his face before she slipped into the home he shared with Sara.

She closed the door behind her, not wanting Reid to see what Connor had done. Broken glass and roses littered the floor not too far into the apartment. Beneath them, she could make out a stain of some sort, which would most likely turn out to be blood, but she couldn't be sure. Beyond that was another stain; this one was obviously blood. Next to it was a pile of women's clothing. Sloane's heart ached for Sara. The woman hadn't deserved any of this.

A trail of blood led down the hall. Sloane couldn't tell if it was from someone being dragged or from someone crawling away, but she held out hope it was the latter. She wanted to believe that Sara had put up a fight, that she'd made him work for the kill.

As she moved into the apartment, Sloane skirted around the broken glass and blood the best she could. Evidence wouldn't matter too much in this case, not with the note from Connor all but saying he killed her. Even knowing that she still didn't want to compromise anything they could gather. Something in this apartment could tie Connor to other murders around the country. The more they could pile on him, the better. Once she caught him, he'd never see the light of day. The thought of her tormentor rotting away in prison made her smile.

The bastard would pay for everything he'd done. She'd make sure of it.

The blood trail led to the bedroom on the left at the end of the hall. Sloane steadied herself, preparing her brain and emotions for what she was about to see. There was no doubt in her mind that it was terrible. He'd stripped Sara down, cut her, chased after her, probably toyed with her. The man was a monster.

As she stepped into the bedroom, Sloane heard the door to the apartment open and the sound of Cade dropping a ton of expletives. He only knew half of it. An empty carton of Chinese food on the stained bedspread and the bottle of beer on the nightstand told a story that proved just how evil Connor was. The man had a meal while Sara bled out. Who did such a thing?

Anger coursed through her as she walked around the side of the bed where she expected to find Sara but only found more blood soaking into the floor. A smear of red led under the bed, so she crouched down to check underneath it and wished she hadn't. She didn't need to get too close of a look to know that there was no saving Sara Larson. Reid's would-be fiance was dead, and it was all Sloane's fault. She started to back her way out of the room when a piece of paper on the bed next to the food carton caught her eye.

It didn't matter that she knew better. Every instinct in her body told her whatever Connor had left behind was for her eyes only. This was how she was going to stop him. He'd left her a breadcrumb, and all she had to do was follow it.

She picked the note up, ignoring the specks of blood on the paper that had been hastily ripped out of a notebook. Cade's footsteps were heavy in the hall, so she shoved the note in her pocket before reading it. If he saw it, he'd take it away from her, and he'd try to stop her from going after Connor. She couldn't let that happen.

"Holy fuck," Cade muttered as he stepped into the room next to her.

"She's under the bed," was all she could say in return.

Words failed her as the severity of the situation hit her so forcefully she nearly dropped to her knees. She stared at Cade as he crouched down to check under the bed, more expletives dropping from his lips as he took in the scene. More footsteps sounded out through the apartment, the backup they needed and probably Reid. She couldn't stop him from entering the room and seeing what Connor had done to his girlfriend.

What she could do was stop Connor from hurting anyone else. In the chaos that erupted as more people filed into the bedroom, Sloane slipped out. She went completely unnoticed as she made her way back down the hall and into the living room. The roses she'd all but ignored before were trampled; their broken petals were strewn over the room, mixing with the blood. It was eerie and unsettling and fueled the fire burning inside of her.

Pulling the note out of her pocket, she read it and immediately knew where she needed to go. Connor wanted a face-off with his little sister. Soon he'd be reminded of the old saying, be careful what you wish for. She was going to make him sorry.

Sorry that he ever set his sights on her. Sorry that he hurt people she cared about.

It was ironic he'd picked the spot he did. For only the second time in her life, she was looking for vengeance. She didn't plan to give her brother a chance. He wasn't going to prison, and he wouldn't get a trial.

Connor DiSanto was going to see exactly what Sloane was capable of. And he was going to be more than sorry he'd ever heard the name Isabelle DiSanto.

She was her mother's daughter, after all. It was about time she started to channel some of that crazy bitch energy.

CHAPTER THIRTY-NINE

Cade paced along the small strip of the uncontaminated floor in front of the couch in Reid and Sara's apartment, his hands balled up in fists in his pants pockets. Reid sat on one end of the sofa, his head in his hands, his shoulders shaking as he cried. It had taken every ounce of strength Cade had to pull Reid from his bedroom and back down the hall. The last thing he needed was to see the mess left behind by Connor DiSanto. It wouldn't do him any good to see what the killer had done to Sara's body. That wasn't a picture anyone needed to have in their head, let alone the man who loved her.

"How did he even get up here?" Diane asked, her voice stern yet filled with compassion.

She wanted answers, but she didn't want to upset her agent any more than he already was. And it wasn't like they could get Reid to leave. They'd tried, and short of arresting the man, he wasn't going anywhere until Connor was in custody. Cade couldn't blame him, and neither could Diane.

"Apparently, he flashed a badge at the doorman and told him he was here at Reid's request."

Before he could say anything else, a couple more people made their way into the apartment. Cade recognized the man in the lead as Dr. Miller, the medical examiner he'd met while working the Mommy Murderer case. He was followed by two other men, one pushing a gurney, the other carrying a bag similar to the one the doctor was holding. He pointed down the hall, then looked over at his boss.

"Go, I'll stay with him," she said before moving over to take a seat on the couch next to Reid.

He couldn't imagine what the other man was going through. How did someone come back from the brutal murder of someone they loved? Would he ever be the same again? And what about Emily and Tally, and even Sloane. While she didn't know Sara well, he knew Sloane would blame herself for what happened to her. The guilt would eat at her far worse than the guilt she felt over Richard.

"Are we free to move things around?" Dr. Miller asked him as soon as he joined them in the room.

"Yeah. The ERT is done here. I had them work this room first so you could rearrange things if you needed to. I know it will be easier to get to her if you can remove the mattress and box spring."

Dr. Miller nodded then instructed his two assistants to get to work moving the furniture. The bed had already been stripped of the bedspread and pillows. Each had been bagged and tagged for processing along with the beer bottle and the empty carton of Chinese food. The fact that Connor had sat on the bed eating a meal while Sara was dying made Cade sick to his stomach.

In all of his years with the FBI, he'd witnessed some terrible shit. Still, for some reason, that simple act had Cade questioning everything he knew or believed about serial killers and the DiSanto family in particular. Connor was turning out to be far more sinister and fucked in the head than either of his parents, which didn't bode well for them moving forward.

Cade moved out of the way as the two men, who hadn't said a word since they entered the apartment, finally moved the bed frame out of the way. His stomach rolled as he got his first good look at Sara. Seeing her in the full light of the bedroom without the shade of the mattress covering her made bile rise in Cade's throat. It hadn't been that long ago that he'd spent the evening eating and drinking and laughing with this woman, now here she was, naked, slashed all to hell, her glassy eyes locked on the ceiling.

"Holy shit," the doctor murmured next to him. "Sorry, that wasn't very professional of me."

Cade shook his head. "You took the words right out of my mouth."

The other man moved toward the body, then crouched down beside her. Cade tried to remind himself that she was just another victim so he could focus on the doctor's observations. That was easier said than done. It felt wrong to be standing in the room with his partner's naked girlfriend, even if she was dead.

"My guess is the wound to the throat will be the official cause of death, but she wouldn't have lasted long with all of these other wounds," the doctor said as he lifted her enough he could see beneath her. "The blood pool we passed in the living room was indicative of another major wound, and it looks like there's one here on her back. Eventually, she would have bled out from that one or choked on her own blood. Either way, it would have been a much slower death than the one she was given."

"Why would he do that?" Cade asked though the question was more for himself than anyone else.

He ran a hand over his face, not wanting to ask his next question. It was bad enough that Connor had sliced her up, but if he'd touched her in any other way...he couldn't even bring himself to think about it.

"Is there any sign of sexual assault?" he asked finally, wanting to get it out before it was too late.

He averted his eyes as the doctor checked, then let out the breath he didn't realize he was holding when he got the answer he was hoping for.

"I don't see anything, but of course, I can't say for sure until we get her on the table."

Cade nodded. "Thank you. I'll leave you to it then. Her boyfriend is out there on the couch, so if you could..."

"We will."

Cade nodded again, then left the room, and the horror of seeing someone he knew laid out on the floor next to the medical examiner. All of his years of training and being the first on scene hadn't prepared him for what he was dealing with. He could only imagine how Sloane was taking it. He walked back into the living room, where Diane still comforted Reid, and looked around for Sloane. She had been unusually quiet since she'd left the bedroom, which worried him.

When he didn't see her in the living room or kitchen, he stepped outside into the hallway where an agent stood guard. He looked up and down the long expanse of the building and shook his head when he didn't see her. Pulling his phone out of his pocket, he went to key in his passcode when he saw something on the floor halfway between the apartment and the elevator.

It could have been nothing, just a piece of garbage from another tenant, but Cade's gut told him otherwise. Specks of rusty red dotted the edge of the paper, and when he squatted down to pick it up, he saw the unmistakable scrawl of Connor DiSanto.

"Son of a bitch," Cade growled as he picked up the note addressed to Isabelle.

He marched back into the apartment, note in hand, anger and fear warring inside of him. He should've known she'd do something stupid. That was her MO, after all. Rushing head first into danger by herself. Her safety, hell, her life, not even a blip on her radar. All she cared about was justice for whoever she was trying to protect.

"She's gone," she said as he thrust the note at Diane.

Reid snatched it out of his hand first so he could read it out loud.

"My dearest Isabelle. Did you like what I left for you? I promise I didn't let her suffer too long. She deserved so much better than what you made me do to her. Yet another innocent life lost because you were too full of yourself to face me. It's time, baby sister. Time for us to finally have our moment. I want to see what you're capable of. You showed the world once before. Find me in that spot, and you can try to show the world once again. If you don't show up, well, I can't be held responsible for what I do next. Your big brother."

"What the fuck does that mean?" Diane asked as she grabbed the note from Reid. "Where does he want her to meet him? And how does she plan on getting there?"

"She's got the keys to the car and one hell of a head start. She could be anywhere by now," Cade sighed. "Can we trace her phone?"

Reid shook his head. "She's probably turned that off by now, but we can track the car. She doesn't know I activated the tracker on it when I rented it."

Diane laughed. "Smart man. You knew something like this would happen eventually."

"She's always been a wild card. I just wanted to plan for the inevitable as best I could," Reid admitted.

"Good job. Let me get Lily and Brian on this, and we'll go save Sloane from herself," Diane said, then excused herself to make the phone call.

"Let's go," Reid said as he stood and strode toward the door.

"Go where?" Cade asked. "We don't know where she is."

"Yes, we do, and I want to get there before the cavalry."

Cade sighed. "You're not thinking clearly, Reid. We'll go after Sloane, but you will not do anything to DiSanto before backup arrives. Don't throw your life away because of him."

"What life, Cade? What life do I have without Sara? Are you coming, or do you want to show up and find Sloane the same way we found Sara?"

Before Cade could answer, Reid was stalking out of the apartment and down the hall. Cade had to nearly jog to keep up, though they ended up being held up by the elevator. Once inside, Cade tried to ignore part of Reid's declaration. Instead, he focused on reminding the man he did have something to live for even with Sara gone.

"Don't forget about Tally and Emily. Remember your niece and your sister when we get to wherever you think Sloane is. They wouldn't want you to throw it all away for this murdering asshole."

Reid didn't say anything, though Cade knew his words sank in. Sara was important to the other man, but Tally and Emily were his flesh and blood, and he'd fight for them even if it meant living in a world where the woman he loved was dead.

In the lobby, Reid talked one of the agents into giving him the keys to their vehicle. Before Cade knew it, they were on the road, speeding toward a situation that was untenable at best. He just hoped they'd get to Sloane before she did something she couldn't come back from. Or before Connor got his wish and removed his sister from his path of destruction forever.

CHAPTER

FORTY

She knew what she was doing was beyond stupid. Who in their right mind would run off to meet their serial killer brother in the woods without a weapon and without backup? No one.

Only someone certifiable would do what Sloane was doing. Whatever happened next, only one of them would make it out of the confrontation alive. She knew that with every fiber of her being.

Though maybe neither of them would live through their showdown. That scenario would probably work better for everyone involved. No one would ever have to worry about the DiSanto kids again.

But that still left Rosalie out there, killing people whenever the mood struck. Sloane had to take her down too. She had to make it through whatever hell Connor had planned so she could bring Rosalie to justice once and for all. Maybe that would be the battle that ended in both of their deaths. If that was how she went out, Sloane could live with that.

The drive to the woods where she killed the murdering pedophile years earlier was almost peaceful. She let her mind wander. If this was her last drive, she wanted to think about the pleasant things she would leave behind. Tally's smiling face was the first thing that came to mind. Her giggles made Sloane smile. Emily came next, the best friend a girl could ever have. She was going to be devastated when she learned about Sara's murder. And it would be even worse if Sloane didn't make it out alive, but her pain wasn't enough to stop Sloane from doing what she knew she had to do.

Her favorite girls were followed up by Cade. The man had worked his way into her life and stolen a piece of her. She didn't know if that piece was from her heart or soul, but she knew if she lived through her time with Connor, she was going to miss the hell out of Cade when everything else was said and done. If they were two other people living very different lives, maybe they'd have a shot at making it work. But after everything that'd happened, she didn't deserve happiness. She didn't deserve love or friendship or family, all things she could possibly find if she allowed herself to be with Cade.

She parked her car in the same spot she'd left it years ago so she could save a little girl. The sense of déjà vu that settled over her was oddly comforting, though this time, she was running in blind, unarmed, and the only person in immediate danger was her.

For a second, she contemplated calling Cade to tell him where she was. She'd dropped the note at some point, though she didn't know if it was inside Reid's apartment building or somewhere else. Even if Cade did find the letter, he wouldn't know what Connor meant. He wouldn't know to follow her to the woods. Reid might, though. But that was only if he was in the frame of mind to even read the note, let alone decipher it.

Instead of calling him, she turned her phone on so he could track it. At least then, eventually, he'd find her. Whether it would be in time, she didn't know. She hoped so, though. As she started toward the woods, she realized she wasn't ready to die, and she really didn't want to kill Connor. She hated him for what he'd done, and she could kill him if she had to, but she didn't want to. She didn't want to be like everyone else in her family. She didn't want to be a murderer.

Some would argue she already was. And maybe they were right, but she didn't want to be. Was there a difference? Did it matter? Maybe she should turn back and wait for Cade and Reid and whoever else to show up. Sloane knew she was making a mistake marching into the woods to face her brother, but part of her felt like she had no choice. Someone had to stop him. He was her flesh and blood so the responsibility fell to her.

The further she moved into the woods, the thicker the dread felt. Her legs grew heavy as she considered what was going to happen. She was unarmed, and she was unprepared. Connor had the upper hand. He had all the advantages. If he wanted to, he could kill her the second he saw her, but she knew that wasn't the way he'd take her out.

No, Connor DiSanto would act like every stereotypical villain there ever was. He'd want to tell her how and why and then make her relive the things he'd done to the people she cared about. He'd tell her what he planned on doing to the others once he was through with her. He'd make her last moments hell to pay her back for whatever she'd done to mess up his life, which from the sound of it, was just being born.

Like she had a choice in the matter.

She needed to turn back, but she knew they'd lose this chance at Connor if she did that. He'd run. He'd find another victim and blame Sloane for their death. What if that victim was Tally or Emily or even Reid. She couldn't let that happen. She couldn't let him get away.

When she made it to the clearing, she marched right in like it was her domain. She'd vowed to herself she wouldn't show fear. From that moment, all he would remember was how strong she was, how she didn't back down even though she didn't have a chance.

"I'm here, asshole. Let's get this over with," she yelled.

Sloane had expected him to be right there waiting for her arrival. The fact that he wasn't, worried her. Where the hell was he? Could she have been wrong about the meeting place? Or had he lured her there for another reason? Maybe he'd done it to get her away from Cade and Reid. Perhaps they were his target instead.

"Fuck," she grumbled before turning around in a circle, peering into the darkness between the trees.

When she'd started into the woods, darkness hadn't completely fallen, but now, especially given how deep she was, it was getting more challenging to see by the second. Sloane pulled her phone out of her pocket and turned on the flashlight, giving her a chance to see what surrounded her. This time, she turned slower, examining each void, each tree.

All she saw were the beady eyes of birds watching her every move.

Where the fuck was he?

"What kind of cowardly bullshit is this? Are you too afraid to face me?" she taunted him, hoping he was out there hiding. "I'm an unarmed woman. I should be an easy target for you."

She waited for several excruciatingly long minutes before she turned back toward the way she came. She had one last taunt to throw out. If he was out there watching and waiting, this would be the one to spur him into action. It had to be.

"I can see now why mom and dad threw you away."

A rustle of leaves came from her left, but before she could turn in that direction, something hard and heavy connected with her temple. As her eyes fluttered shut and true darkness descended on her, she heard him laugh. She knew it would work. She just wished she'd thought her plan through a little more before throwing those words in his face. Maybe when she woke up, she'd have the chance.

CHAPTER FORTY-ONE

"You really are a stupid bitch, aren't you? Or do you just have some sort of death wish?"

When she didn't respond, Connor smacked her hard across the face, hoping the pain would wake her up. He didn't think he hit her that hard when he punched her out earlier, but she'd been out a lot longer than he needed her to be. All he'd wanted to do was knock her out long enough to tie her up without having a fight on his hands. Once she was down, he'd dragged her over to a nearby tree, then propped her up against it. He used a rope to secure her to the tree, keeping her arms tight against her body so she couldn't lash out at him when she woke up. Her legs would be a problem if he got too close to the front of her, but it wouldn't be easy to kick at him while sitting on the ground with her feet tied together.

"Wakey, wakey little sis. It's time for you to pay for what you've done to me."

He waited for a response or any sign she was awake and got nothing again. He smacked her across the face a second time, then stood up so he could kick her in the side. Sloane grunted as his foot connected with her ribs.

"I sure hope you weren't faking being unconscious. It would be foolish to play games with me."

"What the fuck do you want from me?"

A spark of anticipation coursed through Connor as his gaze met hers. She looked so much like their mother, a fact she probably wouldn't appreciate hearing. The ungrateful little bitch had done everything she could to distance herself from her family, including choosing an idiotic name.

"Why didn't you want what you were given? Why did you take it for granted?" he asked, though neither question had been one he planned on asking.

"Because I'm not a psychopath or sociopath."

He growled at her. How dare she disparage their family like that. They weren't crazy. Well, maybe a little crazy, but they were just doing what they were made to do—culling the herd, so to speak. Survival of the fittest and all that. The bitch in front of him was weak. She didn't deserve to be alive. She should've died years ago instead of their father.

He still didn't understand why they'd chosen her over him. If they'd just kept him instead of throwing him away, Michael would still be alive. Maybe their mother wouldn't have had to hide in the shadows pretending to be dead, living under a dumbass name instead of her rightful one. Isabelle was the reason for everything terrible that had ever happened to the DiSanto family.

"You're worthless, yet she still protects you. I don't fucking get it. Why would she waste her time on you when she has me?"

"Why would she waste her time on you when you're clearly fucking nuts?"

Connor's knee connected with her chin, sending her head snapping to the left. He needed to be careful not to knock her out again. He would have to make do with body shots for the rest of the night, at least until he was finished with her. He couldn't risk knocking her out again. He needed her awake for what he had planned.

"That might be true, but I'd rather be crazy than dumb," he told her. "I knew you'd be stupid enough to come out here alone, but I expected you to have a weapon, so maybe you aren't as predictable as I thought you were. But you're dumber, so I'm not sure which is worse."

"Maybe I'm not alone."

He laughed. "Oh, come on now, we both know you are. I followed you here from your ex's apartment, and you didn't even know you had a tail. How the hell did you make it in the FBI as long as you did?"

"Can we just get on with whatever you plan to do with me? I don't fucking care who you are, and I don't care about our fucked up family heritage either. You can have the DiSanto name and the love of our mother or whatever it is you're hoping to get out of this. I want nothing to do with any of it."

"You selfish little bitch. How can you turn your back on our family? They loved you and raised you."

"They murdered people in cold blood. Your beloved father tried to kill me."

"Because you were a disappointment to him. If mom hadn't killed him, I bet he would have come looking for me. He would have wanted someone to walk in his footsteps."

His bitch sister shook her head. "He wanted Rosalie all to himself. You're a little right, though. He wanted me to become like them, but he would've been just as happy with me out of the way. I don't think you would've been any different. There was a reason they didn't keep you around after all."

Connor ground his teeth together. He knew she was trying to bait him, but he couldn't let that happen. He would not let her push his buttons. At least not until he was ready to lose control.

"Do you know why they abandoned me?"

He didn't think she had the answers he was looking for, but it didn't hurt to ask. Or maybe it would. If she knew about his existence and knew why their parents had left him behind all those years ago, he'd be hurt, but he'd also be angry. So fucking angry.

"I didn't even know you existed until yesterday. Why haven't you asked your darling mother why she gave you up?"

"I have," he snarled, then tried to compose himself. "But she refuses to tell me anything. All she ever does is talk about you. Her precious fucking Isabelle. Even though you've betrayed her over and over, she's still devoted to you. She told me to leave you alone. She didn't want me to meet you."

"And how is any of that my fault?"

"Why did they love you more than me? Why wasn't I good enough?"

"I don't fucking know. I don't care either. I wish they had kept you and left me behind. Or hell, not had me at all. I didn't want that life. I didn't want to be put in the position they put me in. All I wanted was an ordinary mom and dad who loved me and didn't fucking kill people for fun."

Connor paced along the clearing in front of her. Darkness had overtaken them, but the lanterns he'd set out on either side of her lit the area up enough. All he needed was to be able to see her. Everything else that went bump in the dark wasn't his concern. He watched her struggle against the rope, even though it was a waste of energy. Why was he holding on to her? What was he waiting for? She didn't have anything he needed. In the long run, he was just wasting time; time that he didn't necessarily have. For all he knew, her friends weren't far behind them. They could show up any minute, and he'd lose his chance to be rid of his competition once and for all.

"I should just end it and be rid of you," he said as he moved toward her, giving her right wrist a shift kick as he got closer. "Once you're out of the way, she'll have to put me first."

The bitch at his feet laughed. "You think that's going to happen? If you kill me, she's going to hate you. She'll resent you until she finally decides to kill you. But hey, what's stopping you? Why don't we just get this over with?"

"You don't know what you're talking about. She loves me."

"Does she? Enough to forgive you for taking out her 'precious fucking Isabelle'? I'm guessing no. But I could be wrong. Do you really want to chance it?"

"Fuck. I don't know," Connor mumbled as he pulled the knife he'd used on Sara out of his pocket.

Blood coated the blade, the sight giving him a boost in his confidence he apparently needed. He didn't know why he was allowing her to get to him. His mother loved him enough to forgive him. He was sure of it.

Wasn't he?

Fuck it. Even if she didn't, he would show her that she picked the wrong kid. If she wanted to kill him for taking out his stupid sister, then he'd have to beat her to the punch. She was old, and he knew all of her tricks. It would be fitting for him to wipe out all of the remaining DiSanto family members so he could reign supreme as the heir to their evil legacy. He wanted it so badly he could taste it. He wasn't going to let anyone stand in his way; even the woman who brought him into this world.

"Fuck you, and fuck her, too. If she hates me for what I'm about to do, so be it. I'll just have to send her to hell right after you."

Sloane laughed, but she wasn't the only one. Another, more sinister sounding laugh echoed through the clearing behind him. He whipped around, the knife in his left hand pressed against his sister's neck.

"Hello, son. It looks like it's time for mommy to dole out some punishments."

CHAPTER FORTY-TWO

"That's what you think, you old bitch. I don't care what you want. We're not playing your game anymore. We're playing mine."

For the first time since he met his mother, he felt invincible. This was his calling. He wasn't meant to merely get her approval. His purpose in life was to become her, the leader of the DiSanto family. That time had come, he didn't need her anymore.

His mother scoffed, which only made him angry. His blood felt like boiling acid in his veins, and his heart was beating a painful rhythm against his ribs. Why had it taken him so long to realize he was the one in charge? He held all of the power. Not her, not her stupid daughter.

"It's so cute you think so, baby. I get that you're feeling a certain way, right now, but you know you aren't going to kill your sister. I won't allow it. I want my babies to get along. I want us to be one big happy family."

"That's never going to happen. She wants nothing to do with you or our family."

She shrugged. "Maybe, maybe not. She hasn't had a chance to be part of the family in twenty years. Maybe we give her some time to see how far we've come. Maybe she's had a change of heart."

Sloane didn't say anything to back him up or to contradict him. To their mother, her silence spoke volumes, but Connor knew better. He knew she was only being quiet to buy herself some time. She wanted their mother to think she planned on being the doting daughter once again. They were going to work against him.

Fucking bitches thought they were going to be in charge and tell him what to do. They thought wrong.

He dug the tip of the knife into the top of Sloane's shoulder. Her cries of pain were music to his ears. On the other hand, their mother didn't seem happy with the mewling sounds she was making. She took a step toward them, then another. The second she got too close, Connor pushed down on the knife, eliciting another cry of anguish from Sloane.

"Stop. Connor, just stop it, okay. We can work this out. I promise. Just leave your sister alone. We don't need her to come between us."

It was his turn to scoff. "Maybe you should've thought about that before you forbade me to go look for her and then demanded I leave her alone when I just started having fun. It got this far because of you, and now you're trying to play nice. It's too little too late, mother dear."

"Oh, Connor. I never thought you'd be so dumb. Do you really think you can win here? Do you not remember who I am?"

He jammed the knife deeper into Sloane's right shoulder, her screams echoing off of the trees around them. He could see the blood soaking through her clothing in the lantern light. Pain was etched across her face. It made him unbelievably happy to be the reason she was suffering. The glare his mother was sending his way only made him happier.

He'd spent so long wanting her approval, and now...well, now, he no longer gave a fuck what she wanted or how she felt. It was a weird sensation. One he liked very much.

Connor had always felt like he was in his element when he was killing, and now he'd found an extra level to the excitement he felt whenever he held a knife against another person's skin. He'd found his place in the world, and it wasn't at his mother's side. It was in front of her, showing her just what kind of damage he could do.

"Tell me why you left me behind. Tell me why you chose her over me."

"I don't owe you anything, Connor."

He waved the knife out in front of him, then brought it back down to Sloane. He traced the tip along her jawline just deep enough to draw blood, but not so deep he hit bone. Anger flared to life in his mother's eyes as she saw more of her daughter's blood being spilled.

"Yes, you fucking do. You owe me everything, yet all I'm asking for is the truth. All I want to know is why I wasn't good enough."

Something flickered across Grace's face, but he wasn't sure he recognized it. At least not on her. It kinda reminded him of the compassion he used to see on his adopted mother's face when he was an awkward little boy. Whatever it was, he wasn't sure if he liked it or not.

"Oh, sweet boy. You were good enough. It was your parents that weren't. Or rather, it was me. I didn't know for sure who you belonged to, and I couldn't bear to ask your daddy to raise another man's child. We didn't have DNA tests back then. So I did the hardest thing I've ever had to do, and I left you behind. I didn't know for sure that you were Michael's until I found you through the ancestry website. I used your dad's sister's DNA to look for you."

"Who else could have been my father?"

Whatever she'd been feeling seconds before was gone, replaced by the mother he'd grown to love. She didn't like his question at all.

"It doesn't matter. They're long gone, and we know now that Michael was your father. That's all that matters."

"But..."

"No. I'm done talking about this. Now that the truth is out, can we move on? Can we leave this place and go back to the life we were living before? Let's just leave Isabelle here and move on. We don't need her."

He shook his head, slowly swiping the knife along Sloane's neck, once again just enough to draw blood but not do any real damage. It wasn't time for that yet.

"As long as she's alive, you're always going to wish I was her. But she doesn't want us. She isn't like us. Why should I live in her shadow?"

"You won't. I promise."

"You're a fucking liar. I can see it all over your face. You're trying to tell me what I want to hear, so your precious Isabelle, Sloane, whatever the fuck we should call her, can get away unscathed. Well, I'm done with your lies. I'm going to kill her no matter what you say, and if that bothers you, well, once I'm done with her, we can figure it out. Maybe I'll just have to take care of you too."

"Oh, dear boy, you should never have shown your hand like that."

"Why? It doesn't matter if you know my plan. Only one of us will be walking out of this clearing."

"Funny that you think that one person will be you. I lived through being shot and plummeting into a raging river. I'm also the only one with a gun. How do you think you're going to win when all you have is a knife?"

"You'd shoot me when my knife is pressed against your precious daughter's carotid?"

She shrugged. "Just because I don't want you to kill her doesn't mean I care if she lives or dies. If you cut her throat when I shoot you, well, then she's collateral damage. No harm, no foul. I agreed only one of us is walking out of here, and I meant it."

Connor didn't believe her. After all the times she pleaded with him to leave Sloane alone, and now she was okay if her daughter died? She was lying. Again. Why couldn't she just be straight with him? Why did she think she needed to manipulate him with her lies and bullshit?

Obviously, he needed to focus on his mother. Sloane was tied to a tree. Killing her first served no purpose other than his mom getting to watch the life drain from her daughter's eyes. And while it would be fun to watch her suffer through that, though he knew she'd try to hide her pain, he'd rather take out the more significant threat first. She said she had a gun, but she'd yet to produce it. Could she have been stupid enough to come after him without a weapon too? Or was she hoping the threat of a gun, when she had a different weapon on her, would keep him in line?

It didn't matter. He wasn't going to let her idle threats stop him. He was the DiSanto heir. He would take their legacy, and he would surpass everything his parents were known for. The weirdos and groupies that loved serial killers would worship him in ways they never did his parents. He was what they'd been waiting for. He was what they'd hoped his sister would become.

Someday he'd show them all that he was the best. It was just too bad his mother wouldn't be alive long enough to see it.

Stepping away from Sloane, he moved toward their mother. Her expression didn't change as he walked toward her. She didn't pull a gun or any other weapon out of her pocket even though he was mere steps away from slitting her throat. She'd resigned herself to her fate. She was ready for him to take up the mantle.

"I won't let you down," he said as he looked down at her, his knife a few inches from her throat.

"You already have," she told him before she moved quicker than anyone her age should be able to.

It took his brain a few seconds to process what happened, and even then, everything seemed to be happening to someone else. His vision blurred as he dropped to his knees. A weird warmth coated his chest in rivulets which confused him. He didn't know what to make of it until he started choking. It felt like he was drowning. He couldn't breathe.

As he fell to the ground at his mother's feet, he looked up at her. He couldn't make out her face through the fog of death, but there was no mistaking the obnoxious laughter. He hated that it was the last sound he ever heard.

As the darkness pulled him under, the last thing he remembered thinking was that the goddamn bitch had won.

CHAPTER

FORTY-THREE

"Holy shit."

Sloane struggled against the rope tied around her as she watched Connor slump to the ground. She couldn't hear anything over the thudding of her heart, but she knew her turn was next. Their mother had just slit his throat like it was nothing. She'd taken the life of a child she'd brought into the world with a smile on her face.

Holy fuck.

Fear sent a chill down Sloane's spine. She was next, and why wouldn't she be. Deciding to get rid of both of her kids in one fell swoop would probably make her life a lot easier. Why keep Sloane around when Connor was the one just like her?

There was no reason to continue to leave her alive, especially since Rosalie had to know Sloane wouldn't stop hunting for her once she was free. There was no love lost between them. No loyalty. And at the moment, Sloane was a sitting duck. There was nothing she could do physically to try to prolong her life.

Yet, maybe there was still a way out of the situation. Sloane knew Cade and Reid had to be on their way. Could she keep her mom occupied long enough for them to arrive? Sloane had to believe they were close by. That was the only way she was going to make it through whatever Rosalie had in mind for her.

The older woman bent down and wiped her knife on the back of Connor's jacket, then stood up, her gaze landing on Sloane. A shudder ran through her as her mom started walking toward her.

"I can see the fear in your eyes, sweetheart. Don't worry. I'm not going to hurt you."

"How can I believe anything you say? You just killed your own son," Sloane countered. "Hell, how do I even know you're truly Rosalie? You look nothing like her."

"Don't be obtuse, Isabelle. You know who I am. Appearances can change, but the bond between a mother and a daughter never fades."

"Seriously?" she didn't even bother to hold back her laughter.

It didn't matter that she was vulnerable or that Rosalie had the upper hand. What she was saying was downright ridiculous. There was never much of a bond between them. Maybe when she was a small child, but then again, what would she have known about bonds or any of that nonsense. Like most kids, she thought her parents were the best there were. They took her on trips and showed her parts of the country most kids would never see. They had fun making memories, and every night when they put her to bed, they told her they loved her.

Then they went out and murdered some innocent that made the mistake of catching their eye. Men, women, it didn't matter. They all bled the same. They all sent the same thrill through her parents as they succumbed to their wounds, the light draining from their eyes.

"I never could've endured all of these years with my old face. I was one of the FBI's most wanted after all," she laughed. "Even if that wasn't the case, I would've needed a nip here and a tuck there eventually. I'd never be able to seduce the young ones looking my actual age."

"So you got a brand new face so you could get laid?"

Sloane knew the comment would piss her off. That was one thing she'd been very clear about once her father was gone, and it was just the two of them. Rosalie DiSanto was never above using her beauty and sexuality to get what she wanted. Sloane had no doubt she'd used those gifts more times than either of them could count over the last couple of decades. It was the only way she could have stayed hidden for as long as she had.

"You're trying my patience. You know very well it's never been about the carnal act itself, even when it's fun. Sex is about survival. You'd be much better off if you'd used the gifts you were given. You're a gorgeous, confident, strong woman, but you could be so much more if you just spread your legs every once in a while for the right man."

Sloane bit back a laugh. "That's some excellent motherly advice there, Rosalie. I don't know how I survived all of these years without it."

"You really are a brat, aren't you?"

"I'd rather be a brat than a crazy ass bitch."

Anger passed over Rosalie's face, but it was fleeting. She never allowed her emotions to show for long. That would give people too much power over her.

"So you have a death wish, little one?"

"Using pet names from my childhood isn't going to endear me to you. We are not family. We are nothing. If you're not going to set me free, then you might as well kill me. This will be the only chance you have to take me out where I can't fight back," Sloane paused, her lips curling into a smirk she knew would piss Rosalie off. "The question is, are you a coward like your pitiful son, or would you rather see who comes out victorious after a fair fight?"

"You ungrateful little bitch. I killed my son for you, and this is how you repay me?"

"We both know he would've killed you the first chance he got. Don't fool yourself into believing he loved you and was an obedient son. He wanted us both out of the way. As soon as I was gone, you were going to be next. You did us both a favor by showing up here and ridding the world of your crazy ass spawn."

Rosalie took a step toward her, then another until she was close enough that Sloane could see the anger and sorrow dueling within her eyes. This was it. She was finally going to die. It was weird because she didn't feel anything other than maybe a bit of relief. Otherwise, she was numb. As long as she didn't let herself think about Tally or Emily or Cade.

Her fate was inevitable. Thinking about the people she loved wouldn't change anything. It would only make it worse.

"It was my hubris that ruined us. Your father and I were perfect the way we were, but I stupidly thought we needed someone to add to our family, but all bringing you into our lives did was end us all. We could've been great. We should've been great, but you wrecked everything."

"Why have another kid when you already had one you threw away? You never even gave Connor a chance. How would another kid be any better than the last?And if I ruined everything, why did you let me live all these years?"

"I told you why we gave your brother up. That's a mistake I'll regret for the rest of my life, but it was the best decision I could make at the time. I let you live because I knew you were being watched by the FBI. It would've been too hard to get to you."

"Bullshit."

"Fine. You're right. I might have let you live because a part of me was hoping you'd be the one to change our family legacy, but I knew it wasn't possible. You're just as fucked up as the rest of your family. I blame my parents," she said softly, then shook her head. "Still, I'm not sure how two people from the same parents could be so damn different. You're such a disappointment, Isabelle."

"I've been hearing that a lot lately."

"Connor might have had a screw loose, but at least he loved his family. He was devoted to us, loyal. I should've let your father kill you. Then he and your brother would still be alive, and we'd be out there doing what the DiSantos do best."

"Sometimes, I wish you had let him kill me," Sloane admitted, though she wasn't sure why.

Rosalie didn't deserve to know about her deep-rooted regret. Not that her parents should've been left unchecked to continue their murderous ways, but she would've been saved from so much pain and heartache if her life would've ended when she was thirteen.

"If it's death you want, little one, that can be arranged. But not like this. I think I'd rather you go down fighting. By the time I'm done with you, you're going to wish you'd let me put you out of your misery while you were tied to this damn tree. I'm going to ruin you, Isabelle. I'm going to ruin everything you hold dear."

"I'm not worried about what you have planned. I'm going to do everything I can to take you down with me, Rosalie. You won't win. Even if I die."

"That's where you're wrong. I'm going to make you suffer. Nobody in your world is safe. Not your men. Not your best friend or her beautiful little girl. Before I'm done, you will be ripped wide open, your guts on display for everyone to see. The world will know who you really are, Isabelle. They will know your weaknesses. They will know you're a disloyal piece of shit. And then they will watch you die."

"Us. They'll watch us die," Sloane vowed. "I'm not afraid of death, Rosalie. When all is said and done, the world will be free of the DiSanto legacy, and that is fine by me."

The sound of her name being yelled from somewhere in the woods around them had both of them whipping their heads around. Relief flooded her body. They were so close, yet still far enough away that Rosalie could change her mind and kill Sloane before they got there. She didn't think she'd do it, but the fear was still there, slowly sucking away at her faith.

She wanted out of the woods, away from Connor's dead body and her crazy mother. While she still felt like her death was inevitable, she wanted more time. She wanted a chance to make Rosalie pay for everything she'd done to her and the innocent people she'd killed along the way. She wanted Rosalie to pay for everything Connor had done; for taking Sara away from Reid. The DiSanto legacy started with Rosalie, and she would be the one to answer for all of their wrongdoings. Even Sloane's.

Her entire body throbbed from the damage that Connor had done both earlier and since she'd been in the woods. It melted into one giant pain threatening her vision and consciousness. She needed medical attention, and now that she knew the cavalry was close, her body wanted to shut down to preserve whatever energy she had left. But she had to fight against it until Rosalie fled. She was already vulnerable enough; passing out would only make things worse.

Cade's voice rang out, the sound of it giving her the last bit of strength she needed to face the woman who'd brought her into the world. She drew her gaze up to meet Rosalie's and put every ounce of malice and determination she could force into it.

"They're almost here, mother. You gonna stick around so they can finally arrest you?"

Rosalie smiled, and despite the face not being the same, Sloane recognized it as the unhinged smile her mother used to give her after her father's death. The one that said she was in for a rude awakening.

"Oh, little one, you know I can't let them catch me just yet. I have so much planned for you. I can't let your boyfriends ruin things."

Rosalie took another two steps toward Sloane, then bent down to place a kiss on her cheek.

"I'll see you soon, Isabelle. That's a promise," she whispered before taking off in the opposite direction of where Cade's voice had come from moments before.

"Sloane, Sloane...shit, get a medic in here."

Cade's voice was louder now, but everything in front of her began to blur. She felt someone working on the ropes behind her and knew someone was kneeling in front of her trying to get her attention, but she could barely make anything out. Her eyelids started to fall, her head lolling to the side.

As everything started to fade away, she heard someone say it was over. If she could have spoken, she would have warned them that the nightmare was just beginning. Instead, she let the darkness take over, chasing away the pain.

Later.

She could tell them everything was about to get a hell of a lot worse, later.

◆ ◆ ◆

Did you enjoy Heir to Evil? If you have time, please leave a review on your favorite retailer or Goodreads. I really appreciate it!
Thank you for reading!

Acknowledgments

I hate to say that this book was fun to write, but it was...except for that one chapter. Poor Sara. Poor Reid.

I really have had the best time writing this series. This has been a dream come true and I can't wait to keep going. I just can't believe Sloane's journey is almost over. I have to thank all of you for reading this series and loving it as much as I do. This has been a wild ride and I'm so honored that you've come along with me.

This book, this series, wouldn't be what it is if I didn't have such an awesome team. Taracina, Christina, and Sami, I wouldn't be able to do this without you. And a huge shoutout to April Hoffman for bringing Sloane, Cade, and the rest of the characters to life. I never thought I would do audiobooks, but I am so glad I took a chance and snagged your amazing skills.

As always, I need to thank my family. Without their support I wouldn't be who I am today. I love you guys more than I can say.

Thank you all for reading. Now go wish Sloane some luck. I think she's going to need it.

About the Author

Paris Hansen was born and raised in Seattle, Washington. She started telling stories at a young age, garnering invitations to writing conferences while in elementary school. Being an author was always her number one aspiration, but as a kid, she also thought being a lawyer or an actress might be cool. As a teenager, she realized she was far better behind the scenes than in front of a crowd and put all of her focus on being a writer.

When not writing, Paris devours as many books as she can get her hands on. After a long day at work, unwinding with a good book, a glass of wine and a decent TV show is her idea of a great evening.

She also loves cupcakes, sexy heroes and popcorn, but not always in that order.

Connect with Paris

E-Mail: paris@parishansen.com
Facebook: https://www.facebook.com/AuthorParisHansen/
Website/Newsletter: http://www.ParisHansen.com
Instagram: https://www.instagram.com/authorparishansen

Made in the USA
Monee, IL
04 December 2023

48095606R00194